John D Felter

The Brother's Watchword

John D Felter

The Brother's Watchword

ISBN/EAN: 9783744650083

Printed in Europe, USA, Canada, Australia, Japan

Cover: Foto ©Andreas Hilbeck / pixelio.de

More available books at **www.hansebooks.com**

THE

BROTHER'S WATCHWORD.

NEW YORK:

ROBERT CARTER & BROTHERS,

No. 530 BROADWAY.

1863.

STEREOTYPED BY
SMITH & McDOUGAL
84 Beekman-st., N. Y.

PRINTED BY
E. O. JENKINS,

CONTENTS.

THE BROTHER'S WATCHWORD.

I.

THE LITTLE SISTER.

"There are in this loud stunning tide
Of human care and crime,
With whom the melodies abide
Of th' everlasting chime."

HE afternoon of a short and chill November day was fast fading into twilight. It was useless straining her eyes any longer through the evening shadow, and the dull heavy mist which accompanied it; so Georgina Archdale rose from her seat in the large bay-window, and began, though at first with rather a reluctant air, to pull down blinds and close the shutters. Those were small hands to lift that creaking bar, and pull the heavy crimson curtains; but they moved steadily and dexterously, as though well accustomed to the task; and, when the last fold was settled and arranged quite to her satisfaction, she tripped lightly across the room, and subjected the fire to the same energetic arrangement, heaping on fresh coals, till the glowing flames brightened up with their dancing, flickering light the very remotest corner of the apartment. Then a

1*

capacious easy-chair was pulled out to one side of the fire-place, and a little round table placed just in front. A small porcelain lamp, ready trimmed, but not lighted, together with a newspaper and half-a-dozen unopened letters, were duly arranged on the table: a pair of slippers embroidered on dark purple cloth were slipped just inside the bronze fender; and then the preparations seemed complete.

"He must be here now soon, I should fancy;" and with the words the little figure tripped again across the room, disappeared behind the curtains, and the shutters were heard rattling again. But looking out was more hopeless now than before: the mist had become far denser, and nothing but darkness at all perceptible; so with a slight shiver —for after the hot fire the very atmosphere of the window seemed chilly—Georgina was contented to replace the bar finally, and take up a more comfortable position on a low stool, at the opposite side of the fire-place.

A book lay open on her knees, its pages illuminated by the firelight, and she tried to read; but her attention was not much fixed. At every fancied sound she started and listened, then, when it died away, turned to her book again, and read, or appeared to do so. Thus half an hour passed; and then it was no mere illusion; horses' feet were distinctly heard coming up the road, then a stoppage, the swing of an iron gate, and steps a little slower;

a confused clattering outside the house, and then the well-known lengthened rap at the front door. Another minute, and the object of so much preparation and expectation appeared in the library.

The book dropped from Georgina's lap, as she rose to greet him. The very tall, manly figure, half hid in cloaks and wraps, which he had not tarried in the hall to disburden himself of, stooped to meet the little upstretched face, on which was bestowed a hearty kiss. There were no ecstatic expressions of joy on either side, as might have been expected from the eager waiting of the younger one; not a word indeed passed further than the murmured, heartfelt "God bless you, darling," which accompanied the first embrace, until the travelling gear was all removed, and the brother seated by the fireside in the comfortable position his little sister had assigned him. The tall form seemed more approachable then; she came and stood by his side; and, as he passed his arm around her shoulder, he said tenderly,

"And have you been very lonely, little Georgie?"

"No," she answered. But the tone seemed to belie the word; and, as he turned to look into her face, he saw the large eyes brimming full of tears, which would force their way down the child's cheek notwithstanding the smile which at the same time lighted up her pale face.

"There have not been many of these, I hope,"

he said rather gravely, but drawing her nearer as he spoke, "or I shall not like to leave you again."

"No, brother dear, not one until now, except indeed the very morning you went; but you know it is the first time we have been parted since"—here she stopped.

"I know it, Georgie," he said: "in the world where he is gone there will be no partings or separations at all for ever; it will be one long unbroken meeting. You must think of that dear, when you feel lonely here."

"I have tried, brother," she murmured softly; "and I think I have realized it a little since you have been away."

He kissed her again very fondly; and then a servant entered to say that dinner was waiting.

"Ah! I forgot," the little girl exclaimed, as she took his hand to the dining-room, "all about dinner; and how hungry you must be! why you have been travelling all the afternoon."

"Exactly, my dear; and I am rather hungry, and very glad to find myself at home once more."

On returning to the library, after dinner, they found the lamps lighted. The brother took up his former position, and began opening and perusing the letters which had arrived during his absence. Georgie drew her low stool from the place she had before occupied, to her brother's side, and sat there quietly working, with an air of happy repose on her features, very different now in their expression from what they were an hour or two before.

Let us take a nearer view of Leonard Archdale as he sits for those few minutes, busily engaged with the contents of his epistles. Very tall, and slight rather than the contrary, but neither thin nor stooping. His face is not handsome, but grave and earnest in its expression—almost stern, indeed, in its seriousness; his presence altogether such that the most giddy and unthinking would hesitate before speaking light or foolish words in his hearing. The glance of the sober gray eye was slumbering just now; but when awakened it kindled and penetrated so that the boldest quailed beneath it; and none that saw that spirit once aroused, aroused on behalf of justice, or humanity, or truth, would wish to regard him as their adversary. But the serious sobriety of countenance and demeanor was not misplaced; for Leonard Archdale was a clergyman. Of his age it seemed difficult, even at a lengthened glance, to form any correct estimate. People in general set him down as somewhere bordering on thirty; had Georgie been asked, she might have said somewhat less. His voice—and there is much in voice—seemed to accord well with his countenance; it was low, but deep, and clear, and musical; and when he spoke, you felt that all he said came just from the heart. It would seem that he had ever fixed and clear before his mental vision that sacred motto, "Let your speech be always with grace," and the account that all must render for every idle word. So amid strangers he passed for a man reserved and taciturn; among his nearer relations as one somewhat too strict and censorious in his notions, but nevertheless worthy of such an amount of respect and deference as they would accord to any other; but by his parishioners, among whom he lived, and preached, and labored, he was looked up to as a perfect model of devotedness, piety, and wisdom of every kind; his advice and counsel sought on every needed occasion, and received with the utmost affection and reverence.

In these latter feelings, as may well be imagined, his little sister largely participated; to her he was every thing, supplying at the same time the place of parents, sister, and brother. All these precious relationships she had once enjoyed; but one after another each beloved one had been taken from her; and now for the last two years these two had been left alone, the eldest and youngest of a once united and loving family. The father was the last one taken; and his death was a sudden and frightful one. He was returning home from an afternoon's drive with his little girl, when one of the horses, startled by an apparent danger, took fright, and set off at an alarming speed. The father, forgetful of the danger he was incurring, and thinking only of his child, jumped from his seat, and attempted to arrest the progress of the affrighted animals; but in vain; a more desperate plunge knocked him to

the ground : both horse and carriage passed over
his head, and left him there a lifeless corpse. The
child was saved; but the shock had been well nigh
too much for her: a dangerous illness succeeded,
from which she was long in recovering, and which
left her in a sort of nervous, sensitive state, very
unlike her former self for many months. It was
during this long illness that the links which bound
her to her brother were fastened so strongly. For-
merly she had loved him indeed, but at a distance
—not with the love she bore her father; there was
a little awe mixed up with it. He had appeared
to her very grave and unapproachable, wrapped up
in his books and studies; and then such a differ-
ence in age. But now every thing was laid aside
—studies, books, friendly engagements, and all for
her—all, that he might soothe and interest that little
pale mournful child, who for many weeks after her
father's death was never seen to smile. And in
time his efforts succeeded; a quiet calm followed
the first bursts of passionate feeling, when, after a
long confinement up stairs, Georgie came down to
take her usual place in the now diminished household, and to fulfil her daily tasks and duties. And
by degrees, too, a returning interest in life and its
pursuits came back; her brother, by his kind and
judicious management, gradually led her not indeed
to forget the past, but to look on it through the softened, hallowed light of submission. "The stroke,
though severe and agonizing, was sent by a Father's

hand, kind and always wise; and that Father was her Father, more tender, more loving by far than the earthly one taken from her." The words sank into the child's heart: she felt and believed them; and from that time her step grew lighter, and her countenance was no longer clouded and mournful. "Her Father in heaven" she could now look up to with a trusting, submissive heart, and give thanks even for her last great grief; for it had led her nearer to Him.

Leonard Archdale had been ordained not long before his father's death; and, about six months after that event, he went to take possession of the living at Beechwood, given him, notwithstanding his extreme youth, by the Bishop of U——, a distant relative, who well knew his worth and active energy. So they left the old home, and with it much that was bitter in the way of association from the loss of many dear ones; and now they had found a new, and in most respects a happy one, in the rectory of Beechwood, an unpretending village in one of the midland counties. The brother and sister had but few relatives: the nearest was Sir William Archdale, their father's elder brother. He had a large family; and with them, at the time my tale commences, Leonard had been spending a day or two, in his way from London, where he had been called on urgent business a week beforehand.

When the last letter was finished, Mr. Archdale turned to his little sister—"Well, Georgie," he said, "we were so busy during dinner discussing home affairs, that you seem to have forgotten to ask me any particulars about my adventures."

"Yes, I have lots of things to ask about when you are quite ready," she answered; and dropping her work, she drew still closer to his side, folded her arms across his knee, and looked up in his face.

"Begin, then, dear; what is the first?"

"Well, I hardly know where to begin," she replied, laughing: "I want to hear about the wedding, when Cousin Clara is to be married, how you liked Mr. Isbel, whether my other cousins seem sorry to lose her, and a great many things besides."

Leonard smiled. "I suppose I may as well, then, begin with the most important piece of news first. The wedding comes off the week before Christmas; and you are invited to go, and act the part of a bridesmaid I suppose, on the occasion."

"O, Leonard!" exclaimed she, her face lighting up for a moment, but instantly becoming sobered again; "but I am not going."

"Why not, my dear? Yes, I have promised you should."

"O, Leonard!" was all she said again, in a tone of mingled surprise and sorrow.

"Do you not like to go, Georgie? I am sorry, dear; but I thought now you might not mind."

"For some things I shall like it, Leonard," she answered, after a little; "you will be there, of course, because you are going to help to marry

2

Clara, and so it will not seem so bad as going away from home."

" I shall only be there a very little of the time; you know I can not be spared."

"Then how long am I to stay?" she inquired rather mournfully.

" A month was the shortest time they would hear of; so I said I would try and spare you as long as that. But, Georgie, darling, come, tell me why it is you don't like going to Leighton; so many cousins, and your uncle and aunt longing to see you; I am only afraid you will be a little spoiled, and unwilling to come back to your lonely bachelor-brother again."

" Leonard, you must not say so," she replied.

" Tell me your reasons then, dear; have you any besides not liking to leave me ?"

" Yes, one or two," she answered, rather evasively, and looking down as she spoke.

" Tell me them."

"I think I had rather not, Leonard, if you don't mind."

"I do mind, Georgie, dear; I want to know." He spoke very kindly but decidedly; and the little girl never thought of refusing when he spoke so.

" I am afraid it will be very gay there," she said in a low tone; "I shall have to stay over Christmas; and perhaps there will be parties and company; and, brother, you remember your sermon last Sunday ?"

"Which one?" he asked.

"About walking with God; and you said how much more difficult it was when we are in worldly company, or among people that do not love God most of all; and I felt happy then, because I was not exposed to that temptation; and I do not want to be, dear Leonard."

"My love," said Leonard gravely, "you are very right, and far be it from me to put you in the way of any temptation which might lead you aside from a close walk with God; but, Georgie, dear, do you expect never to come in contact with the world?"

"I must, I suppose, some day," she answered doubtfully.

"Yes, dear, you must; but I want you to remember that there is such a thing as being *in* the world, but not *of* it; and when you find yourself thrown among those who love the world better than God, you must pray for grace to show by your daily walk and demeanor how far more satisfying and enduring your pleasures are than those which they look upon as such. Which do you think would be the most valued and honored soldier—one that had been exposed to many hard-fought battles and dangerous assaults from cruel and malignant enemies, or one who had lived quietly in his tent all his life, without so much as ever having seen the foe, from the fear of being wounded, or proving cowardly at the last?"

"O, the first, dear Leonard; but the tent does seem the safest place for the weak ones."

"Listen, Georgie," her brother said, taking a small volume from his pocket, and reading: 'The conquering commander triumpheth; yet had he not conquered unless he had fought; and, the more peril there was in the battle, so much the more joy is there in the triumph.'* You would like to have the joy of triumphing at last, would you not?"

"O yes: but I am so weak, so constantly turning aside, even here."

"I know it; and did I not feel persuaded that you have an arm stronger than your own to lean on, I would not wish you even to approach the enemy's grounds. I do think you will find Leighton Hall quite different from any thing you have been accustomed to; more time and thought given to things of no real value, and heaven and its realities thrown into the background. But you will have the same strength there as here, if you seek it. You must pray, and I shall pray for you, dearest, that, during the short time you are there, you may be enabled to let your little light shine before men, and to keep your garments unspotted from the world."

The little girl looked up again into her brother's face as he spoke: it was more than usually grave and earnest; and she felt that, if that calm serious presence were always near her, she should be in less danger of going astray. Perhaps he guessed a

* St. Augustine's Confessions.

little what was passing in her mind; for he repeated slowly and impressively those words, " The joy of the Lord is your strength ;" and she felt that any thing human, however excellent, was far too weak to lean upon—that whatever strength she needed must come from on high.

After a few minutes' silence, Leonard asked, " Was that your only other reason, Georgie ?"

She colored. " O there was another ; but it was a very wrong and wicked one; so do not ask me to tell."

" Is that any reason you should hide it from me ?"

" No," she replied ; and then with a great effort, and hiding her head upon her folded arms as she pronounced the words, " My cousins are all so beautiful !" And then she added—for Leonard was silent for some moments—"O, brother, do not despise me ; you wished me to tell you all ; and the thought was there, so I could not deceive you."

Mr. Archdale felt very far from despising the little pale and now weeping face that rested on his knee; but he did feel some surprise, never having guessed for a moment that such thoughts were passing in her breast. He said gently at last, " ' Even the ornament of a meek and quiet spirit, which is in the sight of God of great price.' I do not despise you in the least, Georgie ; I only thank you for the confidence you have placed in me. Your cousins are no doubt outwardly much more beauti-

ful than you ; but, as long as you are adorned with
that ornament of which St. Peter speaks, it matters
very little whether your face be plain or handsome ; and all the beauty in the world is vain and
contemptible without it. You know this, Georgie,
as well as I do, and feel it too, I think."

"Yes, yes," was the answer between her tears ;
"and O, Leonard, I do feel sorry for having indulged in such thoughts."

"Lay this, with all your other feelings of sin, at
the foot of the cross, dear Georgie ; and you need
not think it a strange thing that has happened to
you. Our hearts are prone to every kind of sin,
and that of pride overtakes us in a thousand ways ;
a desire to be admired and thought well of by
others is one of the most common. Young as you
are, I know you often find this, and it is a thing you
must specially watch and strive against. Pray that
you may be willing to be thought little, even nothing of, in keeping close to God, rather than be
courted and esteemed by your fellow-creatures in a
path of careless unwatchfulness."

II.

A WORD IN SEASON.

"The tears we shed for sin,
  When heaven alone can see,
Leave truer peace within
  Than worldly smiles, which cannot be
Lit up, my God, with smiles from thee."
                                    MONSELL.

AFTER his sister had left him for the night, Leonard Archdale sat for a long time in rather an anxious fit of meditation. The conversation which had just passed had somewhat unsettled his mind as to the desirableness of the step he had taken in consenting to Georgina's visiting his uncle's family, even for the short time mentioned. He had seemed at the time in a manner forced to agree to the proposal; and even now he felt that it could not be set aside, notwithstanding the evident shrinking both had to the temporary separation, and the trial he felt it would be to one whose principles had never before had occasion to be tried, and consequently might prove weak and easily overcome. He would have saved her this her first initiation into the ways of the world, as they are called, had it been in his power; but, on lengthened consideration, he felt it was not.

Sir William Archdale, his uncle, was joint guardian with himself to Georgina; and many many times since her father's death had he urged the wish that part of her time should be spent at his own country residence, Leighton Hall; or, if not a regular portion of each year, that at any rate she should make a lengthened visit, and become more acquainted with her cousins, of whom during all her life she had seen but very little. Leonard, however, had hitherto managed to decline all these invitations. There was the plea of ill-health; for, at the best of times, Georgie was not strong, and the air of Beechwood seemed to agree with her. Then his own isolated position, with no one but herself to bear him company—it would seem hard to deprive him of her. And, lastly, the little girl's extreme reluctance to the thought of leaving home and him; all these excuses had hitherto served; and Georgie had not yet seen Leighton.

But, during his last visit, Leonard had been afresh assailed with new and very urgent entreaties on the visiting question, and found that none of the former excuses were at all admissible. Sir William, indeed, grew warm on the subject.

"It is all very well, Leonard," he said to him, "this plan of yours of bringing up your sister by herself, in that remote corner of the country, without a creature of her own station to associate with; but a little bit selfish at bottom. We want to enjoy a little of her company as well as yourself;

and, besides, this recluse system does not answer. If she is never to see any thing of the world beyond Beechwood, the young lady will be a perfect ascetic, and be troubled before long with fits of melancholy, and morbid notions of every description. You must let her free a little, indeed you must, if you ever wish her to make any thing of a figure in the world."

"That is the last thing I desire for her," said Leonard, shortly. But his uncle appeared not to notice the shade on his brow, and continued:

"And, as for her health, why, the change would do her an immensity of good: pure air, and a healthy place this, Leonard. You say she is looking pale: a month or two here would soon bring the rose into her cheeks, I'll answer for it. Then, 'tis the best possible place to be ill in. Dr. Selfield in the house every other day to see your aunt, so that if any thing was the matter it could soon be set right. You seem afraid to trust her among us, eh, Leonard?"

He was about to reply, when the entrance of other members of the family put an end to the conversation for that evening. The following morning, however, it was renewed; and, finding that Sir William was determined to gain his point, and that farther objection might appear at the very least ungrateful, if not leading to more serious consequences, Mr. Archdale at last gave way, and promised that the long talked of visit should be made, and

Georgina should accompany him to Leighton in
about a month's time; when, as the little girl herself had expressed it, he was to return to help to
marry Clara.

Of course this would involve her being one of
the younger bridesmaids; and the cousins were
well pleased with the arrangement.

Leonard himself could only promise to remain
till the day after the wedding; but Georgie he said
he would leave behind for a month, that being the
longest time he could possibly consent to spare her.
With this understanding he was allowed to depart
peaceably; though Sir William assured him that
the visit should be repeated in the summer, and for
a much longer period. Leonard's anxiety extended not so far as that; it was the first touch of as-
similation that he dreaded most; and now the
sooner that was passed the better.

"I breathe more freely!" exclaimed Frances
Archdale, snatching up the third volume of a novel,
and throwing herself into a capacious easy-chair by
the side of the fire. The words were spoken just
as the front door closed, and the carriage, which was
conveying Leonard to the station, drove rapidly
down the avenue leading from Leighton Hall. The
speaker was a tall and very handsome girl, Sir
William's second daughter; and she addressed herself to her elder sister, who was engaged with
rather a complex pattern of embroidery, and who

only looked up and smiled at the words and the mock sigh which accompanied them.

"I don't know how you have felt," she continued, in the same gay, rattling tone; "but, as for me, I have scarcely dared speak, move, or look, the last day or two, for fear of bringing down some tremendous reprimand on my innocent head from his stern majesty who has just departed. I have been very nearly having it too, I am certain, more than once or twice. He gave such an intense look last night when I unluckily mentioned the word 'ball,' that I made good my escape, and took care to avoid a tête-à-tête afterwards. Clara, can you endure such fearfully grave good people ?"

"Leonard is wonderfully clever," was her sister's reply.

"Yes, I know that, of course; but it only makes it all the worse, because he prides himself on being so much more learned than the rest of the world, and sits up in his stateliness and silence as though one was not worth being spoken to."

"I don't think Leonard is vain, or even proud," said Clara. "And how can you talk of silence? Why, I thought Dr. Welldon and he would never have left off with their discussions last night; and really he argued admirably."

"That may be; because he considers Dr. Welldon as a being not quite so contemptible as mankind in general, and so he gave himself the trouble to be a little sociable with him."

"He chatted with papa, too, pleasantly enough; and mamma said she quite enjoyed the half hour he sat with her," Clara replied, without looking up from her work.

"Clara," exclaimed Frances, growing impatient at the pertinacity with which her sister defended one who was not there to defend himself, "you know this is all nonsense, and that in the bottom of your heart you dislike Leonard Archdale, with his strict notions and censorious ways, as thoroughly as I do."

Clara colored a little. She did not wish to be untruthful; and perhaps, at the very bottom of her heart, as her sister said, she did dislike, or at any rate had disliked him as much as she. But she was feeling rather differently just now, and answered, warmly, "Well, and if I do, it is not a particular sign of good sense or taste, perhaps; but it is not that. I have no feeling of positive dislike, but that of most entire uncongeniality. We live in two completely different worlds. I, in one of enjoyment, of gaiety, and pleasure of any kind; he in a higher, I own, and *perhaps* a not less happy one, of thought, and intellect, and religion. Yes, real religion, I believe," she added thoughtfully. "And that is what makes him so different from the rest of us. For my own part I can not enter into it. I never did, and never shall, I am afraid, be able to like it; and yet, in him it attracts me. There is always something of repose and fascina tion in his presence, though I always feel so immensely far below him, and can not help thinking also, as you say, that he considers himself very many degrees above us. But, perhaps, we are wrong in this: he is naturally so reserved. And only think what troubles he has gone through—enough to make any one sober and religious. Then he is a clergyman; and so it is only proper."

"Well, I should begin to tremble for poor Arthur, if I did not know that matter was settled," said Frances laughingly.

"Ah! there is no occasion to tremble for him." And the sister's face, which had become a little grave and thoughtful, brightened again. "Arthur Isbel and I are most thoroughly congenial. We mean to go through life smoothly and enjoyably, looking only on the bright side of things, and not on what will make us gloomy, and morose, and disagreeable, to other people and ourselves."

"Is Georgie like him?" inquired Frances, after a few moments' silence. "It is to be hoped not, or I pity poor Augusta, as she will have most to do with her, I suppose."

"O, no; at least not when I saw her; but that is three or four years ago now, and she may be altered. Nothing could be merrier and brighter than she was then; but she felt our uncle's death so dreadfully, you know, and has never been thoroughly well since, I believe.

"Poor child! Well, we had better expect the

3

worst, and do our best to enliven her up, if she needs it. But, now for a little quiet. I have been almost dying the last two days to know the end of this tale; but I was obliged to hide away my unfortunate book, for fear of a surprise and reprimand."

. Frances was soon buried in the contents of her book, Clara in her work, and pleasant imaginings of the bright future in store for her, when suddenly and rather noisily the door opened, and a boy, apparently about sixteen years of age, entered the room. He was not a brother of the family, evidently: not one single line or feature bore the slightest resemblance to the countenances of the two beautiful girls whose presence he thus unceremoniously broke in upon. His dress was not of the neatest arrangement—the white turn-down collar being crumpled, and the neck-tie fastened one-sidedly in a knot, and ends flying. The little cap, which he did not trouble himself to doff, was pulled down over his forehead, which otherwise would not have been very distinguishable, from the waves of black hair which overhung it. His complexion was dark, the glance of his eye was restless, and the prevailing expression of his countenance indomitable pride, rendered only more sensitive and keen by the very fact that he was placed in a somewhat dependent situation—a thought ever galling to an uncontrolled and undisciplined nature.

"Where is Leonard Archdale?" he asked in a

tone of forced civility, and glancing round the room as he spoke.

The sisters, who had both looked up on his first entrance, resumed their respective occupations on perceiving who the intruder was; and it was not till he repeated his question yet more impatiently that Frances replied, in a careless way, "I don't know, I'm sure." It was her usual answer to Walter's inquiries: and, whether correct or not, it saved her some trouble.

Clara laughed, and said, "You do, Francie! What are you thinking of?"

Walter's small stock of patience was fast fading away. "Will you tell me or not where Mr. Archdale is?" he exclaimed for the third time.

"I have not the smallest objection to tell you," said his elder cousin; "but one would think you might know as well as the rest of us that he has been gone for the last two hours."

"Gone!" said the boy, in a voice that made his cousin look up. She caught the expression of his face for a moment; it was such a mingling of pain and disappointment that even she might have been troubled for him; but it was only for a moment. The haughty look instantly returned, and, with a muttered "Thanks for your trouble," he quitted the room, slamming the door violently behind him.

"What a clown that boy is!" exclaimed Frances; "think of his coming in here with his cap on, and always disturbing when he isn't wanted."

"He never seems to know, either, the commonest thing that other people do," said Clara. "He won't take the trouble to listen or inquire, and then is cross enough if he is not told. What on earth should he want with Leonard, I wonder?"

Poor Walter! What did he want? That which he would most certainly have obtained, had he found the opportunity of demanding it—counsel, sympathy, a friend. He had not one in the whole wide world; and he had brought his proud heart, which was yet a wise one in some points, to consent to ask advice from one who was the best calculated to bestow it.

It had cost him something to make up his mind; much wavering and doubt and questioning with himself how such a manifestation of confidence would be received; for he knew absolutely nothing of Leonard, had never seen him till within the last two days; during which time not half-a-dozen sentences had passed between them. But he had listened to his words with others, had marked his serious, consistent deportment, and had judged, and rightly too, that there was that in him very different from the rest of the family among whom he was thrown. And so he had determined to seek an interview, lay open his difficulties, and the trying position which he conceived he occupied in his uncle's family, and perhaps confess something of his own delinquencies; for conscience told Walter that his behaviour was not always blameless. He fancied he could take reproof from that calm, dignified, although stern cousin of his, without any very great mortification of his natural pride; and, to carry out his plan, he had hastened home earlier than usual from his tutor in the neighboring town, and, as we have seen, found his opportunity gone.

After leaving the library, he wandered moodily through the house. At the hall door he met his cousin Augusta and her governess just setting out on their usual morning walk. He addressed the former bitterly.

"You might as well have done what I asked you last night: your promises just mean nothing; so I hope you will keep them to yourself in future."

"O! about Leonard; how could I tell when he' was going? You have eyes and ears as well as I," she answered with provoking indifference.

"You expect me to hear all your private arrangements when I am two miles off at Campbell's, I suppose," said Walter, looking up almost fiercely from under his hair and cap. "Well, it is just of a piece with it all; a selfish, conceited set," he murmured, as he pushed his cap still lower over his brows, and walked off in another direction. "And I—I have been a fool for thinking any one belonging to them could be otherwise. I am glad that fellow's gone, after all. I might have said a little too much, and he have gone and betrayed me. There's no trust to be put in one of them—to think how that girl

3*

promised last night that she would let me know if
he left before noon.   O to be free of them all!"

And, to give a turn to his feelings, Walter went
on a visit to the stables, and Turner, the stable-boy.

Clara went up to her room that evening, to dress
for the dancing-party to which her sister had alluded.
There was a parcel, directed to her, lying on the
table.   It was a handsome present from Leonard,
in anticipation of her approaching marriage.   En-
closed in a separate paper were two smaller ar-
ticles, and a letter.   One was a gold locket, containing a beautiful miniature of her aunt, Leonard's
mother, whose name Clara bore, and to whom, as a
child, she had been greatly attached ; the other was
a small Italian psalter, which Mrs. Archdale had
been in the habit of using constantly.   Strange
feelings passed through Clara's mind as she handled
these mementos of one whom she had loved, and
who was passed away.   Not many years since, and
she had been young and beautiful, and full of life
as herself; and now, where was she ?   In the dreary
silent tomb.   Clara thought of nothing beyond that
—at least of nothing more cheering.   A cold,
dreamy, lifeless existence of spirit she might picture ; but from this she shrunk even more than
from the silence and stillness of annihilation.   Who
could say ?   Her aunt had died in the prime of life,
she might be taken off yet earlier.   She had heard
of cases of sudden death ; what if she should not
live even to see her wedding-day !   There was

nothing to make her fancy she should not; but the thought of death came over her, as she gazed on the features of the departed one; and then she could not banish it. It was a thought from which she always shrank; it did not often trouble her; and, when it did, she had generally managed to drown it by company, or entertaining books, or exciting amusements; and she had always found this plan answer; "for the cares of the world, and the deceitfulness of riches, and the lust of other things, entering in," will choke the word, will blunt the arrows of conviction, and the fruit of everlasting life and peace cannot be brought forth.

She took up her cousin's letter, broke the seal, then laid it down again, went to her drawers, and began arranging the dress and ornaments she intended to wear that night. But in vain: she could not rouse herself from the depressing thoughts gathering in her breast. She blamed Leonard for having sent her such wedding gifts, then herself for choosing such a time to examine them. "I might have guessed there would be something gloomy," she murmured inwardly. She returned to the dressing-table, and again took up the letter. "Shall I read it, or burn it?" she thought, glancing at the fire, which at that moment blazed up temptingly. Conscience gained the victory. She unfolded it, and read. The first words were what might have been expected from any one—kind and thoughtful congratulations on the approaching epoch of her life.

Then, in connexion with the smaller gifts he had
sent her, he alluded in touching words to the memory of his mother. " Deeply, bitterly as I have
felt her loss, dear Clara, I would not call her back
from that happy glorious rest on which she has entered. And now, with her calm holy countenance
smiling as it were upon me, I feel emboldened to
ask you if you are prepared, when the conflict of
this life is over, for the rest she now enjoys ? You
do not find it a conflict, perhaps you will tell me.
Ah ! I wish you did. There is no victory without
combat : the sweetest joys are born of trouble and
anguish. Are you living for the glory of God, or
for your own pleasure and gratification merely ?
'I fear hell,' perhaps you will say, 'and I should
like to obtain heaven.' That is not enough, dear
Clara ; with such feelings, instead of longing for the
presence of God, it might be a relief to your mind
to hear that there was no such Being at all, provided
your happiness after death were insured, or, at any
rate, your freedom from punishment. You do not
wish for heaven in order to enjoy communion with
the Highest; for you know his service here is distasteful to you ; you simply desire it as an escape
from the punishment of hell. Am I going too far
in supposing this is the case with you ? Your own
conscience will tell you if I am, and tell you also
that your state is one of fearful danger. And, if
not, let me, in saying Good bye, give you a few
words of blessed invitation and encouragement.

'Return unto the Lord, and he will have mercy upon you; and to our God, for he will abundantly pardon you:' 'When he was yet a great way off, the father saw him, and had compassion:' 'Before ye call, I will answer; while ye are yet speaking, I will hear.' And, should the Holy Spirit of God convince you now of your sin, and your heart whisper in silent anguish, 'What can I do?' let me warn you in the words of a holy man of God, long since gone to his rest, that 'If a traveller sleep or trifle most of the day, he must travel so much the faster in the evening, or fall short of his journey's end.' It may not be evening with you as yet; but still is it not ever true that 'the night cometh?' "

Clara ceased reading, clasped her hands over her eyelids, and burst into a tumult of tears. "It is true—true," she murmured; "my life has been more than wasted. I am not fit for heaven. I cannot with sincerity call God my Father; and yet he is. O Lord!" she prayed, and perhaps it was the first true prayer that she had ever offered, "teach me to love thee; teach me to feel that thou art my Father; help me to live as thy child."

O can we doubt that such prayers are answered? The Father was dealing with his wayward and wandering one in a way which she understood not at first. He was teaching her, and that not by the rough loud tumult of whirlwind and fire, but by the still small voice of parental love to cry, "My Father, thou shalt be the Guide of my youth."

Gaiety and worldly smiles had no attraction for Clara that night. How can they, when the heart is filled with better and nobler longings? Do not the stars grow pale before the light of the rising sun? So must the uncertain flickerings of this world's show and glory fade quite away when the love of God and his Son is revealed to the mental gaze. She sat some time reading the words of her cousin's letter over and over again, and more especially the blessed, precious words which were not his.

Frances entered the room at last, gaily dressed.

"Clara! not ready? The carriage is at the door. What, dearest, are you ill?" she said, seeing, as her sister looked up, traces of tears on her face.

"No, not ill, dear; but I shall stay at home with mamma to-night. You know," she added, smiling rather sadly, "I shall not have many more opportunities: you and Lloyd will go quite well without me."

"What is it, dear?" said Frances; for with all her faults she was an affectionate girl; "I am certain something has happened."

Clara put Leonard's letter into her sister's hand. She glanced rapidly over the first page.

"Ah! well; I'll read it another time. He has been lecturing you instead of me, it appears. What a shame! And you, like a dear foolish girl, have been making your eyes red, and not fit to be seen —all about nothing, I dare say."

"Hush hush!" said Clara, entreatingly; "and do go, dear Francie—hark! Lloyd is calling you."

III.

NEW SCENES.

"Yet oft these hearts will whisper
    That better 'twould betide
  If we were near the friends we love,
    And watching by their side.
  But sure thou'lt love them dearer, Lord,
    For trusting thee alone !
  And sure thou wilt draw nearer, Lord,
    The farther we are gone !
  Then why be sad ? since thou wilt keep
    Watch o'er them day by day ;
  Since thou wilt soothe them when they weep,
    And hear us when we pray."
                                    MONSELL.

"MAY I go into the village with you this morning, Leonard ?" asked Georgina, as she put
away the books she had been employed
with for some hours.

She always spent her mornings with her brother
in the library. He studied, and she studied too, he
often ceasing from his work to direct hers, and she
at times plodding on alone when he appeared so absorbed that she thought it almost cruel to disturb
him. His afternoons he devoted to visiting his
schools and parishioners, Georgie often accompanying him to the houses of the poorer ones, and helping in the school.

" Yes, by all means, dear," her brother answered.
" Do you wish to go anywhere in particular?"

"I should like to call on Margaret, and tell her
all about it—about my intended visit, you know, I
mean," seeing her brother looked somewhat at a
loss to comprehend her allusion.

"Very well; that will do nicely. I have to go
across the common to see old John Hilman. You
and Margaret will want a long talk no doubt; so I
can call for you on my return."

"Thank you," said Georgina; "I will be ready
in a minute."

It was a brighter morning than there had been
for some days past; the sun had succeeded in pen-
etrating through the misty atmosphere, and it
seemed almost pleasant without doors. Georgina
was in spirits at having her brother once more with
her; she had found her every-day walks very dull
and uninteresting without him; and during his absence Margaret had been feeble, and so unable to
accompany her.

She had been obliged to content herself, for protection's sake, with the company of the housekeeper,
Mrs. Airey, a stiff and rather unsociable dame, with
whom Georgina had never as yet been able to feel
quite at ease, partly owing to her own natural reserve, partly to the taciturn and somewhat morose
temperament of the good woman herself.

They passed through the garden shrubbery at the
back of the rectory, out into the open road. A

slight turn brought them into the principal street of the village. Street, however, it might scarcely be called; a long wide lane, with cottages here and there on either side, being a more suitable definition. It must have been a pleasant spot in summer time ; the large spreading trees, now so bare and leafless, gave promise of what a refreshing sight they might present when clothed with verdure, and the little garden-plots in front of nearly every house told plainly that the inhabitants of Beechwood were not deficient in that perception common alike to high and low, rich and poor—the natural love of flowers.

The brother and sister proceeded a full quarter of a mile up the straggling village, and there stopped at the gate of a little trellised pleasant-looking house, standing some way back from the road. Rose Cottage it was called, and doubtless during some seasons of the year well merited its name, though now not a single leaf gave evidence of what might be.

They parted here. Georgie ran up the garden-walk ; and her brother called after her, " In rather more than an hour, Georgie; my love to Mrs. Murray and Margaret."

The door was opened before she reached the house; and in another minute she found herself in the snug sitting-room with Margaret, and her mother.

Margaret Murray had since Georgina's arrival in Beechwood been her constant and only friend. Rather her senior in age, and with a character more

4

matured and tried, she nevertheless resembled Georgina in many points. Both were naturally reserved and timid; both had always loved books and study better than amusement; and, perhaps partly from the very fact of having seen so little of it, and partly from having, young as they both were, their thoughts and highest affections set on objects not of this earth's giving, both had an undefinable dread of entering into the world; and nothing seemed more desirable to either than the prospect of living on, in the quiet retirement of Beechwood, each with the friend who was dearest to her on earth.

Mrs. Murray had been a widow for many years. Her husband, major Murray, had died in India, where also Margaret was born, who inherited, as is so often the case, the frail, delicate constitution of English children born under a tropical sun. Margaret's education had been entirely carried on by her mother, who was a woman of remarkable talent and natural endowments. Since Georgina had come to Beechwood, she also had shared in Mrs. Murray's kindly instruction. Masters there were none in the neighborhood; so Mr. Archdale had thankfully accepted her offer of helping his sister in the musical and drawing department; and, as Georgina inherited much of his own natural ability, she was a very satisfactory pupil; and association in their afternoon pursuits strengthened the friendship which soon had formed between the two young girls.

Mrs. Murray was a truly Christian woman; and her first care from the very hour of her child's birth had been, not that she should make a distinguished and brilliant figure in the world, but that her heart should be, while young, given up to God, and her whole life a preparation for eternity. And, O, they err who say that parents' prayers and tears and efforts are unavailing before God, and that early religious training is futile and unsatisfactory at best! There are indeed numerous and painful instances of the children of some of God's most devoted servants growing up to be the sorrow and affliction of those who gave them birth; but does it not more frequently result from the lack of prayer and watchfulness, and judicious restraint, rather than from the excess of it?

Mrs. Murray soon left the girls to themselves; and then the younger disclosed the great piece of intelligence, which was received with as much surprise and regret by Margaret as it before had been by Georgina. But on talking it over quietly between themselves the thing soon appeared somewhat less formidable. "Such a short time—and her brother to be with her partly."

"Only a day or two just at first, dear; because you know he must come home on the Saturday; but he will come and fetch me, and perhaps stay a little longer then."

"We can write to one another," suggested Margaret; "I am fond of having letters."

"I never get any," replied Georgina. "Yes, that will be delightful. Suppose you write every day, dear; then it will hardly seem like being away from you."

"I am afraid I shall not be able, quite so often," said Margaret; "but I will try once or twice a week, at any rate."

"Thank you; and," said the other, speaking rather low, and pressing the hand she held more tightly, "you know what I shall need most of all, dear Margaret. Leonard talked to me last night so kindly, so cheeringly; and he said he would pray for me. Will you too, dear?"

"Yes, Georgie, I always do."

"But especially. O Margaret, do you know, after all, I have such a dread of going to Leighton? Strange faces, strange ways; and it takes me so long to know a person. And I am sure I shall feel so differently from them all. I know I shall be afraid of my uncle and my cousins, and of their governess. She is French, you know; and perhaps my fear of them may lead me to do things which are not right."

Margaret kissed her seriously.

"I should feel very much like you, Georgie dear; and I don't exactly know what to say to help you, except that our fear of God ought to be greater than our fear of any one besides. I don't exactly mean fear either, but our love to him, and desire to please him; and I think when we feel really anxious to serve him most of all, he will be sure to help us." And then she added less seriously, "And I am sure you need not be afraid of the French governess. Mamma had one once; and she often tells me about her, and how dearly she loved her."

Just then Mr. Archdale's figure was seen approaching the gate.

"Do ask him to come in," Margaret said; "mamma would so like it." But he walked up the little garden without invitation; and Georgie ran to open the door and call Mrs. Murray.

"Well, Margaret," he said, walking up to the fire near which she was standing, and taking both her hands in his, "you are better, I hope."

"Yes, much, thank you," she answered.

"And have you been able to work at all, since I have been away?"

She caught his meaning instantly, and looked up to him with something of the love, though with more of reverence, than Georgie would have shown.

"Not much, I am afraid, Mr. Archdale. I seem to have had so few opportunities."

"Not very manifest ones, perhaps, but still always some opportunities. 'The trivial round, the common task'—you know the rest."

"O yes; and those little daily trials and self-denyings are sometimes the most difficult, do you not think?" she said, timidly. "At least it is where *I* fail so very, very often."

4*

"Indeed I do, Margaret; and yet, when the walk is quite close with God, even they are easy."

Mrs. Murray came in just then with Georgina, and greeted Leonard kindly, telling him that for even those few days they had missed him, and were thankful to welcome his face again.

"I just looked in," he said, "to give you another pensioner, that is, if you are at liberty to take one. Poor old Hilman, across the common: he is very ailing, nearly blind, and no one at all to look after him. His daughter-in-law, who lives in our village, goes over every day for an hour or two; but for all besides he is dependent on strangers. He is a good man, and would feel most thankful if you or Margaret would sometimes go and read with him for half-an-hour. I think you would soon feel interested in him; and perhaps you would kindly see to his being supplied with soup, or anything else necessary, and let me know."

"I will." Mrs. Murray answered, "and thank you for mentioning him. How did you leave all your friends, Mr. Archdale? sir William and lady Archdale?"

"My aunt is much the same as when I last saw her, quite the invalid, and confined to her own rooms, except on very rare occasions when she takes a short drive, cushioned up in the carriage: she is just the same as ever—very sweet and gentle."

"Ah! I should scarcely know her now," said

Mrs. Murray: "it is so many years since we met; but have they not now living with them a son of captain Lockyer, her brother-in-law?"

"They have," said Leonard.

"And what sort of a youth is he? I knew his dear mamma so well, much more intimately than lady Archdale, and a sweeter, more beautiful creature I never saw. Is he like her?"

Leonard shook his head gravely. "I did not see much of him, but fear from what sir William says that he is anything but what he should be, and that they may have trouble with him. He appears to associate very little with the rest of the family; and there is a kind of sullen indifference about him, even in the little that I observed, which is very unpleasing."

"What profession is he to follow?" she inquired. "He must be sixteen or seventeen years old now, I should think?"

"I don't know," Leonard replied seriously: "with such a disposition as his, it seems difficult to know exactly what to decide on. I did not like to say much: I fancy there is an uncomfortable feeling on both sides; still, I feel for the boy."

"Poor fellow!" said Mrs. Murray. "I shall always feel an interest in him for his mother's sake. Is he dark? His father was such a tall handsome man."

"Yes, very dark, gloomy-looking, repulsive, I might almost say, in his manner, but fine features.

However, as I said before, I scarcely saw him except just at meals. I should have liked a little
talk with him ; but my time was so very limited :
Georgina will tell us more particulars of all when
she returns. I have promised her to them for a
few weeks after her cousin's wedding."

" Have you indeed ?" said Mrs. Murray. " Well,
I hope the visit may be a pleasant one in every
respect."

" I am afraid we neither of us anticipate it as
such," said her brother; " I cannot bear parting
with her; and she feels it a great trouble to go.
But I trust it will be for the best. Are you ready,
dear ?" he continued, turning to his sister, who was
looking at a new drawing with Margaret.

" Yes, whenever you are," she answered. " Margaret is coming to us to-morrow, if she is better,
for the day."

" That is well," replied Leonard, and they took
leave.

Georgie's last day at Beechwood came only too
soon. Margaret and her mamma spent the evening before at the rectory. Had it been a parting
for many years, it could scarcely have been con-
templated more sorrowfully. The girls sat together on a low seat near the fire, Margaret's arm
passed round her friend, and her thoughtful eyes
gazing down upon her, full of love and affection.
Leonard stood at the other side of the fire, his
elbow resting on the chimney-piece, his eyes turned

on the same object as were Margaret's. Painful thoughts were in his heart: none could look on his countenance or attitude and doubt it.

Mrs. Murray was seated near. Her eyes wandered from one to the other of the little group, and then rested on the fire, but her face was not sad. She rose at last, and, going to the organ, commenced a touching little air which was familiar to them all:

> " Saviour and Lord of all,
> We lift our hearts to thee:
> Guide us and guard us
> Where'er we be.
>
> When we are full of grief,
> Victims of anxious fear,
> Save us, O save us!
> Jesus, be near!
>
> Brighten the darkest hour,
> Till our last hour be come;
> Then, in thy power,
> O take us home."

She accompanied the music with her soft clear voice; and the spell of sadness and dejection seemed instantly broken. One by one, Mr. Archdale first, then Margaret, and then Georgina herself, all joined in, till the walls of the room seemed to re-echo the sweet strains of that parting melody. When it was ended, Georgie rang the bell, and the servants assembled for the accustomed evening worship. The final parting afterwards was not so

sad and tearful as the former part of the evening
had promised; and, as Leonard shook hands with
Mrs. Murray, he said, "Thank you. You have
given me another lesson to-night. I am ashamed
of my despondency and distrust. The future
seems hallowed now; or at least my dread of it is
gone."

It was quite evening ere the travellers reached
Leighton Hall. The carriage had been sent for
them to the railway-station at Barnes, from which
place sir William Archdale's country-seat was
about three miles distant.

Georgie's heart beat more quickly as they stopped at the first lodge, and then proceeded rapidly
up the broad drive leading through the park.

"We could see the house now, if it were light,"
remarked Leonard presently. He lowered one
window for a moment; and Georgie stretched out
her head into the frosty air, and could just distin-
guish an ill-defined black square of building, with
lights gleaming here and there.

It must have appeared formidable to her; for
she speedily drew in her head, leaned back again
in the carriage by Leonard's side, and sighed heavily.

"What makes this strange oppression at my
heart?" she murmured. "Dear Leonard, can it
be all timidity?"

"Perhaps not," he answered musingly; for he
felt the oppression too. His tone was too ab-

stracted for her to say more; and, after a few minutes of perfect silence on both sides, the carriage stopped.

The hall-door was quickly opened; and servants appeared on the steps with lights, and assisted the travellers to dismount.

Tired and weary with the long journey, an unusual thing for her, Georgie, who shielded herself by her brother's side, took not much heed of the objects around her. The spacious hall, with its surrounding gallery, hung with massively-framed pictures; the wide marble staircase; the statues, holding in their hands elegant lamps, from which jets of gas-light brightly issued—all seemed to pass unnoticed before her eyes; and she awoke first to a sense of the reality of her position on finding herself in a large and richly-furnished apartment. Sounds of music, singing, and conversation, mingled with peals of laughter, broke upon her ear as the door opened, but ceased when the company within became aware of her own and her brother's presence.

"Come at last," exclaimed several voices almost simultaneously; and the next moment Georgina felt herself seized upon by one or two soft pairs of hands, parted from her brother's sheltering arm, to which her own clung almost nervously, and conveyed to the upper part of the room, where a large fire was blazing, around which a group of ladies and gentlemen were assembled.

What an ordeal for the poor, timid, bashful Georgie! There she stood, very pale, before that great blaze of gas and firelight, the little purple-velvet bonnet pushed back from her forehead, and locks of fair hair straying down, one hand still held between those of a tall and dignified gentleman, who she is informed is her uncle, the other nervously engaged in unfastening the buttons of her fur-trimmed jacket, the heat of which is becoming oppressive in that warm light room.

Who might be relations, and who strangers, she is as yet perfectly unaware; but the next minute Leonard comes to her relief, saying, cheerfully, "Now before Georgie is further bewildered, we must give her some formal introductions. This, dear, is your cousin Clara."

A very lovely form which had been the first to rise and welcome Leonard, and now walked with him towards the fire, bent down to the low couch where sir William had seated Georgina, and kissed her fondly. But she did not speak; and no one but Leonard and one other remarked that a tear trembled in her beautiful dark eye, as she turned away and quietly glided from the room.

Then Frances—as beautiful and more so than Clara, roses entwined in her hair, and a complexion as fresh and fair as they—she, too, kissed her cousin affectionately, and then introduced her brother that was to be, Arthur Isbel, a pale thoughtful looking man, with a wide intellectual forehead, and pleasant smile hovering about his lips.

"And here is Augusta, your friend that is to be," said sir William, as a tall and fashionable girl of about fifteen, very handsome, but with no small degree of would-be condescension in her tone and manner, came forward, and placed her blooming cheek for a moment by the side of Georgie's pale one.

"My friend!" whispered Georgie's heart, unconsciously, and a vision of Margaret, gentle, lovely, retiring, passed before her mind and for a while so occupied it, that the names of half-a-dozen strangers who were staying at Leighton in anticipation of the wedding fell unheeded on her ear, as they were introduced one by one, by her uncle or Frances.

But who was that tall, haughty young man, with the proud soldier-bearing, and scornful upper lip, who lounges at the farther side of the fire-place, eyeing the little girl so deliberately, as she sits calm and still outwardly, but with a fluttering heart, receiving her first cold dreaded lesson of the world? That is her cousin Lloyd; and at a murmured "Really, Lloyd, it is quite rude," from his sister Frances, he makes the effort of crossing the room, and extending a very white hand, with a very sparkling diamond on the little finger thereof, to his young cousin, informing her at the same time, in a few words, whether mockingly or in earnest she could not possibly tell, that he was charmed with this op-

5

portunity of making her acquaintance, and trusted at the same time that the feeling was reciprocal.

Something in his tone or manner, however, seemed to disturb Georgina's equilibrium. She made a nervous effort to reply, which only brought a tinge of color to her face, as she fancied she remarked her cousin's lips curl yet more with but half-suppressed amusement or disdain. Then, giving her another deliberate and most comprehensive glance from head to foot, he turned away to the piano where Miss Elmore was resuming the song which the entrance of the cousins had interrupted.

At the same moment Clara reappeared, and invited Georgina to come up stairs to her aunt's boudoir, there to be introduced to lady Archdale, and partake of some refreshment which had been prepared for her.

"And perhaps, dear," she added, "you may like to say good-night to Leonard, as you are looking quite fatigued from your journey; and mamma thinks you had better go to bed as soon as possible."

Georgie obeyed instinctively; and, kissing her brother, she proceeded to wish good night to such of her new friends as were near, receiving from sir William a very hearty embrace as he told her good-humoredly he should expect those pale cheeks to look very differently in the course of a few days. She then followed her cousin out of the room.

Half way along the gallery they were met by a dark and gloomy looking youth with his hat on, and a plaid flung across his shoulders.

"Walter," exclaimed Clara, "where *are* you going?"

"No concern of yours," he replied, as he pushed past.

"Stop a moment, Walter," his cousin added, at the same time seizing the end of his shawl. "Here is Georgina Archdale; she will like to speak to you; and Leonard is in the drawing-room; they are just come."

Had he not been thus forcibly detained, it was evident that Walter would have paid no attention to his cousin's words. As it was, he just stopped a moment, glanced at Georgina, made a cold constrained bow, without noticing the hand which was half extended towards him; and murmuring "How do you do?" in an unintelligible tone, he unceremoniously pulled his plaid, the fringe of which Clara still held, from between her fingers, and hurried on.

"Is that Walter?" asked Georgie in a tone of compassion.

"Yes," replied Clara, with a low remorseful sigh. Poor Clara! Among other long neglected duties which for the past few weeks she had been earnestly striving to perform was that of showing kindness to Walter. But it was too late. Walter had become hardened and indifferent, and repelled with bitterness now any slight attention and kindness which at his first coming he might have welcomed.

And Clara mourned inwardly; for she knew that she was only reaping the fruits of that which she herself had sown.

Lady Archdale received her niece with the utmost kindness; and Georgie fancied that in that quiet room, with her gentle, loving, invalid aunt for a companion, she should feel more at home than in the show and excitement of busier life below. And so in after days she found it.

The next day but one was the wedding. Georgina could never exactly tell how she passed through it. The long, tedious dressing, the drive to church with Augusta and two gentlemen strangers, who were talking nonsense the whole time, the solemn service, rendered yet more solemn by Leonard's earnest serious words and deportment, the company, the breakfast, the parting with Clara, which seemed to her so sad and mournful, but which scarcely disturbed the gaiety and mirth going on around—all seemed more like a troubled unreal dream, than a true life scene in which she herself was acting, so little accustomed was she as yet to the ways and manners of the world.

Leonard left not long after the departure of the bride and bridegroom, but not before Clara, in a few earnest thankful words, had told him that his faithful warning had not been unheeded; that new thoughts and feelings, to which before she had been a stranger, had arisen within her heart; that she trusted she could now call God her Father, and feel now towards him as a very erring and wandering indeed, but yet a loving child, and that in these feelings Arthur fully participated. She had shown him Leonard's letter; and the light that had dawned so suddenly on her had been breaking slowly, but surely, on his heart too. "And we both desire your prayers, dear Leonard," Clara added, "tha. we may be enabled to live for God *now*, though so much of our past lives has been given up to the foolish empty pleasures of the world."

Leonard's heart thrilled gratefully within him. He had marked a change in his cousin from the first moment of his arrival. He could not doubt the reality of the work; and, with Clara's words yet fresh upon his ear, he was able to say farewell to his sister, and leave her there in that whirl of dissipation and gaiety with calmness, and an assured trust that she would be "kept by the mighty power of God." Georgie, too, bore up most heroically.

The amusements at Leighton were terminated by a splendid ball, to which all the gentry and aristocracy for miles round were invited. At this, of course, Georgie declined being present; and all she knew of the night's proceedings was the meeting her cousin Lloyd in full. uniform, as, after saying "Good night" to lady Archdale, she was proceeding to her own room, and receiving from him what

5*

appeared to her a look of most superlative pity. Then, half an hour later, a vision of two very beautiful beings in rustling white silks, and wreaths of roses and lilies in their hair and dresses, "just come in," as they gaily remarked, " to show themselves." They had never thought of those solemn words, "She that liveth in pleasure," not in sin, or sloth, or deceit; but " she that liveth in pleasure is—dead while she liveth." Georgie knew them well, and had often pondered them ; and now she murmured a prayer for her beautiful thoughtless cousins, ere she turned her head upon the pillow, and slep peacefully.

IV.

SYMPATHY.

"Sow with a generous hand,
Pause not for toil and pain;
Weary not through the heat of summer,
Weary not through the cold spring rain;
But wait till the autumn comes
For the sheaves of golden grain."

THE days after her brother's departure passed rather wearisomely to Georgina. There was so little congeniality between her cousins and the young people who remained with them a time after the wedding, and herself. Their way of spending their time was so totally different from anything she had been accustomed to: this, added to her own natural diffidence and reserve, made her, at the end of the first ten days, as far from feeling at home at Leighton as on the first evening of her arrival.

There was, as she anticipated, a great deal of gaiety and company just at the time: parties at home or abroad almost every evening, and a great part of every day occupied in preparations, or in talk over what had happened on the preceding one. Not, however, that Georgina mingled in any of these pursuits: it being an understood thing that she was delicate and unfit for much excitement, and very evident also that she had no taste that way, she was left just to follow her own inclinations; and these led her to spend her time partly alone, partly in the nursery with her younger cousins, whom she found more pleasant companions than the elder ones, and partly with her gentle invalid aunt, who always welcomed her to her room. Every morning, after the first few days, during which she had not been well enough to bear it, Georgie sat an hour or two with her, reading her the psalms and lessons for the day, and talking to her about her brother and home. Lady Archdale at length seemed quite to cling to her little niece: her quiet gentle manners suited her; and, never having received much show of affection from her own children, she welcomed it the more in Georgie.

Mademoiselle Victoire was gone home for the holidays; so that Augusta had more liberty than usual, went out whenever she was allowed to go, and at home-parties presented herself in the drawing-room at as early an hour as possible. Here Georgina also came when she could find no pretext for absenting herself; but she did not excite much notice on such occasions: she sat in some quiet nook by herself at her work-frame; and, as soon as coffee had been handed round, and her usual hour for retiring came, she slipped away, very often unnoticed.

True, on one or two occasions she had felt anxious to break through her great natural timidity, and, unsolicited, endeavor to win the regard of one whom no one else appeared to trouble himself about; and this was when Walter, who, like herself, though from different motives, seemed to think it a necessity to appear at times among his uncle's family, formed one of the party. It made her loving heart feel sorry to see him aloof from the rest when all appeared so gay and cheerful. She saw plainly that it was not that he could not have enjoyed himself; for, though he sat gloomily apart with a book with which he was supposed to be occupied before him, her quick observation told her that was not the case. At times, when anything in the conversation struck him, or a more thrilling tone of music broke upon his ear, the large proud restless eyes would be raised suddenly, and a vehement glance thrown upon the speaker or performer, but only for a moment: before he thought it possible that it could be noticed, they were bent again; but Georgie could see how the brow seemed to contract, and the lips press closer together, and how very often, for an hour after, no page of the book was turned. She saw that he was unhappy, that no one appeared to notice it, and that all spoke of and to him carelessly and unkindly; but she saw also, and that but too plainly, how little effort he made to gain their regard— how, shutting himself up in a barrier of contemptuous pride and ill humor, he only made the breach between himself and those around him grow wider from day to day. Perhaps it was a sort of fellow-feeling that made her take so much interest in Walter and his proceedings as she found herself doing. Certainly there was nothing in his behavior to her to attract : she saw but little of him, though he was at home for the holidays; and, when she did speak to him, or, as she had ventured to do on one or two occasions, show him little attentions which she thought might please, she met with such ungracious rebuffs that she felt quite afraid to repeat them. Their position in the family too was by no means alike. Every one treated her with kindness and consideration, and it was simply because they thought it more pleasant to her feelings that she was allowed to keep so much in the background. Her quiet nook was often approached during the evening by one and another : her uncle, with whom she was already a favorite, would pinch her pale cheeks, and ask her when the roses were coming ; Frances and her young friends would patronizingly admire her work, or invite her to share in some game or dance; and even the tall moustached cousin, who still continued to inspire her with as much awe as at first, would occasionally approach, look down upon her from his military stateliness for a minute or two, make some compliment which Georgie thought had very little meaning in it, and then withdraw, leaving the little pale face very much tinged with color.

So Georgie felt that in many things she could not sympathize with Walter, even were he disposed to allow her; but still in some points they were alike. He was an orphan; and so was she. He, in all that large family seemed to have no real friend; nor had she. He, for some reason or other, appeared to have no taste or inclination for the gaiety and amusements which were constantly going on around him; and this also was the case with her. And she often did feel how pleased and thankful she should be, if in any way it were possible for her to gladden Walter's life. She had too humble an opinion of herself to imagine she could do much: she was not old enough or clever enough to be his friend; and yet, if he would let her, she could love him and be kind to him; and, were she in his place, she knew that even a kind word would be cheering to her; but he was so determinately cold and indifferent, that she felt it most difficult to know how to begin.

One thing, however, Georgie did—she prayed for Walter. One who seemed so unhappy, so almost mysteriously unsociable, so shut out from all sympathy and affection as he, and one who she greatly feared never prayed for himself—surely he needed the prayers of others; and so, night after night, when she had retired to her room, and morning after morning as she rose from sleep, before entering on the duties of a fresh day, she joined to her other petitions at the throne of heavenly love aud mercy a very earnest prayer for Walter, and that, if it pleased her heavenly Father, she might be made, before she left that roof, the means, in some way or other, of comforting and gladdening his cheerless shadowed life. And often, as she prayed, a peaceful happy assurance that her prayer was heard, and would in due time be answered, came into her soul; and at such times she could not but give thanks that, when cut off from every other source, the blessed privilege of prayer still remains.

Day after day passed on, and Georgie found herself no nearer the attainment of her object than at first, in fact rather farther from it. With the other members of the family she was gradually becoming a little more familiar; but Walter still remained so coldly inaccessible, that she almost began to fear her month's visit would pass, and her desire remain unsatisfied.

One evening—how well she remembered it for long after!—she came down into the drawing-room as usual: there was a large party that night; and the ladies were not yet come in from the dining-room. The lamps were lighted, and showed her that the only occupant of the room as she entered was her cousin Walter. He was seated in his usual attitude at a distant table, and looking more miserably depressed than she had ever before observed him. "Perhaps this may be my time," she thought to herself; and, summoning up all her

little courage, and glancing a thought of prayer to
her Father in heaven, she went up to where Walter
was sitting. The step was so light that he might
not have heard her approach; for he took no notice,
not so much as raising his eyes from his book.
She laid one little white hand on his shoulder, and
said in a timid half supplicatory tone, "Dear Walter, are you unhappy?"

O how witheringly to all her hopes did the answer come!

"And supposing I am, is that any business of
yours? Will no one leave me to myself?" And
as he spoke, the little hand was roughly shaken off
from his shoulder. The look that accompanied the
words seemed to rivet the child to the spot where
she was standing; it took from her the power of
speech, and, for some moments, of action as well;
and it was a strange sight to see those two—she in
her pure white dress, with a face in which fear, compassion, and entreaty were strangely blended, looking down on him who in all the pride and bitterness
of his passion yet could hardly meet the touching
guilelessness of her glance; nevertheless for one
moment their eyes met; and then all Georgie's
courage gave way; she felt the hot tears rush to
her eyelids, and pressing the hand which had been
so rudely repulsed before them, to hide them from
him, she glided from the room. What a night of
bitter mortification and self-reproach was that to
Walter! He retired to his chamber when the

6

cheerless evening was over, but not to rest. That soft gentle touch upon his arm, how like his mother's! and yet he had repelled it. That kind, loving, earnest glance, how exactly corrésponding to many he had been used to receive from that almost idolized parent, who had been taken from him! and yet he had scorned it. Those few timid words, which told in every tone that they were prompted only by love and interest; and he had answered them cruelly, insultingly. What would he not have given to have been able to call back those few short minutes, or to have blotted them from his memory altogether. But this was impossible; and now it was too late; her esteem and love and sympathy were gone for ever; he could not doubt it. She must be more than mortal, he thought, as he tossed restlessly on his bed that night, if she could ever forgive his cruel unkindness, much less ever address him in words of gentleness again. He slept at last, and dreamed that a guardian angel with white and glittering wings was hovering around him, and that that angel had his mother's face and mother's smile, and that he was rejoicing in its presence, and then awoke to the bitter recollection that the one who might perchance have been to him something of a personification of that watching guardian spirit he had repulsed and driven from him at the very time he most needed her aid.

Georgie said meekly, as she knelt in prayer that night before retiring to rest, "Lord, if it be not thy will that I should be the means of comfort or blessing to my poor cousin, grant that I may be content; but, dear Lord, I pray thee give the blessing by some other means if not by me, and O lead him to thee." And then she went to her rest, and slept peacefully.

She knew not then, dear child—and had she known, her course of action would not have been otherwise—how very far from the kingdom, humanly speaking, her cousin was. But she prayed and trusted as though he had been very nigh; and in her own soul, at least, she felt the blessedness of quietly believing.

The whole of the following day she saw nothing of Walter. In the evening all the elder members of the family, and Augusta with them, went to a concert in Barnes; and Georgie, after seeing them all off, returned to the library, and went on with a letter which she was writing to Margaret. She was telling her she hoped this would be the last letter; for in three days Leonard was coming to fetch her, and then there would be the joy of meeting again —O how much better than writing! And she was saying how far less formidable than she had anticipated her visit had proved; how kind all had been to her; "and yet, dear Margaret, in one or two things I have been disappointed; but I will tell you all when we meet." She was just finishing when the door opened, and Walter entered the room. The remembrance of the past night was so painful to her that she could not dare to look at him. She felt the color come into her face; but she forced herself to continue her writing without appearing to observe his presence. He came up, however, and seated himself near her at the writing-table. A few moments passed without a word being spoken; only the sound of Georgie's pen was heard, as it moved nervously along. At length Walter broke the silence; and it was in a tone of such passionate earnestness, that it made his cousin start and the pen drop suddenly from her fingers.

"I see how it is, Georgina," he said; "you disdain me now, like the rest of them; and I can't blame you, for you have reason. My behavior to you has been despicable, mean, ungrateful. I am ashamed of it. I can't ask you to forgive it, for I don't deserve that; but, O just once before you upbraid me, once more before you reproach and hate me as I deserve, lay your hand on my arm as you did last night; speak to me again as you did then; say those kind, gentle words—call me 'dear Walter'—'twas the first time any one did, since my mother's death; and I was wretch enough to repulse you. Won't you," he added, after a pause, in a tone of hopelessness, "can't you forget it all, for one moment?"

Georgie had risen from her seat as he spoke; her large thoughtful eyes beaming with a light almost unnatural to them. She could hardly believe it to be a real ty that Walter was there, speaking those words to her: the impassioned tone did not frighten her: but each fresh sentence pained her very heart. She felt such sorrow, such compassion for his grief. And, when he stopped and paused, the words that rose to her lips in reply could find no utterance.

"Not for one moment?" he repeated.

"For one moment! O Walter, it has been forgiven long ago. I was not angry, dear Walter— only sorry, so sorry to have vexed you. I guessed you were unhappy before. Do you think I would have tried to make you more so? But it was done in thoughtlessness; you must forgive me too, for having troubled you."

"Stop," cried he, "I cannot have you speak so." He stooped his head over his folded arms then; but Georgina could see that he was still violently agitated. She went up to him, and again laid her hand on his shoulder, thinking it might pacify him, and show how truly she forgave all. In a few moments he became more calm; and then, rising and taking the little hand into his own, he kissed it reverentially.

"Then you forgive me, and will be my friend still?" he asked in a low voice.

"Yes: your little sister, if you like," she said. "Only that I am going so soon; but you can come and see us."

"Thank you." Then glancing his eye at the timepiece, "You are busy now," he said.

"No. My letter is just finished."

6*

" Well, then, I will answer your question; that is, if you care about it now: it is the least I can do. I am wretched here, Georgina—unhappy isn't a strong-enough term—so wretched that if it keeps on much longer I won't put up with it, but go where my presence shall not be an infliction to any one. I have been trampled on quite long enough."

Georgina was a little frightened. " What do you mean, Walter?" she asked. " Who tramples on you?"

" Every one; and that just because I am poor. My uncle taunts me with it continually; reminding me, whenever I don't just please him, that I am living on his charity. Lloyd and the girls throw it in my teeth whenever they can find the opportunity; and even the very servants have been taught to look down upon me, because I have no fortune, and am dependent."

" Dreadful!" said Georgie. " But can that be the only reason?"

" O that is reason enough for them," replied Walter. " Money and rank and station and amusements are all they think about here; and if you haven't got the one and don't care about the other, you're not fit for their society—you may go to the dogs, for all they care."

" Hush!" she exclaimed involuntarily.

" It is true," Walter continued, in a vehement tone. " I am proud, I know, and I can't endure it. Though I've no money, I am as good as any of them. My mother was their mother's own sister; but one married a poor officer, and the other a rich baronet; and for that and nothing else I am despised and scorned in this way, not even considered worthy to be introduced as their cousin."

Georgie felt almost sorry she had asked Walter anything about his trouble, she seemed so utterly unable to say a word of advice or encouragement.

"Has it always been so?" she asked at last.

"Yes, ever since I came, which is a little more than a year now; and I've borne it pretty patiently; but I shan't much longer."

"Walter! what are you thinking of doing?"

"Taking myself right off, and relieving them of the burden of my support," he answered shortly.

"What! without telling them?" Georgie said. "That would be very wrong." She spoke so gravely and decidedly that Walter feared he had gone rather too far.

"Well, don't you think I have a right?" he said. "Listen: my uncle declares I shall either go into the Church—he has a paltry living somewhere, I believe—or be a lawyer. I am equally determined that I will do neither. I'm not fit for the Church, and never shall be; and the law I hate from the bottom of my heart; and so, as we can't pull together, isn't it much better we should part? They none of them care a straw for me, and would be thankful to get rid of me if they could do it decently; and so, if I take French leave and go, why it would save them further trouble."

He spoke lightly; but Georgie could see that he was feeling more than he chose to own; and that these arguments, though they might have been repeated many times to himself, barely sufficed to satisfy his conscience.

" Is not my uncle your guardian, Walter?"

" Yes."

" Then you ought to obey him in the place of your parents. I am quite sure this plan of yours is very wrong. O don't think of it."

" I never will obey a tyrant," Walter answered sternly.

" What do you wish to do when you grow up?"

" Why, follow my father's profession, to be sure —go into the army."

" And does my uncle know you wish that?"

" Certainly; and that makes him all the more opposed. I spoke to Lloyd about it once too; and he told me to go and get the money to buy my commission. That was a fine speech, wasn't it?"

Georgie was sadly distressed: she did not like the way in which Walter spoke: she felt so surely that there must be some faults with him too; but yet she pitied him so much that she dared not inquire more plainly. There was a pause for some time; and then she said earnestly, " O Walter, I wish you were a Christian!"

" A Christian! what do you take me for then,

Georgie? a Jew, Turk, infidel, or heretic? poor things who are only prayed for once a year!"

"Leonard says," she replied, taking no notice of the bantering tone he used, "that a real Christian is one who is like Christ; who loves him first of all and most of all, and who is always trying to do what pleases him."

"And you don't think I do?"

"I was not thinking so much of that; only real Christians can go to God in their troubles, and ask him to help them; and he always hears their prayers, and sends help in some way or other."

Walter had long ceased to go to God in any way; and he did not give much heed to the words the little girl said, though there was a certain charm in them as coming from her, and a feeling of respect too, which made him hear her patiently.

"I shouldn't mind anything," he said, "if I were only my own master; and that won't be yet for four or five years to come."

She saw that he was anxious to change the subject; that the theme which was all of interest to her was of none to him. But this might be her last opportunity; and would it be faithful to neglect it? "We may not live till then," she said seriously, "dear Walter. The Bible says, 'Seek ye first the kingdom of God and his righteousness'."

"You are a little bit of an enthusiast," was his reply. Then, seeing the tears almost ready to come to her eyes, " No, don't be vexed, Georgina; you are a good true hearted girl, I know. I would not pain you again for anything. I saw from the first, even when I treated you so disgracefully, that you were very different from the rest ; else I could not have spoken as I have to night. Remember, I trust your honor not to repeat it."

" I will remember; only make me one promise, Walter."

" Well ?"

" That you won't think of acting as you talked of, without speaking to my uncle about it."

" I would promise immediately if you were going to be here for a constancy."

The answer could not but give a gleam of pleasure to Georgina; but, had she known how almost prophetic it was, she would not, perhaps, have smiled as she replied, " That won't do."

" Well, I'll not go yet. Good night, Georgie." He shook hands with her for the first time since she came, and then left the room.

Georgie finished her letter to her friend; but, before folding it up, she drew her pen through the sentence, " In one or two things I have been disappointed." Then she went up-stairs, to read awhile to her aunt before going to bed.

V.

SEPARATION.

"When sorrow all our heart would ask,
We need not shun our daily task,
  And bide ourselves for calm.
The herbs we seek to heal our woe
Familiar by our pathway grow:
  Our common air is balm."

KEBLE.

THE expected day arrived at last: the day on which Georgina was to meet her brother after a longer separation than she had ever known before. Could she have foreseen all, she would not have anticipated it so joyously. How well for us is it that many of our most grievous bitter sorrows are totally unknown to us until the very hour for their development is at hand! The thought of them, weighing on our hearts for days, or weeks, or months beforehand, would crush the timid fearing ones to the very earth with anguish, or madden well-nigh to despair the more determined spirits; both of whom are often enabled, from the very suddenness of the affliction, to endure and bear on more manfully, taking hope for their guiding-star, and feeling that, after the first ago-

nizing burst of sorrow is past, the most bitter in-
gredient of the cup is tasted also.   •

Georgina came down to breakfast that morning
with a sunnier smile than usual on her little pale
face; which, however, was by no means so pale as
at the commencement of her visit. Her uncle's
prediction had proved quite correct : there was no
disputing that the air of Barnes agreed with her
most thoroughly.

"Why, you are glad to leave us, you naughty
little puss," he said, as she wished him good
morning.   .

"No, not glad to leave you, uncle ; but glad to
be seeing Leonard again."

"Well, then, you will be satisfied with seeing
Leonard, and be content to let him go off to-
morrow or the next day, and leave you behind ?
Ah! that will be the best plan. Silence gives consent : eh, miss Georgie ?"

"Letters !" cried Lloyd, coming in that moment
with the post-bag. "Who wants any ? Here,
for mamma from Clara: who will take it up ?
From Arthur for you, Francie ; and two more
beside—one for you, Georgie, from the Rev.
Leonard Archdale. The rest for my father, I
declare! Not one for the postman! 'Tis too
bad. Now, put by those long yarns from the El
mores, I entreat you, Frances, and give us a little
breakfast first."

Georgie had taken both her own and her aunt's

letter from her cousin's hand as he spoke. She had lately taken up any morning letters that came for lady Archdale when she went to read with her, after breakfast; so she put that one in her pocket, and commenced opening her own. A little misgiving had arisen in her mind at receiving a letter from her brother the very day on which he was expected. Perhaps it was to put off his coming for a day or two. He was well; for the direction was just as usual. She broke the seal, and read as follows: "My darling Georgie:—I hope to be with you, as I before wrote, to-morrow afternoon. A great trial awaits both you and me. Your uncle will tell you pretty much what it is; and to-morrow evening I shall be able to talk to you myself about it. I know it will be very hard for you to bear, but you know where we have both found strength in former trials, and we must look there now, Georgie, and commit one another to him. I have not time for more, but knew that even a line would be better than nothing from your ever-loving brother."

Poor Georgie grew perfectly dizzy as she read these words. A great trial! He would not have called it so unless it were such indeed. It must mean a longer separation. That was what would be harder for her to bear than anything.

"Uncle, what is it?" she asked, when she could trust herself to look up and speak at all. She did not notice that he was still busy with his letters, she was for the time so thoroughly self-absorbed. He looked up, and at her, almost compassionately; then said, in his usual quick easy tone, "Nothing, my dear child, to distress yourself about. Leonard is perfectly well, and only going on a short trip to India."

"To India!" And her voice died away into nothing, and the color vanished from her cheeks. She could not speak another word, nor ask another question. Plenty were spoken and asked by the other members of the family, who were equally astonished with Georgina to hear the sudden and unlooked-for intelligence. But she stood there silently by her uncle's side, her eyes fixed on the letter which she still held in her hand, and her thoughts fleeting over the weary weeks and months and perhaps years that might intervene before he could possibly return. She did not speculate on the probable causes of his sudden decision: the one thought, that it was a settled sure determination, fell so painfully on her heart that it could give place to nothing else. At length she was roused. Her uncle patted her on the shoulder kindly.

"Come, cheer up, Miss Georgie," he said. "It is only the carrying out of my plan. We will all do our best to make you happy as long as you are with us. And, for my own part, I don't feel very sorry at the turning up of the scheme, since it has such pleasant results. Now, come and have some breakfast, my dear."

As he spoke, the new thought flashed into the little girl's mind that Leighton would be her home during her brother's absence; and mingled feelings rose in her breast at the idea. Her first impulse was to burst into tears: then she felt how ungrateful and annoying to her friends such a display of weakness would appear; and with a great effort she forced the hot tears back to their source, ere one drop fell. But it cost her a considerable struggle; for she had not yet learned to conceal much, poor child; and she dared not trust herself to speak a single word to her uncle in answer to his expressions of kindness, which yet she felt ought to be acknowledged. So she smiled as well as she could, and nearly choked herself in endeavoring to swallow as hearty a breakfast as usual.

At the first opportunity she made her escape from the room, and hastened up stairs with her aunt's letter. She felt as though she could not go through the usual morning' reading, so much did she long to take refuge in her own room, and indulge freely in her grief. On the landing, as she stood a moment pondering what excuse she could possibly make, for she could not tell her sorrow even to her aunt, she suddenly encountered Walter.

"Georgina," he said, "I should be wrong in saying that I am altogether sorry about your trouble; and yet I can't help telling you that, on your own account, I feel very much. It must be very bad to know that you have a great friend, and yet bo separated from him. But you see, Georgie, I am selfish; and your staying will be a little comfort to me."

"O will it, Walter?" she replied. "Being a little comfort to any one will make it easier for me, I think. Thank you for saying so. You are going to school this morning again, are not you?"

"Yes: to Campbell's. Good bye."

Did Georgie's eyes deceive her, or did Walter actually smile? She thought the latter. How strange, that what was such an overwhelming grief to her should make others happy, and cause even her usually gloomy cousin so far to forget himself as to smile! The strangeness of the thing almost made her smile too; and she entered her aunt's room with a far less melancholy face than might have been expected. Lady Archdale wished her good morning very kindly.

"And so I am not going to lose my little reader," she said, taking Georgie's hand, and pressing it fondly. "I am so glad, my love: I should have missed you sadly."

"Thank you, dear auntie. Here is a letter for you from Clara. Shall I wait and read to you when you have finished?"

"Yes, dear child, if you feel able this morning. It must be a great trial to you, parting with your brother, and for so long."

Georgie was thankful to find that her aunt knew

all about it; and yet she could not make up her mind to ask any particulars, though she did long to know how great a time that "so long" meant. But she began wisely to think that it was best not to dwell too much on her own feelings. She gave up all thoughts of evading the accustomed reading; and, reaching the Bible, she sat herself down, and found out her places as usual. And, as she read, she felt the truth of those words, that he that watereth others shall be watered also himself. She had conquered the first impulse of her quick and sensitive nature, in order to minister to the pleasure of another; and now every word she read seemed intended for herself, and fraught with precious comfort and encouragement. The words of the inspired psalmist, written in the time of deep affliction and trouble, fell soothingly now on her ear. "As for me, I will patiently abide alway, and will praise thee more and more. I will go forth in the strength of the Lord God, and make mention of thy righteousness only. O what great troubles and adversities hast thou showed me! and yet didst thou return and refresh me."

"Will you read the evening chapters, darling?" said her aunt. "You will be engaged with Leonard to-night, I hope."

Georgie turned to the place; and again words came as though addressed to her: "Rejoicing in hope, patient in tribulation, continuing instant in prayer." An unchanging ever-accessible Friend would be left her, even when her brother was gone: and O what comfort in the thought that he was ever near, ever waiting to bestow all she could need—patience, hope, and even joy!

She had just finished when Augusta came to call her. "Georgie, Mdlle. Victoire is waiting: she says she supposes you will do your lessons regularly with us now. It is just right, as I only begin to-day."

Georgie tried not to sigh.

"She will have a pleasant pupil, I am quite sure," lady Archdale remarked, as Georgie was leaving her, and, when she was gone, continued to herself with a sigh, "Ah! if only one of mine were like her; but I have greatly erred."

Lessons till one o'clock, then a walk, and then luncheon; when Augusta, herself, and the younger ones dined. Lessons after that till four—the hour at which Georgina expected her brother. She had not throughout the day had a moment's leisure to waste over her own grief: certainly Mdlle. Victoire had returned at the very right time. Georgie found enough to occupy her in the school-room. In some things she was behind her cousin—in music more especially, and French; which, owing to the advantages she had always enjoyed, Augusta spoke with great fluency. Georgie could read and translate perfectly, but could not converse at all; and this was a trial to her, as mademoiselle constantly addressed them in that language, and the

smiles caused by her own somewhat awkward re-
plies were by no means pleasant. She found the
Latin and mathematics and physical geography,
which she had studied under Leonard's auspices,
not at all appreciated; but she could not help feeling grateful for the opportunity thus unexpectedly
afforded her of improvement in those things which
it was impossible she could make much advance in
at Beechwood.

Nevertheless, the thought would come into her
mind from time to time that the mornings spent in
the library at the rectory with her own dear
brother as a teacher were far more pleasant than
these were ever likely to prove, and how lông it
might be before they would come back again!
But she thought of the "patient abiding" of which
she had been reading with her aunt that day; and
again and again she prayed for patience, and trust,
and hope.

Five o'clock came: the lamps were lighted in
the drawing-room, where the family were assemb-
ling for dinner, and waiting Leonard. Georgie had
settled herself at her work-frame: she would try
and please her brother by waiting patiently, and
meeting him as cheerfully as possible. She heard
the carriage drive up, and soon the footman knocked,
and announced her brother's name.

She saw that his eye fell on her, the moment he
entered the room; but he shook hands with sir
William, his cousins, and some visitors staying at

the Hall first; then he came to her. She had been feasting her eyes upon him from the moment he entered : his fine, noble figure, tall as Lloyd, and in her sight how much more beautiful ! his perfect ease, and gracefulness of manner; his beautiful smile. In her sisterly pride she forgot for the instant that she was about to lose him. He pressed her in his arms, and kissed her fondly. "My own darling." Her fortitude well-nigh gave way then; but other eyes were on them; she restrained her feelings, and sat down quietly to her work again. Lloyd took Leonard to his room; and then it was dinner-time. Why did not Frances ask her to come in to dinner with the elders that evening? To sit in the same room with Leonard, to be able to look at him, and listen to his voice, would have been an intense gratification to her, knowing as she did how soon that pleasure would be gone from her. She felt at first as though she had been slighted, but recollected that on one or two former occasions she had declined the invitation when offered to her; so she knew that she must not complain. But the dinner, though in reality earlier, and not so long, seemed to the poor girl an interminable affair; and, by the time the ladies came in, her patience was well-nigh exhausted.

Leonard soon followed them. She had been troubling herself how she should secure some time alone with him, and wondering if he would be able to manage it. But she need not have disquieted herself.

"I am afraid we shall appear rather unsociable," Leonard said, with his grave smile, when his uncle and the rest made their appearance; "but Georgie and I must petition for a little seclusion this evening. We shall have a good deal to talk of."

"To be sure, my dear fellow," said sir William: "it would be strange if you had not, the last night. Frances, my dear, there's a fire in the library ?"

"O, yes, papa. Pray, Leonard, go there as soon as you like."

Georgie had risen. "The last night." Could she have heard rightly ? O she had not anticipated this ! She hardly knew how she left the room; only, when she found herself alone with him, and the door shut, all control and restraint of feeling vanished. She flung herself into his arms, and burst into an agony of tears. " O, Leonard ! Leonard !" He sat down on the sofa, and took her in his arms as if she had been a child, as he had done years before, in times of sorrow ; but he did not speak. It seemed unreasonable to tell her not to give way, when his own heart was heavy and well-nigh overflowing with the same bitter feelings.

" When ?" she asked at length, between her sobs.

" Early to-morrow morning. My darling child, don't distress me more. It is grievous for me, as for you."

" Can I help it ? O Leonard, say something to

comfort me.   Is it utterly impossible to take me
with you ?"

" Utterly, my darling."

Another burst of tears, and then—

· " Will it be very long ?"

" Many months perhaps; but don't think of that.
' As thy days thy strength shall be.'   We must not
look on beyond that, simply believe the promise.
We need much strength to-night, Georgie."

There was a long pause ; during which both lifted
up their hearts in silent prayer to their Father, who
had sent the trial, and who was now sending strength
and patience to bear it.   Georgie grew calm.

" It is pleasant to lie like this, and feel your
strong arm, and see your dear face: it seems so
like old times, Leonard, dear.   But I shall tire you
now, perhaps ; I am so old."

She smiled sadly.

He answered by kissing her fondly; and presently he said :   " Are you comfortable here, little
Georgie ?"

" O they are all very kind: of course it is not
like home ; but I love auntie very much, and uncle
too.''

" And your cousins ?"

" They are all very kind to me, and Mademoi-
elle Victoire teaches me, with Augusta and Carrie,
and little Tom, things you know that I could not
learn very perfectly at Beechwood."

Georgie's quick perception had shown her that

her brother was feeling very much more than she had ever known him before, and on her account. And so what little annoyances and disagreeables she had encountered during her stay, she carefully kept in the background, that he might not be farther distressed by the thought that he was leaving her not thoroughly comfortable.

"Then you think you can be happy here while I am away? There is no other alternative but a school; and that I am sure sir William would not allow for a moment; neither should I like it."

"Will the rectory be shut up?"

"No, darling. Mr. Grove is coming to take the duty during my absence; and he will live there, you know."

"Poor Beechwood."

And Georgie could not restrain a few quiet tears.

"What becomes of Mrs. Airey?"

"She remains there, dear; and the other servants too. I had such messages for you this morning. A great deal of love from Margaret and Mrs. Murray, and a letter from each."

He gave them to her; she put them silently into her pocket, then laid her head on his shoulder again.

"Georgie, darling, how has it been with you in higher things since coming here? Has the inner life advanced? Have you been able to walk wisely and consistently?"

"I have not had so many temptations as I ex-

pected, Leonard. I have been very happy sometimes, but I am afraid not so wise nor so faithful as
I might have been. I cannot feel courage to speak
of those things which are so dear to *me*, to those
who I know do not care about them; and that
seems so wrong."

"It is not always necessary to speak, dearest; as
much, and even more, may be done by a quiet holy
example as by many words. We are to be known
by our fruits, our actions. I don't mean to say we
should allow sin to pass unreproved; but it is difficult for one in your position to speak to those older
than yourself; it would be out of place, and might
be productive of more harm than good. Except in
very extreme cases, silent holiness of behavior,
which will not smile at the unholy or trifling jest,
or join in the worldly or sinful conversation, will
be more becoming, if not more easy for you, my
little sister. But even this is difficult to our poor
cowardly natures; and we need God's grace to assist us every day, every hour."

"Yes, Leonard dear, I know it. You will pray
for me?"

"Yes, every day, my darling. You will never
be much out of my thoughts, and where can I think
of you so happily, with so much love and trust, as
at the throne of grace? You will meet me there
too, Georgie: you know my usual hours, morning
and night."

"Ah! yes: that has been such a pleasure,

knowing that we were praying for one another at the same time; but it must be rather different now."

Leonard sighed as he pressed her hand more closely in his own; then, after a pause, he said: "Do not for any cause neglect your quiet times alone with God, my Georgie. Make time for this duty secure, whatever else you may have to give up. It may be difficult sometimes, perhaps; but you remember the words I quoted to you not long ago: 'It is in the secrecy of the chamber that the battle is lost or won.' O, my darling, I would not have you to be the loser in these great conflicts! You cannot but let your light shine before men so long as you live in the light of your reconciled Father's presence; and that light never shines so sweetly, so brightly, as when quietly waiting on and communing with him alone."

"They have been my happiest times since I came here, dear."

"And they will continue to be so, I trust," Leonard replied. "Georgie, dearest, I have a motto to give you, to think upon when I am gone: you will not be in great danger of going astray, so long as you keep that steadily in your heart, looking on it as the guiding motive of every action—only five words, and you know them very well already—'Seeing him who is invisible.'"

Georgie raised her head suddenly from her brother's shoulder, where it had been leaning, glanced

into his face a look of inexpressible fondness, and
then turning back again, "I understand them now,"
she said : "thank you, dear, dear brother."

Leonard smiled beautifully. " Invisible and yet
to be seen—now by the eye of faith, by-and-by
face to face, and for ever. Georgie, how thankful
we should be for such prospects ! how small earth's
trials appear beside them ! You will not give way
any more, my darling, nor make yourself unhappy
by thinking too much of me, except as being
watched over by the invisible One. And that," he
added, " will not make you unhappy."

Georgie pressed his hand, but did not speak ;
and the remainder of the short evening passed
quickly away, leaving at the close more than half
unsaid that would have been told. Only Georgie
did not forget in the midst of her own sorrow to
think of Walter, and ask her brother to use what
influence he had with sir William in persuading
him to suffer Walter to follow the bent of his own
inclinations, not compelling him to enter upon a
profession for which he entertained such a decided
antipathy, or for which he was so decidedly un-
suited. Leonard promised not to forget ; and
Georgina was satisfied.

Half past nine o'clock struck from the little
time-piece on the mantel ; and then Leonard said,
" Now, Georgie, we must say good-night."

Poor child, she knew that it was not only good-
night that he meant, but a long weary almost

heart-breaking good-bye. They both stood up : she flung her arms around his neck as he stooped towards her, and for some minutes they remained locked in that close embrace. But they did not speak the hard sad word ; and Georgie did not cry again ; only Leonard murmured, as he quietly disengaged himself, the words he ever used on leaving her for however short a season—" God bless you, darling ;" words carelessly and lightly used by many who think not of the deep and solemn meaning conveyed by them, but never so by him ; and this night, to the poor mourning child they seemed to come with fresh power and comfort. Then he took her by the hand, and they left the room together.

VI.

A NEW PROTECTOR.

"So I ask thee for the daily strength,
  To none that ask denied;
And a mind to blend with outward life
  While keeping at thy side;
Content to fill a little space,
  So thou art glorified."

ANON.

NO one would have judged from outward appearances, as the brother and sister entered the drawing-room, of the deep sorrow in the heart of each; nor, from the quiet way in which Georgie said "Good night" all round, and left the room, only lingering a moment at the door, and taking a last look at Leonard, who had already entered into conversation with his uncle, that she was parting with her dearest earthly friend, perhaps for ever. But, when she reached the solitude of her own room, her grief burst forth afresh; and she wept herself to sleep. She had fancied, dear child, that she should not sleep that night; but the fatigue of her sorrow overcame her, and at midnight she was in a deep slumber. Just at that hour the door of her bedroom gently opened, and Leonard entered. He could not deny himself that last look, and thought it just possible she might be awake. But he felt thankful that it was not so ; shading the light of the lamp from her face with one hand, with the other he gently pushed aside a straggling lock from her white forehead, and then bent and kissed it. He saw the traces of tears on her flushed cheeks, the red swollen eye-lids closed so peacefully now, and he knew how much she had suffered, and what she would still have to bear. For a moment his heart failed him. "Should evil befall her!" he thought. But then his path was plain ; the sacrifice must be made, sharp though it were ; and, should the result prove what he hoped, there was great joy and blessing yet in store for her.

Just then she turned in her sleep, and sighed wearily.

"I am disturbing even her slumber," he murmured, and pressing one more kiss upon her brow, he turned away.

Glancing round the room as he left, he saw his sister's little Bible lying open upon her dressing-table. Curiosity prompted him to look ; and he found that the page was opened on the chapter from which he had taken his parting text to her. He took his pencil from his pocket, and drew a line beneath the words. "She will know then that I have seen her once more," he thought; "though she knows not, precious child, the half that I suffer in leaving her."

He left the room quietly, as he had entered. In
8*

the gallery he met Lloyd, on his way to his bed-room, which was just beyond.

"Hey, Leonard!" he exclaimed, "have you lost your way? I ask pardon, I'm sure, for not being more polite in piloting you."

"Thanks," replied the other; "I believe I know my room quite well; but I have just been to have another look at my poor little sister."

Leonard's voice sounded almost harsh, from the effort he was evidently making not to appear moved. Lloyd observed it, though he could not quite understand the feeling: he had no particular love for either of his own sisters; he liked them very well, as handsome, stylish girls; and his vanity was always gratified when he heard them admired, and saw them courted and flattered in society. They belonged to the family of which he was a member, and brought no disgrace upon it from lack of beauty, or elegance, or accomplishments of any kind; and he felt a pride in them on this account. But, as for any particular feeling of affection or sympathy, he did not know what it meant, and would as willingly have parted with either for half-a-dozen years as for the same number of days. For a man of Leonard's talent and self-control to manifest any emotion on such an occasion as the present, he could not quite understand; and yet it touched him, and for a moment he felt quite a compassion for them both.

"Poor girl," he said: "is she in great trouble?"

"Yes, terrible," was Leonard's reply. "Good-
bye, Lloyd; take care of her."

"I will, I promise you," he said warmly; and,
grasping his cousin's hand, they parted.

The next morning found things at Leighton Hall
going on pretty much as ever; only Georgie awoke
with a feeling of heavy oppression on her heart,
which nevertheless she knew must be manfully
struggled against; and Lloyd with a little awkward
feeling of responsibility on his mind, arising from
the promise he had made to his cousin on the previous night.

He fancied, from what Leonard had said, that
Georgie's welfare during his absence was confided
somewhat particularly to himself; and, although
the thought of patronizing any one, more especially
a quiet little girl, who carefully avoided notice from
any one, from himself more particularly, was not
very tasteful to him, yet, in fulfilment of his promise, he felt bound to make some overtures, and try
if he were able, to divert her mind from the depression she must necessarily feel in being thus
suddenly deprived of the only near relative she had.
He felt too that not much had been done as yet to
make Georgie's visit pleasant to her; that his sisters, wrapped up in their own pursuits, had left her
alone, to do as she pleased, and that was all; and
that Mdlle. Victoire, whom he cordially disliked,
was not the one to administer much consolation to
a timid retiring girl like her.

He fancied, too, from the regard which Leonard entertained for her, and from the books which he had once or twice observed her reading, that there was more depth of mind about her than in his own sisters; and he resolutely determined to make the attempt, whether successful or not, to draw his cousin out, make her more at ease in the family, and, he added to himself, if possible, a little brighter, and more like the rest of the world.

So, as the breakfast things were being removed, he approached Georgina, who was turning over the pages of the "Illustrated London News," with a very thoughtful countenance.

" Not much worth looking at in it this morning, is there ?" he asked in a patronizing tone.

Georgie, whose thoughts were very far away, wondering what progress Leonard had already made in his journey, and regretting, as she had not ceased to do since she awoke at six o'clock that morning, that it had not been an hour earlier, and who experienced, as she always did, a considerable amount of nervousness at being addressed by her great cousin, blushed almost crimson, and, mistaking his remark, answered frightenedly, " Yes, very."

" Do you think so ?" Lloyd continued, not at all disconcerted at the very unmeaning response: " Well, perhaps for ladies; but her majesty's movements don't particularly interest me; neither do these fashions," he continued, pointing to the page which just then happened to be uppermost; " but

I suppose you are not exempt from the common frailty of your sex, and like to read about charming *capotes* and becoming *coiffures* as well as the rest of them."

Georgie felt quite perplexed; fashions being the last thing in the world which interested her.

"I think I misunderstood your question," she replied, awkwardly: "I have not been reading about fashions really; I beg your pardon for not listening."

"O, I did'nt ask anything. I only said the paper seemed stupid this morning; don't you think so?"

"It did not interest me much certainly; but I thought perhaps it was my own fault."

Her voice faltered a little here, and tears were almost in her eyes, as she turned away; but her cousin was persevering.

"I think you are fond of drawing and pictures, are you not?"

"Yes, very," she replied, more cheerily.

"I have some which perhaps you might like to look at," he said, "if you will take the trouble to come into my room."

"Thank you; I should like it very much some time."

"Well, come now."

Ill-defined visions of a gentleman's untidy bedroom, and the strangeness of being invited to enter it at such an early hour, more especially by her cousin, who never hardly spoke to her, floated through her mind as she followed Lloyd ; and she did not notice, until they reached the apartment, and he opened the door, that they had mounted no staircase, nor indeed gone in the direction of any of the family sleeping-rooms. Her surprise and admiration were equally great when they entered the apartment..

An exquisitely furnished room it was, large enough for every thing to show to advantage ; but not so much so as to give the idea of discomfort or formal grandeur. The furniture was all of oak, beautifully carved, and the chairs and lounges covered with dark green velvet ; Brussels carpet in green and gold ; and the walls, papered with a rich green flock, were hung round with beautiful pictures in massive gilt frames. Bright glowing paintings they were, principally views from foreign lands, and one or two interiors of splendid cathedrals, with the lights and shadows admirably blended. The windows of the room were low, opening almost to the ground on one side, and on the other out into a beautiful conservatory, gay with camellias, and red and white azaleas. There were oak stands in the other windows too, filled with flowers just coming into bloom, and, had it not been for the large fire which was blazing on the hearth, Georgie might almost have imagined that the season of the year had changed during that short walk from the dining room, and that spring itself was reigning in this pleasant flowery apartment.

She could not repress a cry of admiration as she entered. " O what a beautiful room!"

" This is my sanctum," said Lloyd : "have you never been in here before ?"

" No, though I have often wondered where that conservatory led to. What lovely flowers! Ah! that rare cyclamen : I have one like it at Beechwood. O it is beautiful here !"

Her genuine expressions of delight seemed to gratify Lloyd.

" Now, what do you think of the pictures ?" he said, when he thought she had lingered long enough among the flowers.

She walked with him slowly round the room; he telling her the subjects of the different paintings, and she listening with a fixed, quiet interest, which told how much she enjoyed them. They made the entire round, and stood at last before a pretty landscape-painting of old elm-trees in a park, just tinged with autumnal colors, and the sunlight shining through the branches on the figure of a young girl asleep on the green turf beneath. The light dress and golden hair of the child were in pleasing contrast to the shadows on the old trunks and dark green-sward, and there was a peaceful happy expression on the sleeping countenance that it gave you pleasure to look upon. Beneath the picture was printed the word " Constance."

"That girl is like you," her cousin remarked, after she had been looking at it some time.

"Like me?" Georgie said, and blushing as she spoke: "O, no: she is beautiful."

"That may be: I don't say she is not better-looking; but she resembles you nevertheless, more especially just now, that you have that pretty color in your cheeks: confess now that you see the likeness."

Georgie's only answer was a yet more distressing blush.

"It is not paying the artist much of a compliment," Lloyd said laughingly, "seeing that face was actually taken from your own, and considered by him a pretty fair representation—not exactly as regards feature, but expression."

"What! did you paint that picture?" Georgie exclaimed with great astonishment.

"Yes. Did not you consider me guilty of such things?"

"O no, I had not the least idea you could draw at all. And are all those other bright sunshiny ones yours too? I like them so much; but I had not the least idea——"

"That I spent my time so profitably? Why, what did you suppose that I did all day?"

"Hunting, or shooting, or riding with Frances and the others," she replied simply.

"Thank you for your good opinion," said Lloyd, in a tone of some annoyance; and Georgie began to wish that, notwithstanding the beautiful flowers and paintings, she had not been invited to enter her cousin's sanctum, when he set her mind at ease by adding, in his usual good-humored tone,

"Well, I do indulge in those vanities occasionally. Of course I ride every day; but my mornings are sacred in here, whenever I am at home; and you may imagine I don't waste them, seeing I have done that picture and commenced another since you came."

"You must indeed paint very quickly," Georgie said, turning at the same time away from the elm-trees, of which she had seen quite enough. "Which is the other?"

"I will show you directly; but I want you to give me some little compliment about this one. You see the likeness, do not you?"

Yes; Georgie could not but see it; but something kept her back from saying so. A strange feeling had risen in her breast the last few minutes, one that she had never felt before—a pleased, gratified sensation. That there was anything in her face, which she had always considered so commonplace, to induce Lloyd to bring it into such a beautiful picture, seemed to her strange and unaccountable, and yet rather pleasant. But she did not like to confess this even to herself, and she replied again that she thought it much too good-looking, and that she could not call it a likeness.

9

"You don't seem to understand, Georgie," Lloyd said, looking down upon her scrutinizingly, "that the plainest countenance and the most beautiful may yet have points of resemblance. You are not what is called handsome, I confess: you are too pale. There, now; if you would but keep that color, it would be better—"

"I shall," poor Georgie thought to herself, "if I am talked to like this."

"But there is a kind of quiescence, of repose about your face, especially when the sun shines, which I thought would look well in a picture if I could catch it exactly. I have; and you see how well it has succeeded. This girl is not exactly handsome—"

"Cousin Lloyd, please do not say anything more about it," Georgie said, looking up at him steadily : "which is the other picture?"

Again there was a look of slight annoyance; but he changed the subject immediately, and uncovering a large easel, which stood near, he showed his new drawing. It was at present a mere sketch, of which the subject seemed so unfamiliar to the little girl that she could not at all comprehend its meaning. She was about to ask for an explanation, when there was a quick tap at the door, and Augusta put in her head.

"Georgina, I have been searching for you everywhere. Mdlle. Victoire wants you."

"My compliments," said Lloyd, " and she is engaged at present."

"I had better go perhaps."

"No, no: there is not the least occasion. Georgina is at the beck and call of no one in this house;
and you may tell Mdlle. Victoire so, if you please.
She is not to be plagued with lessons except as she
wishes it."

"I had better go," again interrupted Georgina.
"I cannot talk French at all;" and she sighed.

"No, indeed she cannot," Augusta remarked;
" Mademoiselle says her accent is quite pitiable."

"Trash about accent," Lloyd exclaimed: "if you
and Mdlle. Victoire had both a little more sound
English in your brain, it would be a good thing."

Augusta drew herself up, with a look of supreme
scorn. "You are always finding fault with your
sisters at home," she said. "I shall tell Mdlle.
Victoire and mamma that you don't choose to let
Georgie come to lessons;" and she left the room.

"Do you draw?" Lloyd inquired of Georgie,
when she was gone.

"Yes, a little."

"In what style?"

"Landscapes mostly, and figures in crayons."

"Do you mind fetching me your portfolio?"

"O no; but they are not worth your looking
at."

"Well, I might help you a little. You don't do
anything in water-colors?"

" No ; but I should indeed like, I have longed so
to learn."

" Well, get your portfolio."

He looked them all through carefully.

" Are they entirely your own doing ?" he asked.

" Yes, every stroke.   Mrs. Murray would never
put even a touch: she says it is so untruthful."

He gave her another scrutinizing glance.

" Then you have done remarkably well.   I
thought some one in the family ought to possess the
great gift," he said, as though to himself, and with a
kind of sigh: then to her, " I will teach you to
paint; for I don't think you would worry me with
incessant tongue clack as some do, but go on quietly.
I hate to be talked to, when I am painting.   Come
for an hour or two every morning."

" I am very much obliged to you," Georgie said;
and her eyes glistened with pleasure.   " Do you
mind what time it is ?"

" No; why ?"

" I go to my aunt always after breakfast, and I
should like to go into the school-room till twelve
o'clock.   I am very backward in French, and it is
very kind of Mdlle. Victoire to teach me."

" Well, just as you please.   You can come from
twelve till luncheon.   I shall have time to ride
with Frances and *the others* after that, you know."

" I beg your pardon for saying that.   I did not
intend to be rude.   I meant Miss Davenant and
any other ladies that might be staying here."

"Well, I will overlook it this time. I shall be dreadfully ousy this morning; so come to me to-morrow at twelve o'clock, and don't be late."

"Thank you," Georgie replied in a very grateful tone, as she left the room.

She saw nothing more of Lloyd that day until evening. He did not appear at the luncheon table, and went with Frances, Miss Davenant, and his father to a large dinner party in Barnes in the evening. As Georgina was coming down the wide staircase to her school-room tea, she met him, dressed in full uniform, with his sister by his side splendidly attired, and with pearls and white flowers in her dark hair.

He was talking and laughing with her, and passed on at first without appearing to notice the little slight figure which shrunk back as they swept along. But he suddenly recollected himself; and, stepping back, he said,

"Georgina, why do you never come out with us? You must sometimes: it will do you good."

"O no, thank you," she answered. "I never do. I like to be at home best."

"We shall see about that," he replied; and then in a lower tone, for Frances was waiting, "Good night, Constance."

She blushed and laughed as she returned his good-night; and then he ran down stairs; and the next moment the carriage drove off.

Georgie was thankful when her tea and the evening lessons were over, and she could go up into her own room, and have her happy quiet time, as she called it. But it was at best a mournful time that night. The thought of the preceding evening, Leonard's kind dear face and comforting words listened to for the last time, the sad parting, and the dreary prospect of long separation, could not be dwelt upon without tears and thrilling sorrow. No one could ever replace him to her. Lloyd had shown himself kind to-day, but he could never be like Leonard; and, though she had felt less fear of him this morning, yet still he was so gay, and at times so haughty, that she did not think she could ever quite trust him; and he would very probably soon become tired of noticing her; and her naturally proud spirit shrank from this. She was content to remain always unnoticed; but the thought of being flattered and slighted by turns was very distasteful to her.

This feeling, however, did but pass into her mind and out again. She opened her Bible, and read her evening portions. Then she knelt, and commended herself to her heavenly Father's faithful care and love, praying him to watch over her in her present lonely, isolated position, and grant his peace and rest in her heart, and a pure holy aim to please him and to be like him, and not to care what others thought of her, so that only her actions were pleasing in his sight. And she prayed him to give her grace to crucify all earthly desires, and sinful, unholy feelings that in the midst of her daily walk among others she might let her light shine, and so bring no reproach on the name she bore.

And she did not forget to remember Leonard. As she knelt she held communion with him in spirit, as he had told her; and the thought that he too perchance at that very hour was praying for her strengthened her mind; and she rose from her knees more quieted and refreshed than she had been since hearing the sad news of Leonard's leaving her.

She found Augusta in her aunt's room, where she went to say good night and read as usual. She seemed to have been telling of her, or at least of her cousin's delinquencies in the morning; so when they were left to themselves she mentioned to lady Archdale Lloyd's proposal and inquired whether she felt any objection.

" Not the slightest, my darling child," her aunt replied. " It will be well for him as well as you. He has great natural talent, and has often lamented to me that none in the family sympathized in his favorite pursuit. I have seen you looking at that sometimes," she added, pointing to an exquisite painting, a copy from one of the old masters, which hung opposite her couch: " that is the only religious subject he ever attempted, I believe. He gave it me on my last birthday; and I never tire of looking at it."

" It is indeed beautiful," Georgina said: " I have

often admired it, without having the least idea it was his."

" Your brother was speaking to sir William last night about Walter," lady Archdale said, when Georgie was leaving her, " and saying he thought his disposition and inclinations seemed more adapted to the army than any other profession. Do you know at all, darling? He is a strange, wayward boy, and never says a word to any one of us."

Georgie's heart bounded to think that her brother had not forgotten her request; and she answered eagerly; "O yes, auntie, Walter longs to go into the army; he has told me so, often. Why should he not?"

" There are difficulties in the way, dear child. Your uncle has always so wished him to take orders."

" But," said Georgie timidly, " do you think he is fit for that?"

" No, I am afraid not; but he might improve. Still I do not like thwarting a boy's inclinations so decidedly."

" Does my uncle think of doing anything?"

" I almost think he will. Leonard has promised to be on the look-out; and, if anything very suitable presents itself, I should not wonder if sir William were to buy the commission and let him go."

" O auntie, may I tell Walter?"

" You may speak to him about it, if you like,

dearest; but do not raise his expectations too high. He may have to wait some time. Poor Walter! I love him more than he will believe : he has always been so estranged from us as a family ; and the girls and Lloyd have not acted rightly by him, I know." ·

Georgie saw the hot tears gather in her aunt's eyes. She kissed them away.

" Dear, kind aunt," she murmured. " If he knew you as I do, he would not be able to help loving you."

" You must try and do him good, Georgie darling : you can, I am sure. Good night dear child."

VII.

THE DRAWING LESSON.

"One word, one look, one thought of sin,
Utter'd or glanced, or harbor'd in
  The heart, where Christ should reign,
Tho' mourned and wept, will leave behind
Some moral weakness in the mind—
  Upon the soul some stain."

MONSELL.

GEORGIE tapped at the door of her cousin's studio the next morning, just before the clock struck ten.

"May I come in for a minute?" she said timidly; "I left my pencil here yesterday, I think."

"Certainly," said her cousin, as he opened the door. "I was just beginning to paint. I am going to have a long morning's work."

Georgie glanced at the easel, on which was the same picture that had puzzled her so on the preceding day. This second look did not assist her in making out the subject. There were many figures surrounding what appeared to her a rude stone altar, and by this altar a woman's form was standing. She longed to know what it meant, but could not stay then, as she had promised Augusta to be in the school-room at ten o'clock precisely.

The lessons and French were particularly uninteresting that morning; and very glad she felt when
they were over, though vexed, when she looked at
the time-piece, and found that she was some minutes later than the time Lloyd had fixed for her to
come to him. " How careless he will think me !"
she thought to herself, as she passed hastily through
the corridor. She knocked twice, and waited some
time; but there was no answer. " Perhaps he is
gone out," she thought, " or at any rate does not
like to be disturbed at his painting; so perhaps I
had better venture in." And she entered softly.
She need not have feared disturbing the painter, as
he stood before his easel.

" Can it be Lloyd ?" she wonderingly whispered,
as she looked at her cousin, surprised at the change
which had come over him. The dark blue eyes,
which, beautiful as they were, she had never seen
with otherwise than the most listless expression,
were dilated with a strange light. The short upper
lip was slightly raised, the proud head thrown back;
and the black wavy curls, tossed from the white
forehead, gave a look of eagerness to the young
man's face, which astonished the child as she stood
breathlessly behind him, to look at the painting
which had so entranced the usually indolent and apathetic Lloyd.

It was the same sketch she had seen before; but
the principal figure was now partially completed;
and she saw that the group surrounding it was com-

posed of warriors, some in the prime of life, others old and grey, while there were those who seemed in the earliest youth. They were listening with rapt attention to the maiden who stood before them; for Georgie could almost see her speaking, so faithfully had the artist expressed his idea.

He had represented a scene of olden time in the far Norse land; rocks towering around, their summits capped with snow, and the only verdure the hardy pine and fir, saving that round the Saga's feet bloomed flowers not so beautiful as the lovely form which he had arrayed in snow-white robes, ornamented with borderings of mystic Runic characters. The lady's golden hair streamed down, and surrounded that calm wise face, as with a veil; and as Georgie gazed she distinguished the forms of little children plucking hold of the garments of the wondrous Alruna maiden, whose power was great to influence and rule the hearts of the childlike but mighty Vikings.

She stood there a long time, how long she did not know, till her cousin had put the last touches to the maiden's robe. As he finished he gave a sigh of intense satisfaction, and, stepping back to take a look at his work, he perceived, for the first time, the little girl, who was looking up at him with a face almost as wondering in its expression as those of the children whom he had just outlined in his picture.

"Why, Georgie, how long have you been here?

" She stood there a long time, till her cousin had put the last touches to the maiden's robe."

Brother's Watchword.   p. 108.

I had quite forgotten you; but I have been up in the clouds the last few hours; and you must excuse me."

"O, I don't mind in the least; but how can you paint so beautifully? I have been watching you ever since I came in, and longing to know what your picture means."

"O, only a fanciful sketch of mine," he replied carelessly, as though it was a thing of no interest to him. "I will explain it all to you some day; but I am half-famished now: let us go down to the dining-room. You must have an extra lesson to-morrow;" and he was again his haughty self. But Georgie for the rest of the day saw him only in his studio as she had seen him that morning, radiant and glowing and happy, with his passionate striving after the ideal.

"Ah!" thought she, "he is not satisfied with himself: he wants something higher and better. If only Leonard were here to talk to him?"

The next morning and the appointed hour found Lloyd quite prepared to receive his pupil, and the whole time he devoted to giving her elementary instruction in water-colors. He took an easy sketch, precisely similar to the one he gave her, and drew with her, making her imitate as closely as possible every touch.

"Not that I wish you to be a mere imitator," he said: "but you must get into the style of the thing first, and then you will be able to compose studies for yourself. I see you have it in you.

10

To-morrow you will do this alone, without any assistance or hints from me."

And so she did, perfectly to Lloyd's satisfaction; and from day to day she made such rapid advances that he began to feel proud both of himself as master and of her as pupil, and to congratulate himself on the plan, which had cost him a little at first, of admitting a second inmate to his sanctum.

He found her, as he had hoped, a perfectly quiet little companion. She never spoke at all except about her work, and then not often, unless he called her, or stepped across the room to speak to her; but sometimes, when she had finished her own, he would find her, as he turned, standing wonderingly behind his easel, watching the progress of the beautiful picture, or looking at him with her large thoughtful eyes. His face was so different when he was painting, that she found herself scrutinizing it sometimes when she was hardly aware of it. She fancied that there was something in it beautiful and peaceful then, like Leonard's; and she could not bear, when he had done painting, to see the fine features relax into their usual careless indifferent expression.

One morning, as she was standing thus by his side, looking almost with reverence first at him and then at his picture, he turned round suddenly.

"There, do not stir from that position," he said: "I want a little Constance to complete my group of Norse children; and I will have her now to the life. Quite still, if you please—but, stay: what on earth is become of your hair?"

"O, I am obliged to fasten it up when I am drawing: it comes in my eyes so."

He pulled out the comb rather unceremoniously; and the long bright curls dropped down about her face.

"There: that will do: now look up at the picture again, and don't think about yourself; but admire my beautiful Saga."

It required a little stretch of patience to stand just so for a whole hour and a-half; but she was repaid by Lloyd's thanking her, and telling her she had behaved admirably, and that he should not have to try her endurance in the same way again.

It was a sweet little face that he had painted, much more like the fair child under the elms than herself, Georgie thought, though she hardly liked to pay her cousin the ill compliment of saying she saw no resemblance at all. The shape of the face and the hair, and perhaps the eyes, might be her own; but the beautiful coloring and expression were fanciful certainly, at least as far as she was able to judge.

But Lloyd seemed quite well satisfied, and spent a great deal of time in perfecting the figure; and, as this and other new ones stood out from the canvass, Georgie thought that she had never seen such a surprisingly-beautiful picture in her life before.

Much to Georgie's uneasiness, she soon found that Mdlle. Victoire and Augusta set their faces most determinately against these drawing-lessons, which were becoming so pleasant to her. " They disturbed all her arrangements," the governess said: " she had been forced to change the hour for walking; Georgie's French and practising were terribly neglected; and, if Mr. Lloyd wished to exert his powers of tuition, it would be more seeming to begin at home, and instruct his own sister, who, notwithstanding all her efforts and teaching, had never yet been able to make a perpendicular."

Various unkind and annoying insinuations were thrown out, in Georgie's hearing, till the poor child became distressed and uncomfortable, and felt that if things were to go on peaceably a stop must be put to her lessons. She knew it was a poor return to make to her cousin for his pains, but felt, nevertheless, that she must propose a discontinuance of them; so, summoning up all her resolution, she said to Lloyd one day, after her lesson was finished—

" I am exceedingly obliged to you, cousin Lloyd, for all the trouble you have given yourself about me; but I think perhaps I have had enough lessons."

" What! do you think you have attained perfection?" he answered, drily; " because, if so, you are a little mistaken."

" O, no, don't think of such a thing," she replied, getting very red.

"Well, what do you mean, then?"

"I am afraid it is not quite convenient."

"Well, never mind that," he said, more good-humoredly; "I rather like having you here, because you don't talk and bother one."

"Thank you; but I did not mean quite that, either."

"What on earth do you mean, then?" he exclaimed, impatiently: "Are you tired, or lazy, or what?"

"O, no, no. I don't know whether I ought to tell the reason; but Mdlle. Victoire does not like my coming very much. It disturbs her so about the walk before dinner: she does not like walking after; and now we are obliged to walk then, and she and Augusta told me to tell you so. I did not like to tell you, indeed I did not; but, if you will not mind, I can give them up, though I shall be very sorry."

The poor child stopped here, tears in her eyes from vexation, and nervousness at having to give such a long explanation to her cousin, whose haughty features were working with pride and displeasure. He stamped his foot on the ground as she ceased speaking.

"I have a good mind you shall not set foot within that school-room again," he exclaimed. "Dictating to me, indeed! Not choosing to walk after dinner. It is all that woman's stupid conceit and jealousy; and I will just go and tell her so, and

10*

that she shall not be troubled with your company in future."

His eyes flashed as he spoke, and he strode across the room in high wrath. Georgie was seriously alarmed.

"Don't, don't go, Lloyd, I beg of you!"

He did not appear to listen: she rushed across the room, and, hardly knowing what she was about, seized his hand to detain him.

"O, cousin Lloyd, don't go!"

Her voice was so full of entreaty that he stopped a moment, and looked down upon her.

"It is on your account, Georgie. I am determined your visit here shall not be made miserable to please any one. They have been plaguing you, I am certain; and I might have known it if I had had my eyes open."

"O no, not that; but, Lloyd, some other arrangement might be made. I don't care about walking at all; or I could go in the garden, up and down the terrace by myself, if Mdlle. Victoire would allow me, or have a walk with Walter, when he comes in from Barnes; only don't say anything just now."

"Yes, I shall. Mdlle. Victoire absolutely rules in this house. My mother never interferes; how can she? And Frances is too lazy; but I will have my way this time. You shall not walk with them again just yet; and we shall see how they will like that. You shall go out with Frances and me."

"O, Lloyd," sighed the little girl. But it was too late, her cousin had left the room.

What passed between him and the governess she did not know, only that the latter carried herself more ungraciously and coldly than ever when they next met; and Georgie could hardly wonder, though she knew not what to do to make her feel differently. She could not treat her with more respect and obedience than she had hitherto done; but she saw that from the first, for some reason or other, Mdlle. Victoire had disliked her, looking on her as an intruder in the school-room, and treating her with far less consideration and kindness than she bestowed on her own pupils. Augusta and she were very great friends, kept up a continual gossip in French during their walks, a great deal of which Georgina could not have understood had she listened, about the company who visited at the house, their persons and dress, amusements, novels, and a hundred other things in which she felt no interest; so that these walks had been rather a trial to her than otherwise, especially when neither of the younger children accompanied them. She felt quite at home with them, amusing little Carry by the hour with poems and stories of her home, or things that had interested her when a child of her age; and Tom, by drawing him wonderful pictures of animals and trees and flowers, or patiently teaching him the lessons he had to prepare for his governess, and in which the young gentleman did not feel much interest.

They both loved their cousin Georgie very much: her gentleness and forbearance with their childish ways and faults, so different from Augusta's impatient, domineering temper, had completely won their affections; and in any little trouble she was sure to be sought out and made the confidante; and they found always plenty of sympathy and assistance from her.

That afternoon chanced to be wet, so there was no walking for any one. The following day, at noon, when Georgie was leaving the school-room, as usual, to take her drawing-lesson, she heard mademoiselle, in a very injured tone, tell Augusta to prepare herself for her walk; as Miss Archdale was not to accompany them in future, their company not being considered sufficiently good for her.

"'Tis but another of Lloyd's caprices," said Augusta, scornfully: "he will soon get tired of it."

"I hope he may not," mademoiselle answered; and poor Georgie, who had heard quite enough, hastened from the room.

"I shall tell mamma, if you all talk so unkindly to Georgie," exclaimed Carry: "I am sure she would be very angry. Cousin Georgie is better and kinder by far than any one else in the house."

"I shall punish you severely, if anything you hear in this room is repeated, mademoiselle," returned the governess: "go to your nurse immediately and be dressed, and let me hear no more of such rude speeches."

The child did not dare reply aloud, but muttered to herself as she left the room, " Well, I am not the only one: Lloyd knows she is hot kind; for he told her so yesterday; and I'll speak to him, if I don't to mamma."

Lloyd was so absorbed with his painting when Georgie went into his study, that he did not take the smallest notice of her; so, after standing a few minutes by his side, admiring the progress of the picture, she seated herself in her accustomed place, and went on with her work. He left off by-and-by with a sigh, as he very often did, then came and looked over her shoulder, drew a brush full of paint across a part which did not quite please him, and then went out of the room, humming, in a low clear tone, a song from Tennyson's words, " Break, break, break."

Georgie had become accustomed not to be much surprised at anything he did when in a painting trance, as she called it, and just taking a fresh sheet of paper commenced her sketch again.

Lloyd went into the library, where was Frances in her favorite easy chair, and a heap of books on her lap. He flung himself into a lounge opposite, and drew her attention by a yawn.

" O, Lloyd, how lazy you are !" she exclaimed, looking up from her book and laughing

"I am awfully so, I know; and you r ot much better, by the look of things."

"I beg your pardon: I have read a good part of two volumes, and entertained six tiresome people this morning; and that is no light work."

"Where is Kate Davenant?"

"In bed: she has not been well since the Mary-at's party; she danced too much, I suppose."

"And George Forrester?"

"O, Lloyd, you really are too bad. It is not right to ask people, and then be so rude to them. You never take the slightest pains to entertain that young man—at least of a morning: he has been gone out with papa the last two hours."

"It is very rude and unfeeling to have people here and not nurse them. Poor Kate! all alone and ailing: for shame, Francie; it is really too bad."

"She has her maid, and I have been up twice to inquire for her, and she is coming down to dinner; I am sure I can't do more."

Another yawn from Lloyd, and then the second verse of the song, in the same low tone.

"I say, my dear Fan, do play me that song; it is as beautiful as a picture; I don't tire of hearing it."

"Not just now, if you please, my dear; I so want to finish this before luncheon."

"Ah, I forgot—Frances, you don't mind Georgie's riding with us now and then?"

"O dear no; why, but can she?"

"I should say so; and the reason is that Mddle. Victoire is so stupid, or vicious, or something, that she won't walk after dinner; and so Georgina is either to be done out of that, or of her drawing-hour with me."

"What, are you teaching her to draw?"

"She does not require much teaching; she has it in her, as I have."

"But what can she ride?"

"The black pony, if he is not too fresh."

"Well, let her come. I don't mind at all, only I hope she won't make a figure of herself."

"We won't let her," he said; and getting up stretched himself, went to the piano, and played through his favorite air once, then returned to his study.

"What! did I spoil your picture?" he said, going up to Georgie again. "It was too bad; you were doing it so well."

"O never mind," she replied, "I shall put it with the others."

"Which others?"

"Those that have had black marks across them before," she answered smiling archly.

"How many are there of those?"

"O, five or six, I think; and it is certainly very foolish of me, but I don't like throwing away my first attempts."

"Is that your only reason for not destroying

them ?" he asked, at the same time taking the brush from her fingers and scribbling fantastic figures round the border of the spoiled drawing.

" Yes," she answered simply.

He went on scribbling. Georgie began to collect her pencils and brushes and put away the paints.

" Can you ride?" he asked her, just as she was preparing to leave the room, and without looking up from his occupation.

Her face brightened as it often did when she was pleased, without a smile, and she replied, " O yes."

" Who taught you ?"

" Leonard : we used to have long beautiful rides last summer."

" Do you ride well?'

" I don't know: I am not afraid."

" Well, that is one great thing. Get yourself ready after luncheon, and come and ride with Francie and me, will you?"

"I should like it very much, if I shall not be in your way," she replied, looking down ; " but cousin Frances might not like it."

" O I have asked her; so you need not be modest; have you your habit and all the needful here?"

" Yes, I dare say it was sent with the rest of my things. What time will you be ready ?"

"Let me see—you be in the library a little before three, and I will come and fetch you."

" Thank you," she said again in her grateful tone.

"Here, take your drawing, if you want it, and don't let me spoil any more : seize hold of my hand at another time, and say, ' You shall not.' "

Georgie smiled at the bare idea of her doing such a bold deed, took the drawing and went.   In putting it away she stood a moment examining the strange faces and figures that Lloyd had scribbled around it ; there seemed such talent and power in every stroke of his.

A curious sensation, half pleasurable, half of pain, just as she had experienced before, came over her as she saw that one of these faces was the child under the elm-trees—the Constance as he had called her.   It was very faint and indistinct, but still the same, and a tiny wreath of some sort of flower around the brow.   She felt vexed with herself that such a trivial insignificant circumstance should give her pleasure ; she remembered Leonard's words (.i the night she first heard of her visit to Leighton ; how he had told her that love of esteem and praise was one of her bosom sins ; she had never felt it more than at the present moment ; but she recollected also the precious remedy for this, and all other sins of thought as well as action.   "Lay them," Leonard had said, "at the foot of the cross, and let the Saviour's blood wash them all away."   " Cleanse the thoughts of my heart, O Lord," she murmured, "for thy dear Son's sake ;" and the tempter, who never can withstand the resistance of heartfelt prayer, fled away.

11

Georgie was ready at the appointed hour, had a pleasant ride with her cousins, though a little too shy to feel quite at ease, and demeaned herself entirely to their satisfaction. She had seen but very little of the neighboring country, seldom going beyond the outskirts of the park, excepting on Sundays, when they drove into Barnes once a day to church. She had no idea how beautiful and varied the scenery was; and her cousins were kind in pointing out any particular object or point of view that might interest her. They encountered in the course of their ride many people that they knew. To some of these Georgie was introduced; to others Lloyd and Frances spoke without noticing her, but told her who they were after passing, and then went off into some conversational scandal about one and another, none of which Georgie understood, and to which therefore she paid no attention. But she wondered inwardly how Lloyd, with his rare talent and power of thought, and deep real love for the beautiful, could waste his words on such frivolities. She looked at him again; he was a different man to what the morning saw him : a careless indifference, almost amounting to recklessness, was the expression of his handsome features, and she remembered what her brother had often told her, that beauty and genius and intellect are but dangerous talents when apart from the fear and love of God in the heart.

With Lloyd the one great needful thing was

wanting. The pearl of great price, beside which earth's brightest adornments are as nothing, was not his ; he was not willing to part with all he had, to purchase it. She thought of the young man in the gospel, whom Jesus looked on and loved, and she knew that nothing was too hard for God. " I can pray for him," she thought; and so she did from that day forward.

VIII.

WALTER'S STORY.

"Lord! grant that ever in my heart
  Such dread of sin may be,
That I may never dream of rest
  Or peace, except in thee;
That, 'neath the calmest, brightest sky
  Thy mercy ever gave,
This heart may dread sin's storm, and cry,
  Arise, my God, and save!"

MONSELL.

SINCE that night of explanation, which was yet fresh in the minds of both of them, Walter and Georgina had been friends. Strange as it seemed, she felt more at home with him than with any of the other members of the family, her aunt excepted. She told him all that interested her, her lessons with Lloyd, her French difficulties in the school-room, her letters from Leonard—such parts, at least, as other ears than her own might listen to; and the heart of the wilful impetuous boy expanded to her almost child-like confidences, opening out to hers in return; and life became a somewhat brighter, less cloudy thing than it was before. His grievances were still a subject of bitter complaint; but, as he thought and spoke more on other topics, they seemed to become less, and, since what Georgie had told him in reference to the subject of his future calling, he had ceased to speak so hardly of the family among whom he was thrown. Still, at times, when chafed by any fresh annoyance, he would indulge in very angry invectives against them, and declare that this promise was merely a bait, and that there was no real intention of its being fulfilled.

At such times Georgie had to exert all her influence and powers of entreaty and persuasion to induce him to be patient, and sometimes ventured to tell him that a little more forbearance and consideration on his part might save much vexation and annoyance. She could not direct him for guidance and consolation to the same source that was always so open and welcome to her; she knew that he cared not for it; that God was not to him as a reconciled Father, or at least that he knew him not as such; and, since he had called her an enthusiast, she had felt more fear than before of pressing home to his heart the subject of his soul's salvation, earnestly as she longed to do so.

She knew that there was that in Walter which never would be satisfied, though his earthly prospects might be bright and all that he wished them to be; a craving after some unknown untasted satisfaction, that the fulfilment of earthly hopes alone never can bestow.

With Lloyd the case seemed different. He per-

11*

suaded himself that he was happy; and his easy careless manner told the same tale to those around him. But Walter's restless melancholy face, though lightened up occasionally by the fire of his beautiful black eyes, was enough to speak, without words, that there was no happiness, no. rest nor peace within.

Georgie knew nothing more of his previous history than what he had spontaneously told her on the evening of their first conversation. She longed to hear more, but scarcely liked to ask him, for fear of reviving in his mind some bitter recollections. But, one night, as they sat together in the library, as it often happened they did, and the lessons of each were finished, Georgie said:

"Walter, you know I promised to be your sister as much as I could; and I feel just so now. Do you mind telling me something that I want to know very much, at least if you don't mind talking about it?"

It was evident that the subject was one ever uppermost in Walter's mind, and that Georgie's delicate reservation was at once understood; for he replied—

"Ah! you mean about my mother, I suppose?"

"Yes, I do. You mentioned her name once to me; and I thought perhaps you would have mentioned it again."

"No: it is almost too sacred ever to be breathed in this place," he replied in a deep, troubled tone.

" But I do not mind with you, if you wish it. You have known trouble yourself: it has done you good, and made you what you call a Christian; but it has only hardened me."

" Hush, Walter, I cannot bear to hear you speak so. The trouble was sent in love: I am sure it was, though you have never been able to feel it so. If you only knew what pity God felt all the time he was sending it you, and what love and pity he has for you now, you would not harden your heart against him."

"I do not harden my heart. It is so; and I can't help it. It would be untrue if I said I thought it was love to take from me the dearest, best friends, the only friends I ever had, and leave me poor and dependent and miserable."

"God has not done that, Walter," Georgina answered, seriously, but very affectionately. " He himself is the dearest, best friend we ever can have; and he says, 'I will never leave you, nor forsake you.' I could not be happy for a day, nor for an hour, without knowing that he loved me; and feeling that seems to make up for all. Yes, Walter, I have known trouble like you; but I think I can say truly that I would not wish it to be different now."

Here she stopped, and, hiding her face in her hands, wept silently for some minutes.

Walter was very sorry for her.

"Shall I tell you about mamma?" he said, drawing his chair nearer to where she was sitting, and speaking very gently.

"Yes, do," she answered.

"She was more beautiful, Georgie, than I can possibly tell you. Clara and Frances are beautiful; but, O! they are nothing compared to what she was. Her eyes were dark and bright, and yet so full of love and gentleness that it almost made one weep to look into them; and her voice was like the most exquisite music you ever heard. Sometimes, when Frances is singing, a note will come that reminds me a little of her; and that is one reason why I cannot bear to go into the drawing-room of an evening, because it makes me mad to hear anything she sang, or a voice like hers; and then to know that she is gone. I remember how that voice used to entrance me when I was a mere infant; how I have lain for hours in her arms when I was ailing or languid, and listened to it, and thought that it must be something like heavenly music. And, when I grew older, and was angry or vexed or impatient, how it would soothe me, and in one moment make me quiet and happy again! I remember that when I was about twelve years old, I had a very great illness. I suppose it was fever; for I was insensible for several days; but, when I came to myself the first time, there she was, hanging over me, her beautiful soft eyes looking down upon me, full of sorrow and love. I was too weak to speak to her, though I tried; but I shall never forget the tone in which she said only those three words, "My darling boy." I got better from that moment.

It was a delicious time while I was recovering. She nursed me all day long, giving herself quite up to me, and not going out at all, though she was so admired and courted by every one there, that no party was thought complete without her. O how proud and happy I used to be, as I watched her flit so quietly about the room in her light airy dress, with her sweet beautiful face, and to know that it was I whom she was thinking of; that her heart was full of love and concern for me; that I was uppermost in all her thoughts; for I knew that I was then. Then, when I got much better, and was able to sit out in the verandah, in the cool of the evening, she used to sing to me with that exquisite voice of hers; so that the very servants and natives stood still to listen."

" Where were you then ?" asked Georgina.

" At Calcutta. O those beautiful days of joy!"

Walter's face had been in one continual flush of animation all the time he had been speaking. It seemed as though he was living the time over again, and was happy in it. But, at last, he stopped, and said harshly, " Well, then I lost her."

"Poor Walter!" Georgie exclaimed involuntarily.

He went on in the same tone:

"She was only ill for a day, sickened in the

morning, and died just at sun-set. I was with her all the time. Papa was far in the country, and knew nothing till he returned, and all was over. She was insensible till within about half-an-hour of her death; for it was a dreadful fever; but then she opened her beautiful eyes consciously, and seemed to want me to come nearer. I was not crying then. From the moment the doctors told me there was no hope, I seemed like a person stunned, incapable of showing any emotion at all, and feeling only a kind of stupid despair, which I have known only too well since. I could only stand by the side of her couch, and look at her—that was all. When she beckoned me nearer, I felt my forced calmness giving way; but I dared not sob or shed a tear, or I knew I should be sent away. I put my hand in hers, and she tried to press it; but, O so feebly! Then she whispered, ' My poor Walter: I am afraid for you.' And well she might be, dear mamma, though I hardly understood it then. 'Comfort papa,' she whispered, a few minutes afterwards; and then she never spoke again. A little while afterwards she died; but her last look was at me. I don't remember anything else till papa came back. A great black shadow hung over every thing, and it has never been quite taken away. Of course time has done something to deaden the first dreadful shock, else I could not talk to you about it as I do now; but the shade that darkened my life then can never be effaced.

It wiL dull every thing till the grave—and then perhaps I shall find peace."

Georgie burst into tears. "No, Walter, dear, you won't, till you are reconciled with God. Death can't give you rest till Christ is your friend; and, if he was, why the shadow would be taken away at once, and you might have happiness and peace and joy even here. 'As one whom his mother comforteth, so will I comfort you.' He has said so himself. O, Walter, don't think it unkind in me to say it now—for I feel so much for you—but it is better to live here in misery than to die unprepared."

"Annihilation, a long, deep, unending slumber, is all the death I believe in," Walter said, gloomily; "and I am sure I have often longed for that."

"Hush, hush, Walter!" Georgie exclaimed, "you must not talk so. You will be sorry for every word another day. Besides, I can't bear to hear it. Not believe what God says! not believe the Bible!" And she rose, and looked into his face with a look of intense sorrow.

"*You* need not mind, Georgina. You are all right, you know, however it is; and, if it comfort me to think as I do, why shouldn't I?"

"Because it is such miserable false comfort, and will bring you to despair and wretchedness at last. Walter, what would your poor mamma have said?"

And Georgie hid her face in her hands, and wept again.

"Mamma! Ah! she was more like you. If any one is safe, she is; but there must be a different road for good, and pious, and happy people, and those who are proud and impetuous and unfortunate as I am: why, they can have no two thoughts in common."

"Walter, I can not argue with you. I don't know how. I can only tell you what the Bible says, and beg you to read it for yourself. I do pray for you."

"Do you?" he said, looking up.

"Yes, every day. But that cannot do you much good," she added, sorrowfully, "unless you know what it is to pray for yourself too."

They sat in perfect silence for some time, Georgie's last words seeming to echo from the walls of the room upon the hearts of each. Then Walter stood up. "Good-night, Georgie; I am obliged to go into the drawing-room this evening. There is a gentleman there who knows something about me, lady Archdale said; and she wished me to see him; so I suppose I must go. I will tell you about papa some other time, if you like."

"Yes, I should. Only, Walter, don't give up reading the Bible. Good night, and thank you for all you have told me."

He grasped the little hand firmly, and then went up stairs to arrange his dress. Though it had been very painful, yet Georgie felt thankful for that night's conversation. She was so glad to have been able to speak faithfully to Walter; she had not felt at all afraid, and she knew that her strength had come from above. She was so thankful, too, that he had not been angry or offended with her; the hope of being, under God, a blessing to him was still strong in her heart; and she prayed for him that night more earnestly than ever.

Georgina continued to ride with her cousins most afternoons when it was fine. Sometimes Captain Forrester, a friend of Lloyd's, who was staying at Leighton, for a time, accompanied them, and once or twice Miss Davenant; but she was very delicate, and not able to exert herself much. One afternoon, as they were setting off, Frances said to her brother, "It is no use, Lloyd, putting it off any longer. Lady Legh must be called on; so we had better go this afternoon: it will make us rather later home; but that can't be helped."

Lloyd glanced significantly at Georgina, whom he was just mounting, and who therefore did not observe the motion.

"Well, ' ça ne fait rien.'   Georgie, you don't mind having rather a longer ride, do you? We want to go and make a call, which is too far for an ordinary drive."

"No, not at all," she answered; and the matter was settled.

Fern-Hill-side, the residence of Sir Henry Legh, a young knight, but lately married, was beautifully situated. The mansion, but recently rebuilt, in a modern style of great splendor, was surrounded by lawns and gardens, laid out in exquisite taste, which Georgie could not but admire as they rode up the broad gravel walk. The groom having inquired, and brought word that they were at home, Lloyd assisted his sister to dismount. Then he came to Georgie.

"I had rather stay and ride up and down, if I might;" she asked timidly.

"Nonsense," he said. "What on earth are you thinking of? You must get over your shyness, my little cousin."

He helped her from her horse. Georgina glanced for a moment at Frances. She was standing at the top of the flight of steps, waiting for her; her fine tall figure, set off to advantage by her riding habit, was drawn up; and her beautiful face, slightly flushed by the exercise, looked more handsome than ever. She was holding her dress with one hand, and with the other tapping impatiently against the pillar with her silver-mounted whip. 'What a beautiful brother and sister they are!' Georgie thought, as Lloyd looked proudly on his sister as they entered.

But, if not with equal pride, yet with as much interest, though she knew it not, did his eyes follow the little delicate figure, as, keeping close to the side of her cousin Frances, she entered with her the large, splendid drawing-room.

A satisfied thought passed through his mind.

"I *am* fulfilling her brother's wishes. I am taking care of her," he said to himself. Lloyd, beware! The care that has hitherto been lavished on her has been of a wise and holy nature. She has been helped on in the narrow way; and a brother's prayers and supplications for her have ever been that her garments might be kept unspotted from the world. And your inward thought now is, is it not? that she may with impunity contract some stain—some slight one, you may account it. She is young, and easily led, and timid. You admire her consistency of life, and simple, childlike purity of conversation and thought. But it is a reproach to your conscience, and you would seek to mar it by a nearer contamination with the world, and its vain show and glory. You do not think that you sin in doing so; you wish her life to be made pleasant, and bright, and happy to her; but it is a dangerous mistake. The peace and prosperity of a soul is at stake; and, should you succeed in your endeavors, and draw her into the net which you, half-unknowingly to yourself, have prepared for her, what bitter regret and tears, and agony of self-accusation may be hers!

Lady Legh was all smiles and brilliancy. She chatted pleasantly with Lloyd. Frances was soon busily engaged with Flora Legh, a young sister-in-law who lived at Fern-Hill-side, and was a great friend of the Archdales. Sir Henry endeavored to entertain Georgina by exhibiting a very ex tensive in-door aquarium, of which he was very proud.

"I have succeeded in finding the proper balance," he said. "This water has not been changed for the last three months, and will not be, in all probability, for six more; and you see the fish are perfectly healthy."

Georgie had not the smallest idea what the balance meant, but thought it must be a very convenient thing, as she recollected the fate of various poor gold and silver fish at Beechwood, whose water she and Margaret were changing perpetually, and who had sickened and died off, one by one, to their great sorrow and mortification. She would have liked to inquire what he meant, but her great shyness stood in the way and prevented her. Lloyd called off her attention.

"May I take my cousin round the picture-gallery, lady Legh?" he asked. "There are one or two paintings there I should like her to see."

Frances had often been there before, so she remained with the other ladies in the drawing-room. On their return they found her waiting for them, and just accepting from lady Legh an invitation to a large party she was giving the following week.

"Captain Archdale, we shall see you too, and Mr. Forrester, and your cousin here. My dear," turning to Georgie, "I hope you liked the paintings: we think a great deal of that Cimabue."

"I liked it very much," she answered; "it has been a great treat, seeing them all."

"Yes, this young lady is quite a connoisseur in paintings, if not in aquariums," Sir Henry remarked, laughing. Georgina blushed. She had felt a great interest in the aquarium, though she had not said so; and now she was afraid her apparent indifference had seemed rude or ungrateful. She tried to say so, but very awkwardly, for they were all listening to her. Sir Henry held out his hand good-humoredly.

"Well, we shall see you next Tuesday night. I will not tease you with molluscs and fishes then. You will come?"

"Thank you, I never go out of an evening."

"Well, then, it is time you should begin. I shall not excuse you."

Georgina looked at her cousins for support.

"I had rather not," she said again.

"Nonsense, I will take care of you," said Lloyd, "see you don't dance too much, or get over-heated. I am an admirable chaperon." The ladies laughed. Georgie felt miserable, but could not say another word. They took leave, sir Henry accompanying them to the door.

"Why does not Miss Archdale wish to come, next week?" he asked. "There will be lots of young people."

"O, she is rather strict in her notions, that is all," said Frances. "She does not approve of dancing, I believe."

"Ah, ah!" he said, laughing. Then going up to Georgie, "I have found out your secret, young lady; but I shall not let you off, for all that. A dance now and then would do you all the good in the world. Lloyd," he called out, as they rode off, "I shall trust to your powers of persuasion :" and Georgina heard him laugh again as he went back into the house.

She felt that she must speak at once, trying as it was to her. Besides being particularly distasteful to her, she knew that, if she once gave in, once joined a party of the description of lady Legh's, it would be expected from her in future. The line once crossed, it would be impossible to know where or how to stop. She was so thankful now to have no desires that way, she so dreaded the thought of its ever becoming tasteful to her. She knew that there was a meaning in those words: "If any man is a friend of the world, he is an enemy of God." "Be not conformed to this world :" "Pass the time of your sojourning here in fear ;" and many other passages which came into her mind, even then. And her brother's farewell motto, "Seeing him who is invisible," came forcibly into her mind. Could she bear the thought of being looked upon by Him, when in a scene of dissipation and gaiety, where he was far from the thoughts of all, and where the sudden intimation of his appearing would only beget gloom and horror and despair? She gathered courage to speak—

"Lloyd, I hope I shall not seem rude or ungrateful for their kindness; but I cannot go to lady Legh's party Tuesday evening.

"Nonsense, Georgie," Frances said, in a tone of some annoyance; "what harm can it possibly do you for once? You know we have never wished you to come out much; but, when people ask you in this way, you really must not be so absurd. As though there was any harm in a dance!"

"O leave it to me," said Lloyd; "I am sure she will not be so unkind as to refuse me when I particularly wish it, leaving my promise out of the question."

Georgie thought it best not to say anything more just then; she would be able to speak better to Lloyd when Frances was not present, and she would take the opportunity the next day, at her drawing-lesson. She rode home the rest of the way in silence, but feeling perplexed and uncomfortable.

They reached Leighton quite late. Frances hastened to dress for dinner. Georgie went into the school-room, where she received a reprimand from Mdlle. Victoire for having been so long out. She did not attempt to justify herself, but sat down to her lessons, and studied busily till tea-time.

" And so, you have'been to lady Legh's this afternoon," Augusta began, as they were seated at the tea-table, "and we are all invited there for next Tuesday! I am so glad; it is an age since I have been out; and their parties are always so splendid.

Last time we were not home till nearly three o'clock. I danced twice with sir Henry; he makes much of Frances and me. Did he inquire for me, Georgie? Frances wouldn't tell me."

" Yes, I think he sent his love to you, or something of the kind."

Augusta laughed. "There, I knew he would. O mademoiselle, you should see him; he is the most delightful man, so handsome and agreeable. But you will, Tuesday evening; Georgie and I shall want a chaperon. Frances never looks after one the least; so different from Clara!"

" What! is Georgina going?"

" Yes, I suppose so: she was asked."

" Are you, Miss Archdale?"

" No," Georgie replied very decidedly.

" Well, you will be very rude, and very foolish if you don't, that's all. · Frances said sir Henry asked you particularly; and he 'll not soon forget it, if you refuse him."

"Some people like to be thought particular," mademoiselle remarked in French, and the subject dropped.

Georgie had a trying battle with her cousin the next morning; but in the end she came off victoriously. First, he laughed at her scruples; that was very trying to bear. Then he worked upon her regard for him; he was willing to oblige her in any way; and would she not for one night consent to gratify his wishes? That was harder still for the poor child to resist; but she did. Then he spoke scornfully and almost angrily. What right had a girl like her to set up her opinion above those who were older and wiser? It was nothing but puritanical weakness which she ought to overcome, and just as good as telling them they were a set of wicked sinners together. There was certainly no great virtue in such absurd scruples.

Still there was silence; but a big tear-drop fell upon the picture she was drawing, from underneath the bent eyelids of the steadfast young girl. Lloyd was ashamed of himself.

"Georgie! what! crying? Have I hurt your mind? Is it really so serious a matter as all that?"

She took her handkerchief and dashed it away, and others that were gathering in her eyes as well.

"Forgive me, Lloyd. I don't mean to be ungrateful. It is very kind of you to wish to please me; and I am so sorry."

"Ah! well, I yield this time; but another day, Georgie, I shall expect you to give in. Eh?"

Georgie smiled gratefully through her tears, and was too thankful for the present release to look forward to a future day. Besides which, she remembered the words, "As thy days, thy strength shall be."

Nothing more was said to her on the subject by any of her cousins. On the appointed evening, as she and Walter were sitting together in the library at rather a later tea than usual, Lloyd entered, with a disastrous crack in his white kid glove.

"Here, Georgie, help me out of my trouble, I beg of you—not another pair at hand, and this great hole!"

She fetched her needle and thread instantly, and soon neatly repaired the fracture. He stood watching her, as her small fingers moved busily. She looked so pure and innocent in her clean white dress; and the strong light from the gas-burner fell on her light curls, which hung about her neck, giving them a sort of radiance, such as he had seen abroad in glowing pictures of the Madonna, with the crown of brightness encircling her brows. Her figure seemed but the expression of what there was within —peace and trust.

"You don't seem uncomfortable here," he said, when she had finished the last stitch, and gave it back into his hand with a smile. "And here you are, sending me off to look foolish—'

"You can't, very well," she replied. "Shall I fasten your glove?" she added, as he fidgeted at the button.

("Lloyd, Lloyd!" called Augusta from the hall; "we are all waiting for you.")

"Yes, if you will."

"Had you better put them on at all, just yet? You have a long way to drive."

"Ah! I forgot. Well done, Miss Prudence. How those girls do scream! Walter, aren't you coming?"

Walter glanced at his dress, but deigned no reply.

"Good night, little Georgie, and take care of yourself."

Then he left the room, humming carelessly--

> " And I would that my tongue could utter
> The thoughts that arise in me."

That evening lady Archdale informed Georgina that all the family were going to London in a fortnight's time.

IX.

UNSATISFYING PLEASURES.

"Mark that long dark line of shadows,
  Stretching far into the past;
Every day it seems to lengthen—
  Whither doth it tend at last?
Each one added to the hosts
  From the present moment flies:
These are time's forgotten ghosts,
  Fleeted opportunities."

IT was a beautiful night in the early part of May. A carriage was waiting before the door of a large mansion in Belgravia, in the upper windows of which many lights were burning. But by-and-by they disappeared, and the various occupants emerged from their several rooms. They met in the hall, which was also brilliantly lighted.

Sir William Archdale was waiting there, and Lloyd in his full uniform. Sir William handed his two daughters into the carriage waiting before the door; and then, a little behind, came a pretty graceful figure. Could it possibly be Georgie? Yes, it was. She was dressed in a silk of the most delicate blue: a wreath of forget-me-nots was twined in her fair hair; and her usually pale cheeks were suffused with a delicate color. Lloyd looked down upon her triumphantly as she entered the carriage, and remarked to his father in a tone she could not possibly avoid hearing, " As handsome as any of them, when she is properly dressed." Sir William assented, told Lloyd, as he jumped in after them, to send back the carriage to take him to his club ; and the door closed.

The carriage drove to the Royal Italian Opera. It was a gay and brilliant scene : the music, the singing, the dancing—all was perfect. But one aching heart at least beat there. Yes, under that calm, peaceful, constant face, Georgina Archdale was miserable. Her cousins were all smiles and gaiety; and she smiled too sometimes, but it was not the expression of her heart. They were in lady Legh's box; and sir Henry and his brother and sister were there. He talked and laughed with Georgina, congratulating her on seeing her face there, where he had so little expected. Every word was like a sword in Georgie's breast. Lloyd came and spoke gently to her, pointing out a part in the programme of peculiar beauty, and telling her the names of the principal artists. She did not hear him; or, if heard, the words came unheeded. O for the long weary hours to be passed !

But how came she there, when her heart was so little in it, and every minute so heavy and tiresome that it seemed as an hour ?

The time had come, as Lloyd had expressed it, she must give in. She had made a long resistance,

13

pleaded her distaste and Leonard's disapprobation, and every argument she could make use of; but all to no avail. Her fear of vexing and displeasing Lloyd had been stronger than her powers of resistance; and, though she was doing wrong, and violating her conscience each time, this was not the first, nor the second, nor the third, that she had come into scenes where her heart told her she would not dare to meet the face of her brother, far less the eye of her grieved, but still loving, Heavenly Father.

The only pleasurable result arising from this repeated violation of her principles—for her heart was as far from these scenes as ever—was the sense of her cousin's approval and satisfaction. He had so laid himself out to please her, during their stay in London, giving up all the time he could spare from his duties with his regiment, to show her sights—galleries of paintings, museums, and all that he thought would interest her; but he required in return that she should give up her will on the subject which lay so deeply in her heart, and oblige him by going whither she knew she ought not. And was she happy? Ah, no! far from it. Her quiet times were no longer happy seasons. She observed them as carefully and strictly as before; but the reading of the Scripture and prayer brought no peace nor comfort to her mind. She was walking contrary to God on a point of deep and serious import; and how could she expect his blessing?

She had held out a long time, resisting her cousin's arguments and persuasions very steadily, till on one occasion, when he assumed a very injured and offended manner, and ended by saying that she could not have much regard to her brother's wishes and last words, he having given her specially into his charge. "I may have performed his request very imperfectly, I know," Lloyd had said; "but still I have done so, as far as was in me; and I don't fancy he would consider it a very gracious return for you to make, refusing to gratify me for once in a thing which cannot hurt you in the least. If Leonard had not some species of confidence in me, he would not have spoken as he did."

Georgie's face had kindled as her cousin thus bitterly addressed her: varied emotions contended in her breast. Ungrateful! O she could not endure such an insinuation. She grew very pale; then, looking down upon the floor, she said quietly, "I will go with you, Lloyd."

His handsome features, which were clouded before, brightened instantly: he felt that the victory was gained, little troubling himself at what a cost, and he thanked her repeatedly.

"Now I must be off," he said, taking out his watch. "The men exercise in the park this morning; and I am on duty. To-morrow I shall be free, and we will go, before luncheon, to the Royal Academy again. Good bye, Constance. I am quite proud to think how amiable you have been.

Depend upon it, no one will think the worse of you for giving up your own will occasionally."

"O don't," said Georgina, in a tone almost of pain, as she turned away.

She watched him from the window as he walked down the square, his fine figure drawn up, and towering above the other passers-by. "Constance!" she murmured to herself, as he disappeared from sight. "O, I do not deserve such a name! I have not been constant. I have not held on faith fully. But how could I help it? O Leonard, Leonard!" She went into her own room, and wept long and bitterly. A call from Augusta to prepare for a drive aroused her at last: she washed her face and eyes; and, by the time she was dressed, her countenance was as tranquil and composed as ever. In the evening she found lying on a table in her room, directed to her, a small round box. It contained an elegant wreath of forget-me-nots and a slip of paper in Lloyd's hand-writing, asking her to wear them on the following evening, and one of her pure white dresses that he liked so much.

Georgina looked at the flowers, then at the note, read the latter two or three times, then slowly tore it up and flung it on the fire, watching the pieces as they consumed rapidly in the blaze. Then she closed the box, placing it in her wardrobe, with a sigh. "My heart shrinks from it," she said. "O may I be forgiven!" After the ice had once been broken, it became, as Georgie had feared, an ex pected thing for her to go out, at least to such parties as she was invited to ; but the evening to which at the commencement of the chapter I have referred was the first on which she had visited the Opera.

She had a secret dread of the very name ; but Lloyd had silenced her scruples, and assured her that, if she found anything she objected to, he would not ask her to go again ; but just once she must go, and judge for herself, the singing was so glorious. He went out with Frances, and himself chose the light delicate dress. It suited her fair white complexion ; and he was proud as he looked upon her.

But he saw that she was not happy, that the answers she returned to his questions, and appeals to her taste for admiration, were such as showed her heart was far away. And truly indeed it was! For even there, in the midst of that gay assembly, the gleaming lights, and the thrilling captivating music, her brother's watchword came into her mind, and wounded her very soul as with an arrow : " Seeing him who is invisible." O was this the time and this the place to realize the scrutinizing presence of that omniscient One, to rejoice in that presence, and to expect peace and blessing from it ? Invisible to the natural eye, he was at that very moment watching her : what if he should send the summons to meet him! The bitter anguish of the thought was insupportable, and she grew pale. Lloyd marked it, and inquired if she were feeling unwell.

" No, not that ; but, O Lloyd, do let me go

13*

away from here, I am *so* miserable. Let me go alone—in a cab,'' she urged, but in a low tone, that she might not excite notice.

"My dear Georgie, it is impossible: wait, at least, till we go; there is but another hour."

"I have done wrong in coming, Lloyd. O, could you not take me out ?"

No, the thing was unreasonable ; she must wait for the carriage, unless indeed she felt too ill to stay. At that moment there was a little stir in the box, and an attendant put a note into Lloyd's hand. A sense of impending trouble came over Georgina; her cousins were engrossed with the music and sir Henry; *she* only watched Lloyd's countenance as he read. His first look was at her ; and there was that in his face that she had never seen there before. She started. He raised his finger warningly, then approached Frances, and said, "Georgie is feeling unwell ; and I am going home with her. Sir Henry will see you to the carriage."

"Georgie ill, poor child !" said Frances, as she turned and saw her pale face. "Yes, do go, Lloyd."

They left the box together: In the lobby he put the note into her hands, that she might read it from the light of the gas burner overhead. "I fear lady Archdale is dying. I have sent for sir William; but he has not yet come in. Could you return at once ?"' These were all the words that Georgie could read ; and even these swam before her eyes, and she had to lean against the wall for support.

The note was signed by the family physician in London.

" Now, Georgie, this is dreadful," Lloyd said. " Can you be calm ?"

"Yes," she murmured; "but Francie and Augusta ?"

" They will know it soon enough. It is no use calling them away now." He flung his military cloak around her as he spoke, for she was shivering, and then led her to the carriage. It was a silent agonizing drive. Georgie could not weep, not even shed one tear ; but her heart beat violently as they drove almost furiously into the square. Her cousin whispered, as he handed her out, "I am sorry you went to night against your will, Georgie. You will have to help us all now."

The house was in great excitement. Sir William was not yet returned; and lady Archdale still continued insensible. Georgie, with a breaking heart, hastened to her room ; but the physician, with a grave look, requested that none but sir William might enter until the crisis should be past. " Ah, if I had been at my post, I should not have been sent away," she thought bitterly, as she returned to the drawing-room. Lloyd went in search of his father, and presently returned with him, then went out again on a message from the physician to a friend.

An hour after, the sisters came in. They were surprised to find Georgie dressed, and sitting up. She told them, as calmly and firmly as she was able, of their mother's danger, and begged them, as Lloyd had desired her, not to sit up, as none but those in immediate attendance could be of use. Then she retired to her own chamber; but not to rest. It was a night never to be forgotten by her. On bended knees she returned to her Heavenly Father, and, with his help, made a solemn resolve never again to be led aside from the plain path of known duty into the false allurements of the world, either to please herself or another. She entreated pardon, with many tears for the uneven path she had of late trodden, and grace to keep unspotted from the daily soil of this world's contaminating influence the garments washed clean by the precious blood of the cross. And with great earnestness she prayed for her beloved aunt, that, if Christ's will, she might be spared to them yet a little longer. And when she arose from her knees she sought her Bible, and, in studying its precious words, she found more consolation and happiness to her soul than for many a past week.

And so the time passed, until three o'clock in the morning. The house had seemed very quiet for some time; she longed to know tidings from her aunt's room, and for that purpose stole quietly along the passage, until she arrived at the outside door. She did not knock, fearing the worst, but stood there silently and with clasped hands, waiting till a servant might appear. At length the door opened gently, and the physician came out followed by Lloyd. Both started on seeing the little figure standing so motionless on the landing. She had not changed her evening dress: her cheeks were very pale, and her eyes looked strained and weary. She looked into the doctor's face, and from it gathered strength to ask how was her aunt.

"Better," he replied: "the crisis is passed; and I am going to leave her for a time. And for yourself, young lady," he added, "I think the best place would be bed."

"Georgie, you should not have been sitting up," Lloyd said, "you know I told you—"

"Is this Georgie?" inquired the physician, who was just then turning away. "Lady Archdale has been speaking of Georgie: she seemed to have been expecting you," and he glanced at her full dress. She understood the meaning of that look; and tears gathered in her eyes.

"I may go to her in the morning, may I not?" she added.

"Yes, if you go to bed now, and wake up tomorrow, looking a little less spirit-like," he said, laughing: "Your white face actually frightened me just now."

Georgie thanked him and retreated.

"Is that your sister, captain Archdale?" inquired the physician, as he went down-stairs.

"No, a cousin," Lloyd replied.

"You must be careful of her: she is not fit for much night-work; so don't encourage her in it."

Lloyd's conscience twinged him rather unpleasantly. "It is the rarest thing for her to go out of an evening," he replied: "she has been so excited and alarmed to-night: that makes her paler than usual. You don't think she looks seriously ill?"

"O dear, no: only be a little careful, that's all."

Lady Archdale slowly recovered; and Georgie was a most assiduous little nurse. She sat with her as much as she was allowed, bringing her work and books into her room, and reading or sitting quietly there, just as her aunt was most disposed.

She received about this time a long letter from her brother, who, owing to some lengthened delays at the Cape, had but just arrived in India. He told her that, should all be well, his stay in the country might not exceed three or four months; so that, quite at the end of the autumn, it was possible that under God's blessing, they might meet again. He had received all her letters, which he acknowledged with so much pleasure that Georgie smiled and wept by turns. "And how prospers the inner life, my darling sister, among much that is outwardly more diverting and entangling than you have known before? Well, I trust, from what you write. Keep near to him who is invisible: let not your love for me—which is yet so precious that I would not wish it one iota less—or for any other earthly object or pursuit, draw off your eye from the Saviour. You know already the words of St. Augustine : ' He loveth too little who loves anything beside thee, except he love it for thy sake.' Seek always to feel this, that every other aim and interest and affection be subservient to the great absorbing one—love to Christ, and to the Father through him. We are only happy so long as we realize this : when the world once creeps in, and gets the upper hand, our peace and comfort from that very hour decline, prayer becomes dead and unprofitable, the reading of the Scriptures a wearisome and irksome duty, instead of a delight and a blessing. And so, dear Georgie, I pray that you may be kept in the sunshine of conscious nearness to him who is the centre of all life and peace and happiness, that, crucifying daily the flesh with its affections and lusts, you may be each day more prepared for the eternity which we hope to spend together in his presence."

Georgie knew by experience the truth of her brother's words : her tears flowed afresh as she read them that night in her room ; and, though she felt assured that her past wanderings had been forgiven, yet it made her only the more conscious of her great weakness, and earnest in prayer for grace to withstand all such entanglements in future.

As soon as Lady Archdale was sufficiently recovered to be removed, the family left London ; and all again returned to Leighton, with the excep-

tion of Lloyd, whose duties with his regiment required his presence in town.

Since the night of his mother's alarming illness
he had been very watchful over his cousin, ceasing
every endeavor to persuade her to go where she
knew she could not, with comfort to herself, but
making her daily rides or drives very pleasant, by
visiting various scenes of interest quite new to
Georgie, and where instruction as well as entertainment could be gathered. Of an evening he was
never at home. The sisters returned to their usual
gay life as soon as their mamma was considered
out of danger; and Lloyd was their constant attendant. But often before setting out he would
bring to her in the drawing-room, or in his mother's
room, where Georgina spent much of her time, a
portfolio of drawings, or some new and beautiful
book, which he thought might amuse her; and she
often wondered how it was he knew so well just
what she liked, or found the time and opportunity
to procure it.

But one thing in reference to Lloyd weighed
heavily on Georgina's mind, and the more so because she longed to speak to him of it, and yet
dared not. Lloyd was frequently in the habit of
taking the name of God in vain—not often before
her or his mother, but when in the company of other
gentlemen, or when angry, or in conversation with
those beneath him in station. She longed for courage to ask him to stop, to remind him that the sin

which seemed small in his eyes was as great a breach of the holy perfect law as murder, or theft, or perjury. It always made her start, and the color come to her cheek, when she heard the words escape his lips; and sometimes she said, with a strange feeling of perplexity, " Am I right in liking so well one who from day to day sins so directly against a plain command of God ?"

But then she looked into her own heart, and saw so much that seemed even worse there, that she was ashamed of the thought. " He does it without considering its guilt, and he has had no one to warn him. This surely is a case in which I should not do wrong to speak, should God give me the courage." So she thought to herself, and at the same time laid the matter before her heavenly Father in prayer.

The evening before they left London a fair opportunity presented itself. Lloyd came into the drawing-room where she was collecting some books and other things that were to be taken back to Leighton.

" Georgie," he said, " I have brought you a little souvenir, that you may not quite forget my existence between this and August."

" Thank you, Lloyd; even if I needed presents to keep me from forgetting you, there is not much cause for fear: that beautiful box of colors, the locket with Leonard's hair, my 'Lives of the Painters,' that exquisite statuette of—"

"My dear Constance, pray stop: you know young ladies memories are apt to be treacherous; but see, I have consulted your taste this time, and have brought you a good book. You are fond of all kinds of old-fashioned, outlandish, mystified divines: do you know old Thomas-à-Kempis?"

"Ah, yes, Leonard has one. But, O Lloyd, how beautiful! what a magnificent copy! You surely do not intend it for me?"

"Do you like it? See, it is all got up in the old way—illuminated, and what not."

"It is splendid. I shall value it very much, and read it too." And she turned over the leaves slowly, and with intense pleasure.

Lloyd watched her complacently: he always liked to see her thoroughly pleased. "What are you reading?" he asked at last, as she lingered over a page longer than merely admiring the beautiful illuminated capitals. She pointed rather mildly to the passage which had caught her attention: "If thou seek rest in this life, how wilt thou then attain to the everlasting rest? Dispose not thyself for much rest, but for great patience. Seek true peace not in earth, but in heaven; not in men nor any other creature, but in God alone. For the love of God thou oughtest cheerfully to undergo all things—that is to say, all labor, grief, temptation, vexation, anxiety, necessity, injury, reproof, humiliation, and correction of every kind and degree."

"You intend that for me, I suppose?" Lloyd said.

when he had read it. "You are decidedly disposed to great patience, and would, I believe, endure that long list of calamities in the most magnanimous way."

"O, Lloyd, you do not know me, or you would not think so."

"Yes, I know you very well; you are goodness personified—a little too good; that is all the fault I find with you. It sits very well on you, however; but this quietness and intense abnegation would not suit me. I like to enjoy life thoroughly *now*, while I can, and it is pleasantest, eh, Georgie?"

Georgina could not smile in reply, as he did. Some words came into her mind—"Remember *now* thy Creator, in the days of thy youth, while the evil days come not, nor the years draw nigh, when thou shalt say, I have no pleasure in them." Her heart beat, and the color came into her face; she might ─ithout ostentation make use of this opportunity, for a question had been asked her; but, as she feared and pondered, the occasion vanished.

"Ah, you are too charitable to condemn me, I see, plainly," said her cousin. "Now, good night, little Constance: I shall not say good bye till to-morrow. I shall hardly know myself when you are all gone."

"Did you say it would be August before you came back to Leighton?" she asked, as he left the room.

"Yes: what were you thinking of?"

"Perhaps Leonard may be home by that time," she answered with a sigh.

"Hardly, I should think," replied her cousin; "but do not distress yourself: we will take good care of you;" and then he added to himself, as he went down-stairs, "I believe that child thinks of nothing but Leonard from morning till night."

The next day, about noon, found Georgie seated with her aunt and her attendant in the ladies' compartment of a railway carriage, one side of which was fitted up as a couch, lady Archdale not being equal to anything but a reclining posture.

Carriages met them at Barnes, and early in the evening they arrived at Leighton. It had been an exquisite day; and Georgie had never seen the Hall looking so beautiful before. The trees were still leafless when they left for London: now all was clothed with fresh bright verdure. The slanting shadows of the elm and oak trees in the park lay softly on the green turf, and the few fleecy clouds which travelled softly across the blue sky were reflected in the clear sheet of water which formed a pleasing feature in the grounds of Leighton.

"How lovely it all is!" Georgie could not refrain from exclaiming, as they approached the house.

Augusta, to whom the remark was addressed, answered with a sigh: "It is very well, but nothing after London: it was a dreadful bore to be obliged to come off so soon. 'Tis true the holidays will soon be here, and then the Elmores are com ing, and we shall have archery fêtes, and so on; but I hate the country, especially after London."

" But you know, mignonne, the society of Barnes is nearly equal to that of London," remarked Mdlle. Victoire: "you may be as gay as you please: there is always something going on."

"That may be; but, my dear mademoiselle, you must confess it seems flat at first."

They reached the house just then, and the conversation was interrupted.

" Walter come out to meet us, I declare!" said Augusta: "wonders will never end."

"To meet Georgina, I fancy," said the governess, as Walter handed Georgie out, and followed her into the hall.

14*

X.

UNCONSCIOUS INFLUENCE.

" There are—of beauty rare,
  In holy calm up-growing,
Of minds, whose richness might compare
  E'en with thy deep tints glowing;
Yet all unconscious of the grace they wear,

" Like flowers upon thy spray—
  All lowliness—not sadness:
Bright are their thoughts, and rich, not gay:
  Grave in their very gladness;
Shedding calm summer light over life's changeful day."

                                        S. D.

A FEW days after her return to Leighton
there came to Georgina a letter in her cousin
Lloyd's hand-writing. She opened, and read
as follows: "Dear little Constance,—A friend in
need is a friend indeed; and now I am going to
put your friendship to the test. I want a nice little
sketch of the Hall, done in your very best style.
It may be either pencil or colored, just as you
please; and now, as soon as you have read this, go
out, and reconnoitre as to the best point of view to
take it from. I should advise the end of the farther terrace on the left side of the fountain, close
to the pink acacia: you there get such a good view

of the conservatory and my sanctum. If I recollect rightly, there is a seat somewhere in that neighborhood; and you can have the small easel out there, and work away as well as in-doors. I have been what you would call dreadfully dissipated since you left, until last night, when I had an evening of sober intellectual enjoyment, namely, in hearing one of 'R's' lectures on modern painting. He is a splendid fellow. I could have sat till midnight listening to him. His thoughts are very pictures, bright and glowing and beautiful. Even you would have enjoyed it, little Georgie; and, if I have nothing better to do, I shall certainly visit his lecture-room again. I take it for granted that you miss me very much. I hope, however, that does not prevent your going on with your drawing, and that you make use of my studio for the purpose as much as you please. There is no room in the house like it for good painting light. Write, and tell me what you do in the drawing way. I hope you ride sometimes with Frances and papa, and that Leighton air is getting up your good looks again. In addition to these good wishes, receive the best love of your affectionate cousin, "Lloyd."

Georgina was well pleased to be able to oblige Lloyd in any way, and immediately prepared to carry out his wishes. She found the spot he had selected the very best for the purpose, with Walter's assistance removed her drawing paraphernalia thither, and devoted all her spare time to the work. She made two sketches, one in pencil, the other colored, and despatched them both to Lloyd, by post, about a week after the reception of his letter. She received by return a note full of thanks and praises. The gentleman, he said, to whom one of them had been presented—an artist himself—had expressed his surprise and admiration at the distinguished talent of the fair young painter, and regretted beyond measure that he had not had the honor of an introduction during her late stay in town. "But it is possible," Lloyd added, "that he may yet have that pleasure; as I hope some day to bring him down to Leighton."

Georgie's face flushed a little as she read the flattering epistle; but, when she reached her room, she tore it slowly into pieces, as on one previous occasion, and, lighting a taper, watched the remains as they consumed quite away.

The holidays were now fast approaching, when Mademoiselle Victoire·was to go·to her home in France for two months. Georgie, feeling it just doubtful whether she would find her at Leighton on her return, and, wishing to manifest her perfectly friendly feeling, determined to make her some little parting gift. To accomplish this purpose, a visit to Barnes was necessary; and she hardly knew how to arrange her plan, as on every occasion, except when she rode with her uncle and Frances, mademoiselle accompanied them.

She confided her difficulty to Walter, who, after some little consideration, said, "Will you come with me?"

The only thing of value which Walter possessed in the world was a beautiful black horse, which had been his father's, and which he had brought with him from India. It was a fiery spirited creature, and seemed to have a sort of fellow-feeling with his young master, scarcely allowing any one else to mount him, and receiving even his grooming from the hands of Turner with no very friendly eye. And Walter, though he had been used to persuade himself that his life was one utterly devoid of pleasure, nevertheless experienced a wild melancholy kind of enjoyment in scouring the country for miles round on the back of his favorite steed, always alone; and, when once mounted, never stopping to greet either friend or foe.

Once or twice in her rides with Lloyd and Frances the black horse, with its gloomy eager rider, had galloped past them; but not even the presence of Georgina had availed to draw from Walter word or look of recognition. No wonder, then, that she was somewhat surprised at the proposal.

"Yes, that would do very nicely if my uncle has no objection; but I thought you disliked riding in company with any one, Walter?"

"So I do, with any of them; but I don't mind *you*. You need not ask sir William, however; I will tell Turner to get your horse ready."

"I should not like it exactly without asking him. He will not mind in the least; he is so good to me."

So she went in search of her uncle.

"May I ride into Barnes with Walter this afternoon, uncle, if the pony is not wanted?"

"Wanted, my dear child, who should want it but yourself? But with Walter—" and here he shrugged his shoulders—"he is not fit to take care of you; why not go with your cousin and me?"

"It is a little shopping errand, uncle; and I should not like to detain you."

"Ah! very well, Miss Georgie. Well, take care of yourself; and of him too, you will be obliged to, I fancy. He will be dashing off madly somewhere, if you don't look well after him. Walter is the last person I should choose to ride with, were I in your place."

"He is very kind and obliging to me, dear uncle," Georgina said.

"Well, I am glad of it, my dear girl; but it is the first time I have had that character of Walter."

He had, nevertheless, the curiosity to stand waiting at the window till they rode off, and watched with interest the patronizing air with which Walter mounted his cousin, and then leaped into his own saddle, reining in the fiery animal to keep pace with the little pony, which cantered easily at his side. "There is some good in the wild headstrong boy, after all," he said to himself as he

"Walter reined in the fiery animal to keep pace with her little pony."

Brother's Watchword.   p 166.

turned away; "but strange that it should have been brought out by that quiet sober little maiden."

Georgie selected an elegant writing-case conveniently fitted up, and, after directing it to be sent to her at Leighton, they returned home.

The evening before mademoiselle's departure, she penned a tiny note, slipped it within the desk, and sent it by her maid to the governess's room. The features of the volatile young French woman softened as she read those few simple words: " Dear mademoiselle,—Any acknowledgment I can make for the pains you have taken with my studies must fall very short of what you deserve; but will you accept the accompanying box as a slight token of my gratitude? I hope you will have a very pleasant visit with your friends at home. Forgive anything that may, though unknown to me, have been annoying to you in reference to the disarrangement my drawing-lessons caused. I am sure I would not willingly have caused you any trouble. From your sincere friend, Georgina Emily Archdale."

A few tears gathered in the young lady's eyes.

"She is not then the proud cold-hearted girl I had imagined," she said to herself, and, hastening to Georgina's chamber, she put her arms about her neck with all the impulsive warmth of true French character, confessed with tears that she had judged her wrongly, and treated her with injustice, begging her from henceforward to look upon her as a friend and treat her as such. Georgina warmly responded.

She had not guessed before that there was so much depth of feeling in the head of the gay, and, as she had imagined, frivolous young lady. She felt sorry that she had not known her until now, just on the eve of parting; but she promised to write and tell of her movements should Leonard return before mademoiselle's long holiday was over. And so they parted friends.

It was not to be wondered at that Georgina missed Lloyd very much; more especially after Mademoiselle Victoire's departure, when her whole time was at her own disposal. She had so long been the companion of his studio, had subjected her plans and ideas in drawing so entirely to his direction, and watched his work with so deep, an interest, that Leighton seemed hardly itself without him. Still she was not, on this account, idle; she availed herself of the permission he had given her to occupy his beautiful room, and there she now spent the greater part of her day drawing busily.

She missed his constant advice very much; but he wrote to her very often, made her tell him just what she was doing, and sent down his instructions in such a lucid manner, that, as Georgie said, it was almost as good as having him near her.

His letters were clever and entertaining; but there was a certain tone about them which always gave his cousin an undefined feeling of dissatisfaction; and, after having culled all the information they contained, she almost invariably committed them to the flames. She fancied, from hints that he sometimes threw out, that he was leading a very gay life, more so than ever, she thought; and she would have liked, poor child, to warn him of the danger, and ultimate sorrow and hopelessness of such a course, and to beg him to seek enduring pleasure and satisfaction in Christ, and heavenly things; but—she was afraid. She did not think he would listen to her: might it not be out of her sphere and obtrusive? She erred; but she did not altogether fail in effort. She prayed every day, and that very earnestly, for Lloyd. She longed for his conversion: it seemed the most desirable and eagerly to be sought blessing that could possibly be granted her. Too great a one almost to be expected: perhaps she hardly believed that it ever would be accorded; and, if it might, it would be perhaps by some wonderful, little less than miraculous, interposition or awakening, such as she had read of in the lives of some great saints. The still small voice could scarcely reach his ear, dulled and stifled as it was by the din and noise of this world's busy and distracting pleasures. The arrow must needs be very sharp, she thought, that would penetrate the dense coating of worldly love and ease and indifference which enveloped his soul. The whirlwind and the fire would surely be commissioned to speak to him; and of what use was her tiny effort?

So she thought, poor child, in her lonely musings;

15

but still she prayed, and those prayers were often-times the only earthly bulwark which kept Lloyd from falling grievously.

With the holidays came a great deal of company to the Hall; and Georgina found that she was able to be pretty much to herself. There were fêtes and pic-nics, and archery parties given and re-turned; and sometimes Georgina accompanied her cousins; but for the most part she preferred re-maining at home, her drawing occupying the morn-ing, and her aunt liking her company during the after part of the day. Then she sometimes had a drive with lady Archdale, it being a thing taken for granted now, that Georgie should be her companion on such occasions; and lady Archdale's health seemed strengthened somewhat since her return from London.

Carry also was becoming a firm little attendant upon her cousin. She often crept into her brother's studio as Georgina was there painting before her easel; and would ask, in coaxing tones, if she might stay a little while, it was so dull in the nursery, and Tom was so boisterous. Consent was always given, and pains also taken to encourage in the little girl that taste for drawing which Georgina fancied she already perceived in her. In other things, too, did Georgie become her teacher. She read the scriptures with and to her daily; and the child listened with deepening interest, wondering that the book had never attracted her notice before.

Georgie also commenced reading to her little cousin her own favorite book, "The Pilgrim's Progress," explaining it carefully as she went on, greatly to Carry's delight; and many pleasant readings did they have together on those summer evenings, seated in some shady arbor, or beneath the spreading trees of the park.

At the close of a glorious evening, quite in the beginning of August, it happened that Georgina and her cousin were thus occupied. The sun, very bright before its setting, cast slanting rays of gold through the leaves of the old elm beneath whose shelter, on a rustic bench, Georgie was sitting. Carry was at her feet: her blue eyes upturned towards her cousin with an earnest wondering look, her waving brown curls agitated from time to time by the soft evening breeze. Georgina's voice was low, but very clear and sweet, and it seemed to suit the words that she was reading. There were no others near them, and no outward noise, except the ever-sounding voice of nature, to disturb the solemn impression that those words were calculated to convey.

Georgie ceased reading for a moment. The narrative, although so many times perused, was still so full of solemn pathos to her, and her voice faltered a little. "Now I farther saw that betwixt them and the gate was a river; but there was no bridge to go over; and the river was very deep. At the sight, therefore, of this river the pilgrims were much terrified; but the men that went with them said, You must go through, or you cannot come at the gate."

"But did they?" asked Caroline eagerly. "O how did they get across?"

Georgina went on. With breathless interest the child listened, the expression of her face becoming more and more earnest the while. She heard of Christian's sharp and terrible conflict, the hopeful and comforting words of his fellow-pilgrim, of their safe and glorious landing, and the triumphant greeting which awaited them on the other side.

"Shall *we* have to go over that river, Georgie?" she asked, with tears in her eyes.

"Yes, darling," said her cousin; "but is there anything to fear if Christ is near us, as he was with Christian, and if there is such joy and glory at the end?"

"No, not when we know that he is our friend; but I do not know that. I have been very naughty; I never thought of him at all till you told me of him; and now I so often forget him! O Georgie, I wish I were like you."

"Do not wish that, dear Carry; rather ask to be made like him. He will listen to your prayer, darling. He loves little children, for he died for them."

"Is there any more, Georgie? O it almost makes me want to go to heaven to see that beautiful city, and the King, and the angels."

Georgina read again. "Now, just as the gates were opened to let in the men, I looked in after them; and, behold, the city shone like the sun, the streets also were paved with gold; and in them walked many men with crowns on their heads, palms in their hands, and golden harps to sing praises withal. There were also of them that had wings; and they answered one another without intermission, saying, 'Holy, holy, holy, is the Lord!' And after that they shut up the gates; which, when I had seen, I wished myself among them."

The last words had scarcely passed from Georgie's lips when she felt a firm hand laid upon her shoulder. She started up hastily; but not before Carry had exclaimed, in a tone of surprise and pleasure, "It is Lloyd!"

Georgina was almost too surprised to speak at first.

"Well, Caroline, how are you?" he said, kissing the child. "Constance, did I startle you? You are not glad to see me, it appears?"

"O yes, so glad! but, Lloyd, how did you come? I did not hear you."

She took his hand so warmly, and a glow of such real pleasure came into her face, that he could not doubt the reality of her welcome. He sat down on the bench beside her. "I thought I would take you all by surprise for once," he said.

"Yes, I hardly expected you so soon. I am very

15*

glad you are come. Do they know about it in-
doors? I must go and tell them."

"No such desperate hurry," replied he, rising,
however, listlessly. "What are they all about?"
and there was a touch of impatience in his tone.

"At dinner, I suppose," his cousin answered.
"Shall we go in? I am afraid you are tired."

"Yes, I am, awfully. I have walked from the
station."

"I will run in and give notice," said Caroline;
and she bounded across the park.

Lloyd and Georgie followed more deliberately.

"Georgina, you are looking very well, and as
quiet and well-behaved as ever. But why are you
not in the house dining with the others, like a
reasonable little woman?"

"Because I prefer spending these lovely evenings
out of doors. Don't you think it much more pleasant? Besides, there are a great many people here
now; and you know I am rather shy."

"I wish I knew you were not. I was in hopes of
finding you wiser, little Conny. Have you heard
from Leonard?"

"No; not for some time;" and her face was
clouded instantly.

"You thought he would be back in August?"

"Yes, I did. O I cannot tell you, Lloyd, what
this long, long waiting is."

Lloyd changed the subject immediately; and
soon afterwards they reached the house. The

whole family were charmed at his unexpected appearance. Frances possessed herself of his arm. "O you are a dear good fellow to have come just now. We all wanted you terribly: come in to dinner." She led him off, and Georgie saw nothing more of Lloyd that night.

But the next morning, as soon as breakfast was over, he beckoned her away with his old smile and shrug of ennui, saying, " Now let me see what you have been doing all this while. O how I have longed for my easel !" And the next minute they were on their way to his studio, notwithstanding Frances' cry of shame at his immuring himself, as she called it, for the whole morning.

" Very respectable," he pronounced, as Georgina displayed some drawings on which she had been recently engaged. " But what have we here ?"

As he spoke he uncovered an easel close at hand, on which was a picture in a partially finished state. " My dear girl, what a strange composition ! half saint, half Leonard ! Where have your fancies been wandering ? And not badly done, either."

Georgina's face lightened up even with this somewhat-qualified approbation. " O it is *my* picture, my very own; and do you really think it is like Leonard ? I am so glad."

" Your very own, what do you mean ? Was this strangely solemn face revealed to you in some wonderful dream or vision, and did you arrest the

phantom, and stamp it in reality in the person of
your brother ?"

"Not exactly; and perhaps I was wrong in saying it was entirely my own; for though I have
never seen it, I have read of it."

"Where?" asked Lloyd.

"You would not know the book," she answered.

"Nevertheless I choose to know; and in here,
you know, Conny, I am master."

She colored a little; then, looking down upon
the floor, she repeated, in a clear steady tone, "This
was the fashion of it. It had eyes lifted up to
heaven, the best of books in his hand, the law of
truth was written upon his lips, the world was behind his back: it stood as if it pleaded with men;
and a crown of gold did hang over its head."

"You are a strange girl, and read the strangest
set of books that can be conceived," her cousin said,
after a moment's silence, and rapid glance at the
picture to see whether it agreed in all its description. "But if you mean this as a likeness of Leonard, it will do; and perhaps you will favor *me* with
the next sitting. It will be merely returning a
compliment. Look at my little girl under the
elms, you grow more like her every day."

Georgie had learned to receive her cousin's com-
plimentary speeches with less discomposure than at
first, and she only smiled in reply, asking him at
the same time some question about the background

of her picture. Soon both were busily and silently engaged in their respective work.

Many pleasant mornings passed thus. Lloyd was the same kind and considerate friend as he had been before and during their London visit. But Georgina, who watched him closely, perceived a change in him at other times—a change which did not please her. Though his spirits seemed gay almost to exhilaration in the family circle and in company, yet there were transient gleams of restlessness and dissatisfaction which would gather in a moment across his fine countenance, and as rapidly pass away.

Though his mornings were devoted to his painting and to her, yet in the after-parts of the day she saw but little of him. There were some brother-officers stationed for a time at Barnes, and with them much of his time was spent, and, as Georgie feared, not most profitably. He brought them frequently to the Hall; and there was a great deal of evening amusement and gaiety, in which Georgina very little participated.

Sir Henry Legh, too, was a frequent visitor at Leighton. He had formed a great friendship for Lloyd; and his influence over him seemed, as far as Georgie was able to judge, anything but desirable. He was very gay and reckless: dogs and horses the usual topic of his conversation; and with the exception of his being a connoisseur and admirer of pictures, Georgie discovered not one good trait about him. He invaded Lloyd's studio on two or three occasions, and complimented Georgie very much on the great skill displayed in her drawings; but there was a something in his tone and manner from which she involuntarily shrank and always felt a sort of relief when the room was freed from his presence.

"You don't like Legh," Lloyd said to her, one day, when sir Henry had just paid one of his impromptu visits. Georgina did not answer.

"Tell me your reasons, Georgie," said her cousin. "You have too much good sense to dislike a person without sufficient reason; and I am sure he is always friendly enough to you."

"But do I dislike him?" she asked; for she had never so far analyzed her feelings on the subject. "What makes you think so?"

"Why, your behavior, to be sure : you snub him awfully."

Georgina took a hasty mental retrospection of the past hour, and then said, "If you mean by snubbing that I do not much care to talk to sir Henry Legh, perhaps you are right; but I hope I have not been rude."

"Why don't you care to talk to him? What possible harm do you find in him? He is one of the nicest fellows going."

"He is not what Leonard would call a Christian, or a gentleman," said Georgie, with rather more than her usual boldness.

Lloyd gave a "hem!" of some annoyance

"Leonard again!" he said. "When will you learn, Conny, to think for yourself?"

"I *do* think *that* myself," she replied.

"I wonder you condescend to associate with *me*, then," Lloyd remarked.

"You are a gentleman, and my cousin," she answered quickly, "and very, very kind to me."

"Nay, nay," interrupted Lloyd, "you are mistaken in the obligation. But, Constance, I am sorry you don't like sir Henry. It is his birth-day next week, and he has asked a favor of you."

"Of *me!* and what?" asked Georgie, looking up.

"O never mind till the time comes : 'tis a secret. Those angels supporting the crown are somewhat unethereal, Georgie : you must improve them."

Georgina felt a little uneasy. What might this favor be? and to be gained through the medium of Lloyd! She thought of all the past, and was anxious, then looked up at her cousin's face, so bright, so kind, so true; and the anxiety passed away. Yes, she could trust Lloyd now. He would never, after all that had passed, tempt her to do wrong again.

And, when he smiled and spoke to her again in that deep winning voice of his, softened almost to gentleness in addressing her, she blamed herself that a doubt of his perfect sincerity and friendliness should even have crossed her mind.

XI.

ANGER AND SORROW.

"Or if, for our unworthiness,
Toil, prayer, and watching fail,
In disappointment thou canst bless,
So love of heart prevail.

KEBLE.

"NO, Lloyd, do not ask me any more. I really cannot go; to please sir Henry, or to please even you."

"I have no patience with such absurd affectation. There is more of obstinacy than anything else in such ridiculous and feigned scruples," said Lloyd, with flashing eyes.

Georgina colored, and with difficulty kept down some rising emotion; however she did not reply.

"Tell me again, am I to be made a fool of by you, or not? Once for all, will you go? I told you, you need not dance yourself."

"No," she answered decidedly.

"A regular set of humbugs, yourself and your brother," he muttered angrily.

"What?" said Georgina, on hearing her brother's name.

"Why, Leonard is a humbug for putting such

preposterous notions into your head; and you are one for listening to them," said Lloyd in a tone of bitter scorn, which he knew only too well how to assume at times. He had never, however, used it with her before; and even then, had it been directed only against herself, she might have borne it; but such a speech and such a tone in reference to Leonard, her idolized brother! She lost, for the moment, all sort of self-control, her face glowed, her eyes flashed with passion. Could it possibly be Georgie?

Without waiting one moment to consider her ill-timed words, so bitterly to be regretted afterwards, she exclaimed impetuously, "Lloyd! how can you dare to speak so of Leonard—Leonard, so good, so pure, so holy? you—who are a swearer"—

They had scarcely escaped her lips before she would have given worlds to have recalled them; but it was too late. The blow was too well aimed: she could not, had she studied a whole life-time, have found words more galling, more exasperating to the proud haughty Lloyd. He became perfectly pale with anger; then, unconscious almost of what he was doing, and thinking only of the daring and defiance of the words addressed to him, he raised his hand, and struck his young cousin as she stood there before him, still trembling with excitement and agitation.

"Take that for your impudence—and—go!" he muttered between his clenched teeth.

He need not have added the last word. With a cry less of pain than of intense fear and sorrow, she had rushed from the room before her cousin had time to recollect what he had done. But the dreadful thought came over him the next moment. He called her back once and again; but she heard nothing, saw nothing, felt nothing till she was locked in her own room, and had flung herself in a paroxysm of grief and tears upon the little couch near her bed. "What have I done? What have I done?" she cried between her sobs. "O, is this the end of my concern and interest and prayers for him? To bring reproach upon the name of Christ by my sinful wicked passion! And after his kindness for so many months! Is it possible! O can I, can I have said it?" Yes, her burning cheek gave her back the answer, if nothing else spoke. She hid her face in the cushions, and wept bitterly, passionately, remorsefully. O, to recall the words! But, alas! it was impossible. Whatever she might do or say in apology, they could never be effaced, never forgotten. She remembered the expression of his countenance at the time, and felt that it must be so.

But far worse than her bitter offence against her cousin was the thought of the grievous sin against her heavenly Father. She never remembered being in such a fearful passion before. O was it possible that one really a Christian could act so?

She did not attempt to extenuate or justify her conduct in any way. She knew thât, whatever Lloyd's aggravation had been, her duty remained the same, and that she had grievously, deeply neglected it. O what could she do? Nothing, nothing, but go to God just as she was, lay it before him with all the deep agony of contrition she was feeling, and seek forgiveness. "Lord, my life seems nothing but one long act of failures," she murmured; "and yet I long to please thee. O grant me thy strength, thy grace, thy help."

She remained on her knees a long time; and rose at last, humbled, sorrowful, tearful still; but somewhat lightened of her great load of misery.

A servant tapped at her door at last, telling her that luncheon was waiting. She sent an excuse of violent head-ache, which indeed was so overpowering that she felt scarcely able to lift up her head. Nevertheless she seated herself at her writing-table, and with trembling fingers wrote the following note to her cousin:

"My dear Lloyd,—After asking forgiveness of God, I feel that I cannot rest even a minute without telling you how sorry, how condemned I feel for my wicked passion, and my ungrateful words to you this morning. I hardly like to ask it, but, if you only knew the sorrow I feel, I think you would

forgive me. It was said hastily, and without considering how wrong and unbecoming it was. Can
you forgive me? And, as a sign that you do, will
you speak to me to-morrow morning as usual?
Dear Lloyd, if I had not spoken so rashly and in-
considerately, I might some day have asked you if
you have ever thought of the great sin of taking
God's name in vain; but I meant to have spoken
humbly, as one much younger than yourself. O
do not continue to do so because I have acted so
wickedly; for they are the words of the Bible, and
not mine, " Swear not at all." Believe me, your
affectionate and sorrowful,   GEORGINA."

The little letter was not finished without many
tears. Just after she had sealed it she saw Frances
and Lloyd setting off on their usual afternoon ride;
and the former glanced up at her room, as though
remarking on her absence, for Georgie frequently
accompanied them, as before.

"It is no use sending it yet, then," she murmured;
and, laying herself again upon the sofa, sought to
calm her throbbing, aching head. She slept a little;
and, getting up between five and six o'clock, determined to go and have tea with lady Archdale, as
she sometimes did when not feeling very well.
Headache was not an unusual thing with her; and
she was always suffered to remain, at such times,
quiet and unmolested in the retirement of her own
room. She felt very thankful to encounter, on her

way to her aunt's apartment, Williams, Lloyd's man-servant, who was taking hot water to his master's room, in readiness for his evening toilet.

" Will you give this note to Mr. Lloyd when he comes in, if you please, Williams ?" she said, placing the letter in his hand.

He bowed obsequiously, and promised; then put it into his pocket, and thought no more of it for the next three months.   Poor little Georgie !

" And so my darling has had her sad headache again," said lady Archdale compassionately, as Georgina entered her room.

"It is better now, thank you, auntie ; but I thought I would take tea with you this evening, if you don't mind, and go to bed early."

" I am so glad to have you, my love.   Your little face is all hot and flushed now.   It has been very painful, I am afraid."

" I have been lying down, auntie dear, on the couch, and been to sleep a little while too ; so my face is hot."

" Rest again, dear child, on that lounge : stay, I will ring, and Harbridge shall arrange you."

" No, thank you, dear aunt, I will sit here in my own place till tea : I like that best."

She sat down on a low ottoman by her aunt's sofa, took one of the thin white hands in hers, and began to caress it, leaning her hot cheek against it, and kissing it over again.

" I am afraid you have been grieving about Leon-

16*

ard," said lady Archdale, fondly; for she fancied she felt something like a tear drop upon the hand that Georgie held.

"No, auntie, not particularly. I do indeed long to see him again; and it seems strange I should not hear. I had almost hoped he would be home by this time."

"I did not expect that, darling; and I think you are sure of hearing by the next mail. You must try not to be too anxious. You have been so good and patient hitherto."

Just then Harbridge came in with the tea. Georgie roused herself to pour it out; and in waiting upon her aunt she partially forgot her own troubles. She saw nothing of the rest of the family that evening, but waited anxiously for the morning, half dreading to meet her cousin, but yet trusting and praying that her note might have taken some effect in softening his feelings towards her. That was Tuesday; and he was to leave Leighton on the Thursday till Christmas. It would indeed be sad were he to part from her in anger.

And what had been Lloyd's feelings meanwhile? After Georgie had left the room intense shame and self-reproach had succeeded the first wild impulse of anger. That he should so far have forgotten himself as a man, far more as a gentleman, as to strike a girl, and one too who had ever been so gentle, so meek, so trustful as Georgina; and who now, though her words seemed hard and irritating, yet had only spoken to him the plain undisguised truth, in return for a bitter taunt from him, which his conscience told him was entirely false—it seemed incredible, even to himself, that he could have acted thus; and he felt, for a moment, willing to undergo almost any humiliation to regain his forfeited honor.

He called her back, as we have seen, but received no answer. What was to be done? A servant came just then, and summoned him to the drawing-room. Two of his officer friends were awaiting him there; and, in conversation with them and others of the family, his first bitter feelings of remorse wore off. He was a little uncomfortable on hearing at the luncheon-table that his cousin was ailing, and unable to fill her accustomed place; and yet the idea of meeting publicly, until reconciliation had been made, was so distasteful to him, that he could hardly regret it.

He rode with Frances as usual in the afternoon. Thoughts of the absent one disturbed him very uncomfortably during the ride; though he was, to all appearance, gay as usual.

On his return he hastened to the library.

"She is sure to be there," he thought, "and, good-hearted little creature as she is, will no doubt make some allusion to this stupid affair; and I shall not find much difficulty, I fancy, in setting matters straight again. After all, I only forgot myself for the moment; and she *was* provokingly impudent."

But no Georgina was to be found. After dinner he went to dress for the ball at Sir Henry Legh's, which had occasioned the unfortunate upset, and when ready, again made a visit to the library. But only Walter was there: his great books open before him.

"I say, where is Georgina?" he inquired.

There seemed, to his fancy, a reproachful look in Walter's dark eyes as he answered, "You might know as well as I do, I should think, that she is gone to bed with one of her dreadful headaches."

Lloyd left the room hastily. "Shame," he muttered angrily, and stamping his foot on the hall-floor. "She has gone and told that boy!"

All thoughts of humbling himself, or seeking a reconciliation now completely vanished from Lloyd's breast. The unfounded suspicion that Georgie had confided to Walter the particulars of his morning's passion, took so firm a hold upon his mind, that all his natural pride and arrogance were afresh aroused, and his thoughts towards his now penitent cousin as hard and bitter as shame and mortifying self-reproach might make them.

Breakfast was nearly over, the following morning, when he entered the dining-room. Georgina was there, in her accustomed place, looking much as usual, but her poor heart throbbing with an inward tumult which she could not suppress. Would he notice her? No. With a careless "Good morning" to all, he threw himself into a chair, took up the morning paper, and was soon fully engrossed with it.

He has not forgiven me, then, she thought; and, hastily swallowing the remainder of her breakfast, she left the room as soon as possible. What a wearisome day it was!. Not a word from Lloyd, not a look, nor a glance. When in her presence, he was just as coldly indifferent as though she had not been there, laughing and joking with the others more than was his wont, but studiously ignoring her.

"I could not have said more than I did in my note, yesterday," she repeated to herself many times; "but yet I cannot much wonder. I deserve it; for I have brought it upon myself. And yet I should not have thought him unforgiving, though proud and hasty. And—he leaves to-morrow!" Yes, all preparations for his three months' absence were being made. The whole household seemed busy on his behalf. There were portmanteaus to be packed, books and paintings to be put together, time-tables to be consulted; for Lloyd had altered his journeying plan a little that morning, owing to a pressing letter from an Oxford friend to spend a day with him en route to Dover, where his regiment was stationed for a time. And Georgie, who would so gladly have lent a helping hand, and who knew that in some things no one could assist him so well as herself, dared not even enter his room, or proffer her services. Poor child! had she ventured to do this, all might have been explained, her little tear-stained note been produced from the deep recesses of Williams's pocket, and much pain and trouble have been spared. But she had gone as far as she dared—as far as she thought was right, and now she felt she must bear the consequences.

Lloyd found himself twenty times in the course of the day, upon the point of calling her, to ask some question, to give some parting injunction; but the thought of his insulted honor, as he called it, came into his mind just in time, and he had to seek assistance elsewhere. If she would only just say she was in the wrong, it would be a different thing, he thought; but to have told of it to another, and, above all, to Walter, it was unpardonable. Then, she appeared so studiously to avoid him. Did not this show what she had done, and that she was ashamed of it?

Night came at last; and poor Georgina went sad and mournful to her room. She met Lloyd on the staircase; and he passed her, stern and resentful. She longed just to say "Good night," but dared not. There was the angry scowl of the morning upon his brow, and she could not meet *that.*

"O my sinful passion!" she said again bitterly to herself, "it has cost me very dear, and, worst of all, has brought reproach upon the Name I love." And again she prayed for pardon, and for God's blessing upon her cousin.

The following morning she awoke more calm,

She deemed, and truly too, that perhaps this trouble, bitter as it was, had been sent of God for some wise purpose. She had been liking Lloyd too well. All the attractions of his naturally noble character had been opened up to her; she had studied them, and rejoiced in his talents, and genius, and perhaps his beauty too. She felt in him the sisterly pride that she had in Leonard; and of late, since her fear of him had quite passed away, she had felt a great pleasure in his presence, and quiet enjoyment of all his efforts to please her. She had begun to make an idol of him; and now the dream was all at once dissipated, and that through her own instrumentality. It was very hard to bear; but, as soon as she seemed to see her Father's hand overruling even her sinful failure for her spiritual good, the burden became lighter.

Lloyd was to leave Leighton that afternoon at three o'clock. Just at noon, Georgie, on her way to fetch a book from the school-room, passed by the library door. She heard the voice of lady Legh and her young sister-in-law talking with Frances. At the moment Georgie passed, the latter exclaimed, "O, I must fetch you Lloyd's last drawing: it is scarcely finished, I believe; but he takes it with him this afternoon. It is so beautifully done."

Georgina knew what picture it was—one in oils that Lloyd had been working hard at lately, of cattle drinking at a narrow stream, with flowers and rushes on the br'nk, and waving trees overhead.

She knew how careful he was over it, and almost trembled, as she saw her cousin hasten across the hall, in the direction of his studio, to fetch it.

She was kept in the school-room longer than she at first intended, and it might have been half an hour after, that she re-passed the library. All was quiet there: the guests were gone. "I wonder whether the picture is taken back," she said, with her usual forethought; then went in to see. No; there it lay, to her great alarm, with the bright colors still wet, half on the ledge of the window, which was open, half on a small round table close by. "What would Lloyd say? What a dangerous place!" she exclaimed, mentally, and was hastening across the wide room to rescue it, when, to her extreme fright, she saw the opened window quickly descending. It was not an uncommon thing: the spring was out of repair; one moment more, the heavy frame would fall, and Lloyd's precious gem of a picture be totally ruined. One thing only could be done: she did not stop to consider the danger she should herself incur, though a sense of pleasure in pain suffered to conciliate him, might have glanced through her mind. She rushed across the room, but just in time, and placed her hand upon the sill. The heavy window fell: the painting was unhurt; but the poor, brave little fingers, were crushed terribly. With her right hand she drew the picture quite on the table, then extricated the wounded one, which yet she dared not look at, such a sickly sensation of pain and dizziness was coming over her, but, wrapping it in her handkerchief, with trembling, faltering steps she sought her aunt's chamber.

She felt that now she must have sympathy; and that was the only place where she might find it. In the dressing-room she met her aunt's maid. Startled at her pale face and the drops of blood 'upon her light muslin jacket, Harbridge begged to know what had happened.

"It was the window, Harbridge," she said. "Do you mind looking at my hand, and doing something to it, before I go to auntie? I feel so faint and curious."

She dropped into the nearest seat; and the nurse unwrapped the handkerchief.

"Is it very bad?"

"I am afraid it is, my dear young lady."

"Mr. Selfield will be here soon, will he not? Shall we wait till then?"

"I think it would be better. I will just bathe it a little, and let me give you something to revive you, my poor child," she said compassionately.

"There, I shall not frighten aunt, now, do you think?" Georgie asked languidly, when her dress was a little arranged, and she could walk into the room. "She will let me lie down and be quiet, I know."

Lady Archdale was seriously alarmed. "I trust Mr. Selfield will soon be here," she said; "and till

17

then, my darling, do try and get a little sleep : you look worn and exhausted altogether."

Georgina knew that there was but little chance of sleeping. The pain in her hand was sharper' than any she had ever felt before ; but it was a comfort to lie down in a darkened corner of the room, and close her eyes to everything external.

Two hours passed, but the doctor did not arrive. A little before three o'clock, the door of lady· Archdale's room opened hurriedly, and Lloyd entered.

"Mother, I am come to say good-bye," he exclaimed.

Lady Archdale raised her finger warningly, and said, "Take care," in a low tone.

"What now, mamma? what is the matter?"

"Georgie," she said in a hushed voice.

"Well, and what of Georgie?" He tried to assume an indifferent tone; and he succeeded.

"She has hurt her hand dreadfully, poor child. The library-window has fallen on it, or something of the kind. I have not heard the full particulars yet."

"Nothing but a little graze, I dare say," he answered lightly : "girls make a tremendous fuss about trifles sometimes."

Georgie did not see his face : had she, she might not have been so pained at the indifference of the words. Nor did she know that he walked half across the room towards her, then hesitated a moment, and turned away. What would he not have given to have spoken but two words ere parting? But there she lay, her face pale and still, and her eyes fast closed; and he could not disturb her in sleep.

"Well, good-bye, mamma. I shall look out for first-rate accounts of you. You will see me all right again at Christmas."

He stooped and kissed her; then rising hastily, and with one last glance towards the couch in the corner of the apartment, he left the room.

Georgina listened to his footsteps until they died away in the distance; then, a few minutes after, to the faint sounds of parting and good-byes in the hall below, to the shutting of the front door, and, lastly, to the noise of the carriage-wheels as they rolled quickly down the avenue. Presently after, a short stifled sob came from the little couch. Lady Archdale sighed; for she thought it was drawn forth by pain, but she was mistaken.

Mr. Selfield came at last, and examined the wounded hand. His face told that it was a serious affair. One finger especially was shockingly crushed. He did not say so to Georgina, but told the nurse, after leaving the room, that he should wait until the following day, but that he quite feared the upper joints would have to be taken off.

"My mistress must not know it," said Harbridge.

"No, I will see Miss Archdale in another room

to morrow. I think she seems brave-hearted: it would be as well to tell her the worst perhaps, and prepare her mind for what I fear must happen."

Poor child! she truly had borne it bravely. The dressing was most painful; and, though she had not spoken once, nor given one utterance of pain, fearing to distress her aunt, yet tears forced from her eyes by the sharpness of the suffering dropped silently upon the cushions.

Mr. Selfield was a shrewd and clever man, well-skilled in his profession, and at the same time truly kind-hearted; but his manner was harsh, nay, at times almost surly towards those even of his patients in whom he felt the greatest interest. He had spoken very sharply to Georgina for not giving a better account of the way in which she had injured her hand.

"You must surely have seen that the window was falling," he said; "why could you not have removed your hand?"

"It falls so very quickly at the last," Georgie replied, who, besides her actual unwillingness to enter into full particulars of the case, was so dizzy with pain and faintness, that she had not a very clear recollection of what had happened, and wondered herself, when she came to think of it, why she had not snatched away the painting instead of placing her hand on the sill. She remembered, however, that there was a beautiful alabaster vase of flowers on the small table where the picture lay, and that, had she delayed even a moment in order to remove this vase, the opportunity would have passed, and the painting have been ruined.

Mr. Selfield, however, could not but admire the heroic way in which she bore the pain, and said to her, as he was arranging her hand in a sling, "Now, young lady, you have a bad hand; but it is your own fault, and you must put the best face you can upon it. Go down stairs to tea with your cousins, and try and forget about it; and, if you can't, take the medicine that I shall send you to-night, and you will have some good sleep, I hope. I shall see you again to-morrow at twelve o'clock; so good-bye, and be careful how you trifle with broken windows again."

"Walter," said Georgina, as they sat together in a corner of the drawing-room that evening before a chess-table, which game Walter had suggested as a likely means to make her forget her pain, "I hardly like to think about it, but I am really afraid that I may lose my little finger. I just caught a glance of it once, and of Mr. Selfield's face; and you cannot think how bad it was."

"O Georgie, is it possible?"

"Yes, I think so. Are you afraid of such things?"

"No, not a bit. Will it be any satisfaction to you for me to see Mr. Selfield with you to-morrow morning?"

"Yes, if *that* should happen. I am a little afraid

of him; he speaks so harshly. And he thought
me a great coward for crying this afternoon, I
know."

" What, did you cry?"

"'A little; but I should not perhaps, if you were
there. I don't think, Walter, I can have much
worse pain in it than I have had already, though the
idea shocks me." And this was, in fact, pretty
much the case.

That evening, when Georgie went to her room,
she found a few withered flowers, lying on her writing table, close to her beautiful Thomas-a-Kempis,
two small sprigs of cedar, and a few faded blue
harebells. Strange how they came there; she did
not remember gathering them; but her memory
had been somewhat dulled by pain and other emotions, and she so often plucked flowers, and brought
them to her room, that she might have done so now
and forgotten it.

" Poor faded flowers !" she said sadly, " what are
you like? I love you even in decay; but it is useless treasuring you now."

And with a sigh she swept them together, and
gave them to the servant to carry away. Had she
understood more plainly the language of flowers,
she would not have done so.

They were Lloyd's silent messengers of compunc-
tion and reconciliation.

XII.

LLOYD'S DISCOVERY.

"And wherefore mourn the fading gleam,
    When joys that cannot last decay?
Who mourns when stars, that loveliest seem,
    Grow dim before the rising day?
What though e'en suns no more may shine,
Be there but light, O Lord, from thine."

WALTER sat by her all the time, holding her hand; and on her lap lay an open letter from Leonard, which, as though for the very purpose of cheering her, had arrived that morning. And Georgina did not cry. She was not insensible to the pain: she took no chloroform; but a power and strength greater than her own upheld her. She had prayed very earnestly for it; and it was granted. She had prayed that the presence of the Invisible One might be with her; and so it was. Those around her wondered how she was so calm and still; how that young fragile girl could bear great pain so bravely. They knew not the hidden source of her strength; how that, long before the doctor came, she had prayed for her Saviour's presence, and begged him, in the time of severe trial, not to forsake her. She pleaded before him the promise,

"As thy days thy strength shall be;" and she found it realized.

Mr. Selfield spoke almost kindly to her, as he laid her on the sofa, when it was all over, "You are the bravest young lady I ever met with," he said: "and now you must take care of yourself for the next few days; and then it will be all right again, I hope. I shall look in again in the evening; and Mr. Lockyer will do all he can to amuse you, I am sure. Did you sleep last night?"

"No: scarcely at all."

"Well, you will to-night, I think, if not before."

When he was gone, Walter said, "Georgie, shall I play for you?"

"Yes, if you please," she answered, greatly wondering, at the same time, whether he were able. He went to the piano, and after striking a few chords, as if to try the power of the instrument, he commenced an exquisite air of Mendelssohn's—one of his songs without words. His touch was peculiarly soft and expressive; and, when the air was ended, he went through a series of beautiful variations, which seemed to come into his mind as he sat there; and so wonderful were the taste and execution with which he played, that Georgie raised herself a moment from her couch to see whether it really could be Walter. Yes, there he sat, with his large melancholy eyes turned upwards, and an expression of repose and happiness on his countenance that she had never seen there before.

"Dear Walter," she said, when the last note died away, "how beautiful! Who taught you to play like that?"

"Mamma first," he answered.

"But I have never heard you before."

"No; this is the first time I have touched a piano in this house. I am very glad you like it."

"Where do you practise, then?"

"O, at Campbell's."

"But do my cousins know how beautifully you play?"

"I neither know nor care. I do not fancy I should ever play to please them. But you are to be quiet, you know, Georgie. Shall I go on?"

"O yes," she said, laying herself back again. She shut her eyes, and gave herself up to the full enjoyment of the charming music. It soothed the strained nerves, which had been wound up to the very uttermost from pain and lack of sleep, and in less than half an hour she was in a deep slumber. It was just what Walter had designed; and, when he found his end accomplished, he left the instrument, came and sat near his cousin's sofa, and, taking his little Greek Homer from his pocket, was soon deeply absorbed in its contents.

Frances came softly into the room towards the close of the afternoon. Both she and Augusta had been in great fright all day, and to divert their feelings had gone into Barnes shopping; but Frances was very feeling, though not courageous.

"How is the poor child, Walter?" she whispered. "It was very good of you to be with her. I felt I could not; and poor mamma does not even know what has happened now."

"She has slept the last three hours, I should think. What time is it now?"

"Past five o'clock; and papa expects gentlemen to dinner."

Georgie gave a turn and a slight sigh; then murmured in a low voice, "He won't be angry with me now."

"'Tis that doctor she is thinking of," said Walter. "He scolded her yesterday."

"No, darling," said Frances, stooping down and kissing her, "no one will be angry with you; and Mr. Selfield was not really angry: it is only his manner."

Georgie opened her eyes and smiled.

"What did I say, Frances?"

"You thought some one was angry, dear; but it is a mistake. How is your poor hand?"

"Ah! I was only dreaming—a long, tiresome dream; but it is over now. O, my hand is better. Have I really been asleep?"

"It looks like it," said Frances, holding up her watch. "But I must go now, my dear, and dress for dinner. I will send you something nice, that you can enjoy. I suppose you will go to mamma's room soon?"

"No: she is to go straight to bed from here,

Mr. Selfield said," answered Walter, " and not to get up to-morrow till he has seen her, unless he says differently to-night."

" I must be obedient, I suppose," said Georgie. " If you see auntie, Frances, tell her I am better, if you please."

" I will, dear child. Good bye, for the present." And she flitted gracefully from the róom.

" How pretty Frances is, Walter !" said Georgie, after her cousin was gone. " I could not help wondering what beautiful face it was looking over me when I woke up just now; and it made me smile, although I had had such an uncomfortable dream. I do not think it can be wrong to admire beautiful people ?"

" No, of course not," Walter replied.

" And yet, perhaps, we are disposed to make too much of it. It is a gift from God, like all other things. You have had the charming talent of music given you, Walter ; and Lloyd, of drawing. We ought to use them all for his glory."

" I don't see how beauty can be used to please God."

" I do," said Georgie ; " but never, perhaps, so plainly as this afternoon. Frances' face is enough to cheer any one, however cast down or full of pain one may be. Think how many poor unhappy people she might comfort even by her smiles and kind words. The rich gay people she sees and pleases do not seem to need it; but the poor would value it so."

"I don't think poor people trouble themselves much whether people are handsome or not," said Walter.

"They may not love them any the better; but Leonard says they have just the same natural taste for beautiful things that we have, and that we ought to gratify them as much as we can."

"What! by taking beautiful young ladies to see them?"

"No, Walter," she answered, laughing, "I don't mean exactly that; but the thought came into my mind when Frances was looking at me just now; but I suppose I have not quite well expressed what I meant."

"You have moralized quite enough, I think. Here comes some dinner, or something for you. Shall I feed you, like a baby?"

Georgie laughed again; and so did Walter, as she declined his offer.

"My right hand will answer all needful purposes, I think."

Augusta came frightenedly into the room after dinner. She was surprised to find her cousin so well, and in such good spirits. She sat with her some time. "Mademoiselle Victoire comes the first of October—that will be Monday," she informed her. "She will have been gone nine weeks. Her sister's wedding has taken up such a time."

"I have got quite into lazy habits," Georgie said; "but I shall not be sorry to settle down again."

"I shall," said Augusta. "I never want to settle down again till I am married. Of course I don't want to lose Mdlle. Victoire; but still I can't help being very thankful to think that in about a year I shall be free."

"Another year!" thought Georgina, "what may happen before then!"

"There is Mr. Selfield's ring," said Walter.

"Good night, my dear," exclaimed Augusta, and retreated hastily.

The doctor entered; and Georgina was shortly afterwards despatched to her room. She was surprised to find how weak she was when she attempted to walk. She turned very pale, and was glad to accept of the maid's assistance to help her to her room. Walter was a little frightened; but Mr. Selfield assured him that it was nothing more than was to be expected. "But I think you have been a good nurse," he added: "she seems in good spirits, and doing even better than I hoped. She must be kept amused, but not try her strength much the next few days; and don't let her get low-spirited."

Walter did his best to obey the doctor's injunctions; and so did all the others; and they flattered themselves that they succeeded. She was very patient, never complained, and always seemed quite

18

cheerful when others were present; but an inward sorrow, of which they did not know, still weighed upon her heart heavily; and many a sad tear did she shed in the quiet of her own chamber; many a painful regret did she experience at the recollection of her sinful passion; and what appeared to her, her deep ingratitude came afresh into her mind. "If I were only suffering for well-doing, I should find some comfort," she often said to herself; "but I have done evil, and deserve to suffer. I had so prayed for his conversion; and now he will think that religion is nothing but a name, that there is no reality in the holy obedient serving of God." She felt indeed that her sin was put away for Christ's sake; but that the injury caused by it to the dear name she loved might be lasting; and this thought hovered round her heart incessantly.

About this time she wrote the following letter:

"MY OWN DEAR MARGARET,—It is past the middle of October, but yet I am seated with the window quite wide open, and a mild soft air, almost like spring, blowing in upon me. In my cousin's beautiful studio I am writing—the room I have so often described to you—everything beautiful, in doors and out. Without there is a soft green lawn, bright scarlet geraniums, and purple heliotropes, gay as in the middle of summer, and untouched by the least frost. The fountain is playing in the distance, and the noise of its water sounds cool and refreshing, even in this autumnal month; and the only sign that we are just touching on winter is a few dead leaves, fallen since this morning's sweeping. Trees in the park beyond, with exquisitely colored foliage, green preponderating, but brown and gold intermingled. And in doors, too, dear Margaret, everything is beautiful. All sorts of rich colors, which I like so much ; statuettes, books, drawings ; best of all, that exquisite painting I told you of long ago—the Aruna maiden teaching the bold brave old Norwegians : I know all the history of it now. And every one is so kind to me ! My accident seems to have made them all even kinder than before ; so much more so than I deserve. Mdlle. Victoire reads to me by the hour ; Francie and Augusta talk, and take me pleasant drives in Francie's own pet carriage, with the two white ponies ; and Walter comes in of an evening, and plays to me ; and once or twice Frances has sung as he played, O so beautifully. And so you will think me strangely wilful and contrary, dearest Margaret, when I tell you that I am dull and wearied. Can it be the season of the year infusing something of its sadness and melancholy into my heart ? No, it cannot be ; for, as I said just now, all is brightness and cheerfulness as yet. Margaret dear, I think I am getting home-sick. I long so intensely to see Beechwood once more, to be in the dear quiet library again, and see my brother and you. I have been too long away. I seem growing old very quickly, Margaret. I am changed since I saw you ;

not in my tastes, or my affections, or my shrinking from the noise and confusion of society; but my inner life has been conscious of so many variations. I have striven after much, and have failed so often! yes, the more I have sought, the higher I have aimed, the deeper I seem to have fallen. I want counsel and instruction, and I have no one to whom I can turn. I have prayed so earnestly for patience about Leonard, and the time of his return; and yet on that very point my mind is restless and perplexed. Not only my thoughts, but my words before others, have been impatient, if not complaining. I seem leading a useless life, dear Margaret. I think of you, with your classes, and your poor people, and your visiting, in all of which I once shared, and I long to be with you, and fall again into my former quiet happy life. When I look onward, things appear gloomy. Leonard speaks not a single word of return in his last letter; and then I weary my brain with surmises as to the cause of his leaving England at all. I know this is very wrong; for he asked me if I could trust him about it without knowing, and I told him I could. There is not one, dear Margaret, to whom I can speak, and tell all my troubles, and my inward weariness and anxiety. My dear kind aunt—I feel quite sure she is a true Christian; but she shrinks from speaking on the subject. I often wish I could go to my home above, fly away, and be at rest for ever from the noise and tumult and temptations of outward things,

and the sin and struggles and failures of the inner
life. To feel that the battle is really over, the victory won, the last sin and temptation passed for
ever—O what rest, what peace it must be! And
to be with the Saviour, to feel that we shall no more
grieve him with our forgetfulness, and coldness, and
wanderings, but live in the smile of his approving
presence for ever—how safe, how happy it will be!
It seems more like going home, to me. I have so
many dear ones safely landed there already, only
myself and Leonard to follow them.' But time tells
me, dearest, that I must leave off. One more thing
however, I must say. I know you take an interest
in Walter, and that you have long prayed for him.
I don't know what he is feeling, I have not been
able to speak to him for a long time; but he is very
different, hardly the same as when I saw him first,
ten months ago. He is quite cheerful sometimes,
talks with my cousins, and goes to see aunt every
day. Only yesterday I heard Augusta wondering
to Frances what happy change had come upon Walter; and she quite agreed with her. Only think,
dear, if the greatest, happiest of all changes were
working in his mind. It seems almost too good a
thing to anticipate; but O, nothing is too hard for
our Heavenly Father. Walter would make such a
beautiful earnest Christian; his whole heart goes
where his affection or interests are placed. And so,
my own dear Margaret, do not forget to pray for
him, and for your very loving and affectionate

18*   "GEORGINA."

And was Georgie's life at this time, as she sadly imagined it, a useless and an aimless one? The conversation that was passing in an adjoining room at the very time that she, with tearful eyes, was writing to her friend of her unworthiness and her failures, proved that it was not so. Perhaps it might have cheered her somewhat, could she have heard it.

"Tom, do you ever read the Bible?" asked Carry, as she brought in a fresh supply of mulberry leaves for some silkworms they were rearing.

"No."

"Why not?"

"I don't much care for it."

"You would, though, if you were to read with cousin Georgie every morning, as I do."

"Do you?"

"Yes, and she makes it so interesting; she explains it as we go along, and there are such beautiful stories in the Old Testament, I had not the least idea. Besides, Tom, it is right to read it, you know. It tells us how to go to heaven; and Georgie says that is the most important thing of all."

"I don't want to go there yet," said Tom.

"Ah! but supposing you were to die?"

"I hope I sha'nt," he answered.

"But you may. Georgie had a little brother and sister die before they were as old you; and they both went to heaven, she says, because Christ loved them, and they loved him."

" Is that what makes cousin Georgie look grave and serious so often ?"

" Perhaps it is. You must not ask her, though, Tom; she cried a great deal when she told me; but she said she should see them again some day, and her mamma and her papa too."

" I love her," exclaimed Tom. " But do you think, Carry, she will ever be able to draw and cut out things again. Isn't it dreadful about her poor finger ?"

"Yes, very; but she will be able to draw, I know, as soon as ever her arm comes out of that sling. You see it is the left hand. But I am afraid she won't be able to play."

" The window is mended now," said the boy; and then, after a minute or two, he added, " Do you think she would mind my reading too of a morning ?"

" No. I will ask her." So on the following morning the young untiring teacher had two little pupils instead of one; and with patient delight she labored to make them love that holy book which so long had been precious to her, and that Saviour who loved little children, and had died to save them."

Six weeks after the accident, Georgie's hand was perfectly recovered—disfigured for life, it is true, but painless.

Frances was pitying her one day, and mentioning a clever practitioner in London who manufactured artificial members of every description. She proposed a journey to town to consult him. Georgie declined for the present, then looked at her injured hand, and smiled, anything but sadly, Frances thought, as she surveyed her own beautifully formed hand, and wondered what she should feel were it deformed in a similar manner.

November had set in, bleak and dull and dreary. No, it was not the weather which had weighed on Georgie's spirits, and made her sad and low. She was happier now, though she had received no farther news from Leonard, and nothing more in prospect to cheer her as to his return.

She had received letters from Margaret and Mrs. Murray, too—kind, but wise. Was she not dwelling a little too much on herself, and her own feelings and efforts? forgetting that it is not what we are in ourselves that God regards, but only what we are in Christ; that God may be glorified as much by patient continuance in well-doing when such is the marked-out path, as in more active exertion in his service. And with much love they bid her take courage, and not be cast down, but throw the whole burden of her sorrow and troubles on the arms of her heavenly Father, and wait patiently for him. "Light is sown for the righteous, and joy for the upright in heart," was Mrs. Murray's parting text, and with trust and hope Georgina was going on her way once more. She was like a calm pure moonbeam in the gay flutter of excitement that ever pervaded the atmosphere at Leighton, passing on in it, but not of it; and shedding a steady light which those that noted admired, though they knew not the source whence it came.

"Blessed are the ears," writes one who lived in constant communion with the invisible One, "that gladly receive the pulses of the divine whisper, and give no heed to the many whisperings of the world. Blessed indeed are those ears that listen not after the voice which is sounding without, but for the truth teaching inwardly."

Many voices whispered and sounded in the ears of Georgina—undue love of praise, of learning, and of things beautiful. To such temptations she was peculiarly alive; but the divine power, working and ruling within, was able to close her ear to the fascinations of them, and to cause her to listen anxiously and with diligent heed to voices of softer and more hallowed meaning, wafted from the heavenly country. And well was it that this calm peace was dwelling in and sustaining her heart. Those few tranquil weeks of autumn seemed a kind of lull and preparation for a new and unlooked-for trial, which the snows and frosts of winter and the chime of Christmas bells should unfold in all its bitterness.

"Dear Frances,—I intend to be with you to-morrow evening, by the eight o'clock train, most probably. Let my horse be sent to the station for me, and anything you choose for the traps. Don't stay at home on my account, if you have any engagement, as, if Farrer accompanies me, I may not be in till the next train."

So wrote Lloyd, a week or two before Christmas. He was fumbling over the papers in his writing-desk for a suitable envelope, when his eye fell on a note from Georgina, written to him during his former absence in London. He took it up and looked at the graceful, delicate hand-writing. "Just like her," he said to himself—"everything she does tells what she is like; but I was mistaken in her too. Constance! no: I named her wrongly; or she would not have been unrelenting. She might have accepted my peace-offering: she need not have blazed abroad my foolish passion." "How do you know she did?" whispered a voice which, strange to say, had not spoken before; "it is but your sur- mise, after all." "If not, why did she so scrupu- lously avoid me? not even showing by a word or look that she was willing to be reconciled; better to have reproached me, than such perfect indiffer- ence; I might then have humbled myself." These thoughts passed through his mind as he folded and sealed his letter; then, rising, he pulled the bell to give orders that it might be posted. Williams entered.

"Here, take this quickly to the office: I shall leave early to-morrow, and want you for some other business when you come back. Stay, what have you there?—letters at this time?"

The servant appeared somewhat confused:

"I have to beg your pardon, sir," he said, "and Miss Archdale's, too; but I hope it was nothing of consequence," he added ingenuously.

But Lloyd, who had recognized the long, narrow envelope, and the clear writing, had already snatched the note from the hands of the man-servant, and was hurriedly glancing over its contents. He felt the color mounting to his forehead, and the angry flash of the eye could hardly be restrained; but he would not commit himself before his servant, and inquired, swallowing his temper as well as he was able,

"What is the meaning of this? when was it given you?"

"The evening before we left Leighton, if I remember rightly, sir: you were out at the time. I put it in my pocket and entirely forgot it. I hope, sir, it is of no importance."

"Take the letter," said Lloyd, in a harsh, decided tone; and the man, vexed at his own unfortunate forgetfulness, and his master's evident displeasure, left the room precipitately.

Bitter self-reproach, indignation, shame, and withal a sense of some kind of satisfaction, agitated the young man's breast, as he reperused the little note, unlike the one he had just been reading; for it was stained and blotted by her tears.

"'Passion, ingratitude, wickedness!' no, you are more like an angel," he said. "And what a wretch I have been, accusing you of malice, poor blameless little Constance." A third time he read the note. "She asks me to speak to her: well, you shall know it all soon, Georgie. It was shame that prevented me. But for that man's stupidity, three months—no, not three hours should have passed without your learning how I despised myself, the moment after I had given way to such unpardonable passion."

He sat some time with his head resting on his hand, recalling, as far as he could recollect, the circumstances of his last two days at Leighton. He remembered with regret how he had purposely avoided speaking to her on the morning—passed her without a look or a word at night, and the indifferent expressions he had used with regard to her in his mother's boudoir. She was sleeping, then, however, he consoled himself by imagining. A knock at the door announced the return of his servant. Again he apologized for his remissness, hoping that it was of no real consequence.

"It was a matter that should have been attended to," said Lloyd, with some of his usual hauteur. "When do you say Miss Archdale gave you the letter?"

"I have been thinking, sir, that it was on the Tuesday afternoon, as we left the Thursday;" and then added, for he was beginning to feel his curiosity somewhat awakened, "Howsoever, it was the day but one before the young lady hurt her hand with the picture."

"With what picture?" inquired Lloyd, roused to

forego a little of his accustomed dignity in the interest of the subject: "I thought Miss Archdale hurt her hand by the falling of the window."

. "Yes, sir, and surely enough she did; but I beg your pardon, I thought you might know how; but perhaps the young lady has not told."

"Told what? I don't know what you are talking about. What do you mean about a picture?"

"The picture, sir, as you brought away with you to Oxford. I could not hinder myself from seeing the accident, for I was in the garden close by, gathering flowers for Hilman."

"Just tell me, will you," said Lloyd, speaking as composedly as he could, for he began to guess what yet he hardly dared to think of.

"Well, sir, Miss Frances had just laid the picture half out of the window, to dry, I suppose, and she was walking in the garden with lady Legh; and then Miss Georgina comes into the library. I was just gathering the cloth-of-gold rose then; so, as I said before, sir, I could not avoid seeing her."

Lloyd moved his head imperatively for the servant to proceed with his story.

"Miss Georgina was looking very white and ill, as I thought, sir; but all at once she ran right across the room; and then I saw that the great window was falling. I thought about the picture too, because I knew as you set store by it; but before I could look she had her hand on the sill, and down

19

came the window on it, instead of on the picture; and then, as sure as I live, she smiled, and pulled the picture out. As I said to Mrs. Timmins, I never saw such a thing in a young lady before, and one so delicate and pale-like as she was, too."

Lloyd winced, and his foot moved nervously up and down upon the carpet; but he only said, " Did she seem much hurt at the time?"

" When she got out her hand, sir, the blood dropped down upon her dress, and I thought she looked frightened; but I was called off just then, and never heard much more about it, except that my lady sent word for Turner to go for the doctor directly; and then Mrs. Timmins wrote me word as how she had been forced to have her finger *ampitated;* and I said to myself, 'No wonder.' "

" But why on earth did not all this make you remember the note?" exclaimed Lloyd, whose feelings were becoming almost unendurable.

" Why really, sir, I can't think myself," answered the man, " only I know as I should never have thought of the matter again, if I hadn't been turning out my pockets just now. 'Twas my best livery suit, sir; and I was just brushing it up a bit."

A loud knock and ring was just then heard at the door.

" If that's captain Ross, say that I am particularly engaged," said Lloyd; " and come back in about an hour to do the packing. We must be off by the first train to-morrow morning."

The servant left the room; and Lloyd, resuming his former attitude, murmured in a low remorseful tone, " *Never, never,* shall I be heard to **swear again.**"

XIII

THE FEARFUL ACCIDENT.

"Or we may live to feel 'twas best
  That God denied our prayer,
And tried and prov'd, till we confess'd
That waves and storms which broke our rest,
And toss'd us to our Saviour's breast,
  Our richest blessings were."

MONSELL.

IT so happened that the Leighton party had an engagement on the evening that Lloyd was expected—sir William, his two eldest daughters and Walter, who had become much more sociable of late, and who found, as Georgie told him, that much of his former neglect and discomfort arose from his own moodiness and want of will or tact in accommodating himself to the ways and wishes of the family.

"You must do all the welcoming till we come home," said Frances, gaily, as she flitted into the drawing-room, with her scarlet opera-cloak, and a wreath of holly-berries in her glossy hair; "but don't sit up, you know, dear, later than you like Lloyd will comfort himself with a cigar or a nap, if you are tired, and like to go to bed before we come back. I shall say good-night in case;" and she stooped and kissed her.

Then Walter came in. His hair was brushed off from his wide forehead now; and he never transgressed by wearing his hat in the presence of ladies. The large black eyes flashed less frequently with anger, and were oftener lighted up with a glance of happiness or eager interest.

"A twelvemonth ago, to-night, that I saw you for the first time, Georgie," he said.

"Are things any brighter than they were then with you?" she inquired softly.

"Yes, very much: at least one part of me."

She guessed very well his meaning.

"Ah, Walter, there might be peace and happiness within too, if you really sought it."

"I have been trying for it months past, but it won't come."

"You are looking for it in yourself, perhaps," she replied; "and if so, you will never find it."

"No, not in myself: I have been more like the rest of the world lately, than ever before."

"You will not find it in the world either, or in anything external. Christ says, 'Take my yoke upon you, and you shall find rest unto your souls.' I have often thought of the words—a yoke to carry, and yet rest. And they are true words, too."

"Good night, Georgina."

"Where are you going?"

"To an amateur concert at admiral Blakey's; it is the music I care about, not the company."

"Good night," she replied; and then she leaned her head upon her hand, and tried to finish the letter that she was writing to Margaret. But it would not do: she could not well write that evening: a strange oppression hung over her: each noise without doors, each ring of the bell made her start and change color, though she knew her cousin could not be expected yet. Little Carry came running into the drawing-room to say good night.

"Only a week more to Christmas, Georgie; and Clara and Arthur come on Monday. Is it not delightful?" She received no answer, and looking up saw tears in her cousin's eyes. "Ah! you are thinking about Leonard," she said, "perhaps he may be here too. Mamma says it is quite possible, because a letter may have been lost, or gone wrong: don't cry, dear." Georgie kissed the little affectionate girl. "Why are you sitting in here to-night, when they are all out, and there is no company? I thought you liked the library best."

"Lloyd is coming home, you know, darling."

"Ah, yes, I forgot: he will be pleased to see you waiting for him, because he likes you, Georgie. I heard him telling some one so, one day, and how clever you were; and I said so, too."

"Little flatterer, you should not tell people so to their faces."

"Ah, but I love you;" and she flung her arms

round her cousin's neck, and embraced her most warmly.

"Love is very precious," thought Georgina to herself, when the child was gone : "if I have reaped nothing else since coming here, the affection of this child is worth a long sowing-time."

She sat and waited: the time seemed long. The footman came in to arrange the fire. "Is this time-piece right, Charles ?" she inquired, as it chimed out nine o'clock.

"Yes, miss—exactly, I believe. Will you have supper ?"

"No, I thank you," she answered; and he left the room.

She fancied that she heard the sound of carriage-wheels coming up the drive. "He rides," she thought: "it cannot be he." She walked rather nervously about the room, closed the piano, re-arranged the ornaments scattered on the table, and turned on the gas more brightly.

"I wish the others had been at home," she murmured to herself: "how will he meet me? But I brought it on myself: I must bear the punishment. If he is angry I will explain all—ask his forgiveness. The long absence may have softened him." She stopped her musings suddenly, for there were voices in the hall. "It must be Lloyd; but—" and she started—"there seems strange confusion." With beating heart she left the room, stole down the great stairs, and stood on the landing. What a

sight met her eyes! They were carrying Lloyd in.
A handkerchief was thrown over his face: she could
see that it was saturated with blood: he was quite
motionless: she thought he was dead. She gave
no cry, no shriek, but, following the frightened servants into the nearest room, saw them place him on
the bed, and heard the surgeon asking for water.
She went and fetched some directly; and Mr. Selfield looking up, saw who it was.   ..

"O Miss Georgina," he said, "I am thankful to
see you: I can get nothing done: there is no one
who possesses the slightest degree of capability;"
and Georgie found herself helping and directing with
a composure she herself wondered at; a composure
external truly, but a heart sorrowful, heavy, almost
breaking.

An hour passed: he was insensible still. Would
those eyes never look up again? They were hid
now by the white drooping eyelids, and their heavy
fringes contrasted with the marble face, so still and
quiet in its pure outline. "O, for one look again,"
thought Georgie—"one word to me to say he has
forgiven!" and for a moment her forced calmness
forsook her; and the young girl was almost stifled
with the effort to restrain her feelings.

"You must be calm, indeed, Miss Archdale,"
whispered the surgeon to her. "Lady Archdale
and her daughters are in a pitiable state. I could
on no account allow them to be here; and we must
have some one who is perfectly still and self-pos-

sessed, as the slightest agitation may prove fatal. You can be, if you choose, I know."

"Mr. Selfield, do you think he will die?"

"I cannot tell: he is in very great danger: we must hope," said the surgeon, gravely.

Lloyd lay still: his breathing was heavy and thick: sometimes he murmured. Georgina could not hear what he said, distinctly; but once she fancied that he called her; so she took the burning hand in hers, and said, "Yes, I am here, dear Lloyd, close to you."

No notice was taken, and he did not speak again; but Mr. Selfield looked uneasily at him as he saw a dull stupor coming over him.

"What shall I do?" said he to himself: "he must be awakened from this comatose state. I hope Sir John Cooper will soon be here: it is a fearful responsibility."

One hour passed thus; another and another. Midnight came and went. Not a sound was heard, as the two sat silently by the sick-bed; a strange contrast, truly—the man, past the prime of life, gray, hard in feature, yet with an expression of benevolence and kindliness on his face not often met with in one who had been tossed for many a long day on the tempestuous sea of life; beside him the young girl, a child in years and stature, but a woman in action and thought; and very fair and fragile did that sweet face look, as the dark blue eyes suffused with tears, and the cheeks flushed crimson, as she struggled to repress her emotion, and to stifle the cry of the heart which was beating tumultuously with the burden of sorrow which no others knew. It had wounded her very heart, the parting for three months unreconciled; but to part for ever thus! And the sense of eternity, over the confines of which his spirit, all unprepared, was hovering, came over her soul with an awful reality, such as she had never before experienced. Fervent, agonizing prayers went up from the side of that bed of suffering that night.

Morning broke at last, bright and beautiful, gladdening and refreshing many a weary one; but to Georgina it only brought a realization of the sorrow which was on the household.

And now lady Archdale had summoned up nerve and resolution to enter the chamber, and she insisted that her niece should have some rest. Very reluctantly Georgina was obliged to comply with her aunt's wishes; and she wondered to herself on finding how very weak she was directly she left Lloyd's room. In the gallery she met Walter. He almost started to mark her pale face, swollen eyelids, and trembling steps; and going up he took her hand gently, and led her to the library. A large fire burned upon the hearth, and with its blaze illuminated the room, the shutters of which had not yet been unclosed; for there Walter had kept his nightly watch. He placed her in a large chair near it, for the touch of her hand was cold, and he observed that she shivered; then, telling her hé should bring some breakfast, immediately went out.

Poor Georgina, thus left alone, and at liberty to give free vent to her feelings, leaned back in the chair and wept passionately. The tears seemed to bring some relief. When Walter returned with a tray containing a cup of chocolate and some dry toast, he was glad to see her look more natural, though tearful, sobbing still. He placed the breakfast on a little table near, and gently told her to eat. She obeyed from a strong sense of duty rather than choice; for she felt now that her strength must be kept up if possible. But it was a painful and bitter meal. Walter did not interrupt the silence, but sat gazing into the fire and at her. At length when it was ended, she said,

"Walter, tell me all about it: I have not heard."

He told her then how Lloyd, on his way from the station, had been thrown from his horse. He was riding at more than his usual speed; for the train, Walter said, was late, and he seemed eager to be home. The horse had taken fright, and thrown Lloyd violently, his head striking against a heap of stones by the road-side. When the groom arrived at the spot, his master lay bleeding and insensible. Happily, at that very juncture, Mr. Selfield's carriage drove past, bearing the surgeon, who had been sent for to the Hall to lady Archdale

With the man-servant's assistance, Lloyd was placed in the carriage, and brought slowly home: these were the carriage-wheels Georgina had heard.

The poor girl listened to the account with silent anguish; then again leaned back, and covered her face with her hands, groaning aloud. For a moment it seemed as though her great secret must be disclosed, that she could bear the burden alone no longer, that Walter must know that Lloyd had parted from her in anger. But ah! that would involve inquiries as to the cause; and a word to his disadvantage should never, never cross her lips. The thought silenced her: she only murmured,

"O, Walter, if he should die!"

"What does Mr. Selfield say? Is there hope? Has he spoken?"

"Not once coherently, and not at all for hours. Mr. Selfield thinks there is very little hope: he believes him to be rapidly sinking, I know. But sir John Cooper will be here soon. Walter, I promised aunt to lie down for three or four hours: will you let me know, and have me waked if I am asleep?"

He promised. Then she went to her room, with Mdlle. Victoire's assistance undressed, and soon, poor child, wearied and exhausted with prolonged and painful excitement, fell asleep.

The physician from London, sir John Cooper, arrived in the course of the morning. He, too, shared Mr. Selfield's fears, but approved of all he had done. Nothing more, he said, was wanting : they must only wait for the awakening which might never come on earth. O, how bitterly now did lady Archdale reproach herself for the indolence and apathy which had hindered her from speaking to her son on aught but earthly things ! Now, the mask of reserve fell off, and she saw revealed in true colors how culpable, how negligent she had been : the veil was torn away at once, the barriers of conventionality were pulled down, and she knew at once what she had wasted and misused.

Three days passed thus—three dark and anxious days, counted by weeks instead of hours : they seemed interminable.

As much as they would allow her, Georgina was with her cousin, composed, self-possessed, a treasure to the doctors. None knew or guessed the deep and restless feelings which lay hidden beneath that calm exterior.

. Lloyd had not spoken coherently : he was weaker, stiller than at first. He moaned, O so piteously, it went through Georgie's heart to hear him. He looked so ill, so helpless, as he lay there; but toward the evening of the third day, there came a little change. The strange wild look was no longer in his eyes : he was cooler, and not so restless.

"He is better," whispered sir John Cooper to Mr. Selfield. The latter nodded assent; and in the evening, to Georgina's glad surprise and his mother's joy, he said quite sensibly—

"Mother, has Georgina been here? I thought I saw her a minute ago."

"Yes, my dear," replied lady Archdale, "she is here."

"Let me see her," said Lloyd: "Little Georgie, have you forgotten me?"

"O no, no, dear cousin."

He made a sign as though he would speak a word to her alone. She bent towards him.

"Can you have forgiven all, Constance? I must know before I sleep, and I am tired."

She pressed a kiss upon his white forehead lovingly, as the surest token of reconciliation; for she could not speak.

"Constance still," he repeated, as though to himself, and smiled as he closed his eyes. Georgie retreated to her place behind the curtain, and, taking hold of her aunt's hand, sat silent and thankful, whilst her cousin slept calmly and peacefully for some hours. On awakening, though weak as a babe, he was perfectly collected and reasonable, able to express himself clearly, and so much better that sir John Cooper pronounced all immediate danger passed, but enjoined perfect silence on the part of sufferer and nurses.

"Do not be frightened, lady Archdale," he said, when he was out of the room, "at the inflammation which will probably supervene. Of course I do not for an instant mean to say that *all* danger is over, but I think there are favorable symptoms enough to warrant the hope of your son's recovery. But again I must urge the complete silence which I should wish to be kept in the sick room. Do not allow any other members of your family to see him : your little daughter has shown wonderful presence of mind and self-control : she may be there ; but you will acquiesce in what I say when I tell you life and death may hang upon the necessity of the slightest agitation being avoided." And having concluded this unusually long speech—for the courtly old doctor was a man of proverbially few words—he accepted lady Archdale's offer of refreshment, and in half an hour was on his way to London, promising, however, to return the next day.

Towards evening Lloyd grew feverish and flushed. Georgina was startled to hear him again calling for her, and speaking of days and scenes of which she knew nothing. Mr. Selfield was prepared for this, and, assuring her that there was no fresh cause for apprehension, begged her to retire and secure one night of thorough repose. He then thought it necessary to bleed his patient, as he was afraid of the rush of blood to the brain ; and having done so he had the satisfaction of seeing him more composed and tranquil ; and then, for the first time since he had been summoned to the Hall, he lay down on a sofa in the same room, and endeavored to get a little of the rest which he so much needed, after his indefatigable exertions ; not, however, without leaving in charge a nurse whose experience and vigilance could well be trusted.

The next day Lloyd was much the same—certainly no worse, though he complained much of headache, and was irritable to an excess, allowing no one but Georgina to attend upon him, and refusing to take anything but at her earnest persuasion. Altogether it was a most trying day to the poor girl; and once or twice her firmness was on the point of giving way at his great fretfulness; but she bitterly reproached herself for this, when sir John Cooper said to her in the afternoon—

"You must not be surprised at great irritability in your brother, Miss Archdale : concussion of the brain is always attended by it; he is not responsible for his actions yet; and I know he is suffering very acute pain. So you must bear with his complaints, wearying as they must naturally be. But come, I see you are tired yourself, would you have any objection to showing me your beautiful gardens, of which I have heard so often? A little fresh air will be quite a treat to a man who is shut up in dingy smoky London, as I am. Christmas is strange weather for seeing fine grounds to advantage; but I think that the exercise will do us both good."

Georgina complied, and returned to the house quite invigorated by the walk, which had been made pleasant by the cheerful kindly words of the physician, whom she had undeceived as to her relationship to the family. Then, somehow or other, she had found herself talking to him of her own concerns, her past sorrows, and her brother's absence, her hopes and fears; and insensibly the conversation had led to higher themes—the spirit's nobler longings, and the life to come; and so had she been comforted and refreshed by the friendly counsel and advice which had come from a quarter where she least had expected it. O how unspeakably blessed the tie which, imperceptible to all others, unites in the bonds of sympathy and true affection the hearts of the faithful! No distinction of youth or age, learning or ignorance, wealth or poverty can break it. The chord struck in the heart of one vibrates responsively in the innermost soul of the other.

Hopes, longings, aspirations—all one: one Lord, one faith, one baptism, one God and Father of all —the earthly path perchance very diverse, but the same home in prospect at the end of the journey. The voyage calm and unruffled to the one, to the other cloudy and tempestuous and swelling; but the same haven awaiting each—the same rest, the same joy, the same glory. "And, if here in the Church's low estate the communion of saints be blessed, then how great," writes St. Augustine, "shall the joy be, in the perfect love of the innumerable company of blessed angels and men, when each shall love another even as himself! for every man there shall rejoice as much for the happy estate of each as for his own felicity."

"In quietness and confidence shall be your

strength," whispered Georgie to lady Archdale, as she left her for the night, remarking that her aunt seemed nervous and agitated. "Dearest auntie, God has been better to us than our fears."

"He has indeed, my darling; and O how little have I deserved it! My eldest one, and very fondly loved—but unwisely—I neglected to teach him and the others also, to seek first the kingdom of God and his righteousness. Want of interest and concern myself in former years, and of late, a strange feeling of reserve and fearfulness as to how they might receive it—I have been very unfaithful, Georgie; but I have had a solemn lesson, though at the same time a tender one, to show me my past error and present duty. You must pray for your poor aunt, dear child."

The tears came into Georgina's eyes, as she pressed her aunt's hand.

"And I too have been sadly negligent and un-watchful, dear aunt. I hardly like to think of the past, except as being forgiven for Christ's sake."

"I find peace in that too, Georgie," she replied, kissing her. "Now, dearest, do not sit up more than another hour: it is only on these conditions I leave you. You must save yourself a little for all our sakes."

"Yes, I promise you, auntie; but I must give him his night draught, you see, or he would perhaps be vexed. How strange that he will only take his medicines from one person!"

From that time Lloyd gradually recovered, but very slowly. For some days the progress was so slight that it was scarcely perceptible; but still it was progress. It was a trying time both for himself and his nurses. Great quiet and stillness in the sick room were indispensable; and Lloyd, as he became better, grew yet more restless and fretful, was very exacting in his requirements, and impatient when denied any little wish that he had set his heart upon.

Georgina was the one who seemed best able to manage him. She coaxed him into acquiescence with the doctor's wishes, and gave up to his whims and caprices as far as possible; at the same time steadily refusing to talk more to him than was permitted; and the firm but quiet way in which she put her finger before her lips, when she knew silence was necessary, had more effect upon him than all Mr. Selfield's admonitions, or nurse's forebodings of evil results.

"I know I must be a dreadful bore to you all," he said to her one day. "I feel that I am awfully cross sometimes; but a fellow must be allowed that, when he suffers as I do, and is not even permitted a good story to amuse him. You must be tired enough of sitting in this stupid room, Constance?"

"O, no; I have my work to amuse me, you know · and I only wish I could interest you more;

but Mr. Selfield said I might read a little to you in a day or two."

"O, for that I am always interested when you are in the room; but nurse is such a horrid old croaker, and she makes me cross always when you are away, ready to be smoothed down again on your return. So he said I might be read to?"

"Yes; but—" she continued, hesitatingly, "nothing exciting, such as poetry or novels."

"Nonsense! And that is all I care for. How on earth can it hurt me?"

"Dear Lloyd, you don't want to be worse again; and Mr. Selfield and sir John both said that the least thing exciting to the brain must be avoided, and for that reason you must be good and quiet now. There, let me give you some grapes, and try and have a little sleep, and, after dinner, Francie is to come in, and see you a little."

"Well, then, come and sit here, and give them to me; and, I say, do put down that shutter. I am half blinded with this strong light."

"Poor fellow!" thought Georgina to herself; "he little knows how weak his head must be; why there is scarcely any light in the room as it is." But she did as he told her, and before long he was asleep.

"Let us have our chapters in Lloyd's room to-day," said lady Archdale, a day or two after this conversation, as Georgie came in with her Bible, for her usual morning reading. "I spoke to him about it last night; and he said he should like it."

"Ah! that will be nice," she answered. She had been wanting to propose the very thing herself, but had felt some little difficulty. So every morning and evening she read, and sometimes in the day besides. Lloyd never made any remark upon it. Sometimes he would thank her when she closed the book, but oftener would say nothing at all, but give an impatient sigh, or call for some trifle to be brought him. But he never interrupted her when she was reading; and Georgie sometimes sadly hoped that in his heart he felt more interest than he chose to manifest. So she prayed on, and in her heart thanked God that this opportunity of hearing his word was given to her cousin. "It cannot return void," she said trustingly : "it must accomplish the thing which he pleases, and prosper; for he himself has said it."

When Lloyd became sufficiently recovered, he was taken by day into his own cheerful room; and very much pleased was Georgina when she first saw him established there on a comfortable lounge near the fire. But he seemed low, and out of spirits.

"It may be months before I touch that again," he said, pointing to his easel. "Mr. Selfield has some cram about its hurting my brain, as though that were not sound enough now. Why, if I were a confirmed maniac, he could not talk much worse."

"Well, it is best to be a little too careful, is it not? And now, Lloyd, you must not be gloomy the first time of coming into your nice beautiful room : only look at the flowers."

"I do n't care for flowers just now. I want to paint. I have an idea in my head that I long to carry out."

"You will be able to do so, before very long, I dare say. Shall I read to you a little? or will you have something to take? You must be tired, I know."

"No: I'm not tired—only—" for he caught sight that moment of her pale face, as still and unruffled as his own was discontented, and noticed a little touch of weariness in the calm soft voice—" only, little Constance, shamefully perverse. You must forgive me. Yes, I should like you to read a little presently; but you look so white and tired. Come, and sit down and talk a little." She obeyed him. After a little pause, he began : " Georgina, I have never been able to speak about it yet, but if you knew how I hate myself every time I think of my shameful behaviour to you—this room reminds me."

" O hush, Lloyd! Do not speak of that now— never again."

" You know about it, then ?"

" Yes, Williams told me, the night after your accident, about his forgetting the note. Poor fellow! He was so sorry."

"Sorry! and I was half-mad. Georgie, I said then you were like an angel, and I think so still

And, then, in the face of it all—ah! your poor little hand. If you have forgiven me, I shall never forgive myself. I should have burned that picture, had I known it, at the time."

" What picture ?" asked Georgina quickly. "No one knew, no one saw."

" Yes, Williams saw. I know it all. Can you forgive me, Constance ?"

" Do'n't ask it, Lloyd. You have never given me your forgiveness yet."

He did not answer this; only, after a moment's silence, in a low tone, and with averted face, he said, " I have never sworn since, Georgie, and never intend to. You gained your point, if that is any compensation for all you went through. But, still," he continued, as though anxious now to have a full explanation, " why did you not accept my flowers ! I thought you might have understood."

" What flowers ?" she asked anxiously, and a dim vision of faded flowers in connection with that terrible night gleamed through her mind.

" I put them myself on your table, and fancied they would speak your name, and ask my pardon as plainly as I could."

Georgina could have cried as she remembered their fate.

" It would have saved me a great deal of misery," she said; " but, O Lloyd, it is all passed now. You *will* not speak of it again, will you ?"

" I make no rash promise," he answered. " Is

it not strange, Georgie, that you don't hear from Leonard ?"

The tears, restrained before with difficulty, now dimmed her eyes; "I can't understand it. I try not to think about it too much, but cannot prevent myself."

"I can't think how you take it so patiently; and then I worry you so with my ill-temper."

"Hush, hush! You do not at all. And, besides, Lloyd, after all, it must be right. God is watching over Leonard more carefully than I could, and he will bring him back to me in the right time."

"Well, I wish I were as resigned as you. But I never shall be; so there is an end of the matter. What is that book, Constance, which you were reading to Caroline last summer when I took you by surprise in the park ?"

"I forgot. I thought we were talking. What was it about ?"

"O some *good* book, of course—not exciting; some Hopeful or other; and they appeared just to have forded a river."

"Ah! I recollect: it was 'The Pilgrim's Progress,' was it not ?"

"I don't know; perhaps so."

"Would you like to hear it? It is beautiful."

"I don't care."

Georgina was glad of only this slight encouragement, and hastened to fetch her favorite book, which she was delighted to have the opportunity of reading to her cousin.

From day to day she read, but never to the neglect of the Bible, and Lloyd appeared well pleased. The simple but quaintly-eloquent language impressed him, though the meaning oftentimes seemed a hidden thing. Once he asked Georgina a question as to its signification. "You must imagine yourself talking to Caroline," he said, "I am about as ignorant on the subject as she was, and you were giving her quite a small sermon that day."

Georgina smiled. "The meaning is the most beautiful part," she said: "I should not have understood it as I do, had it not been for Leonard." But she could not quite turn Lloyd into Caroline; and he said nothing more about sermons.

One day, on coming into the room unexpectedly, she found her cousin with the book in his hands. He closed it hastily as she entered, and made an indifferent remark on the fineness of the edition, and the softness and beauty of the plates. But, when she took it up the next time, she found two pages turned down, not by herself. The first pointed to the words, "Flee from the wrath to come;" the other to the passage where Christian is represented as losing his burden at the foot of the cross. Her heart thrilled gratefully. "Can it be that his heart is even now occupied with thoughts of his eternal safety?" she thought.

There was no external manifestation of such being the case, certainly. He was impatient and restless as ever; more so, indeed, complaining sadly of his privations, as he called them, and at the same time so weak that, if he ventured to join in any company, or make the slightest exertion, his increased debility the following day was most painful to witness. His former gay carelessness of manner had quite forsaken him, and the habitual expression of his fine handsome features was weariness and dejection, except when roused to interest either by Georgina's reading, or soothed by the conversation and attentions of his mother and sisters into a temporary forgetfulness of himself.

"This will never do," said Mr. Selfield to lady Archdale, one day, when she had been complaining of his increased dulness and low spirits. "He must have change of air and scene. He should be making more progress now; but it is difficult to know where to send him. London is too exciting just at present; the sea a little too cold; and he should be among friends, too. Miss Georgie, what can you suggest?"

"Beechwood," she replied, in a low tone.

"Yes," said Lady Archdale, "the very place itself. But would he like it?"

"I think so. And I could go and take care of him."

Lloyd entered just then. He raised his eyebrows inquiringly, and asked what they were talking about.

"About sending you off," replied the doctor. "A young lady here has volunteered to go and take care of you, entertain you at her own house, too—will you go?"

"I don't care," said Lloyd. "Better there, perhaps, than anywhere else. I don't wonder," he continued, with more of his old good-humor of manner, "that you are all anxious to get rid of me. I feel a kind of incubus to myself and every one else."

"Not quite that, my dear boy," said his mother; "but a change seems really needful for you. The Rectory is just unoccupied, and Georgie's plan really seems a feasible one."

"You do not want any more of my medicines," continued Mr. Selfield, going up to Lloyd, who had thrown himself upon the sofa, and, laying his hand upon his shoulder, "All you require now is good air, good cheer, and good spirits."

"One more thing still," thought Lloyd, to himself; but he did not say so. "Well, I hope I may pick them up at Beechwood," he replied, carelessly, and with a forced smile.

"I can trust Miss Georgina for doing her part," said Mr. Selfield. "Sir John and I talked seriously of giving her a diploma. She would make a capital doctor." And with this compliment and a bow to all, he took his leave.

The following week saw Georgina, her cousin, and their attendants on the way to Beechwood, with the arrangement that Lady Archdale was to follow when the spring was a little more advanced.

XIV.

PEACE SOUGHT AND FOUND.

'The rest of a happy child
 Led by the Father on,
Feeling his smile and reconciled
 To all that he has done—
Of one who can meekly bend
 'Neath my yoke, with me beside;
Of a soldier who knows how the fight will end
 With a Leader true and tried—
The rest of a subject heart,
 Of its best desires possest:
Come, all that are heavy laden
 And I will give you rest."

THE dear old home again; the village street, all in the dimness and indistinctness of twilight; the neatly-kept cottages; the church; the well-known garden; the clang of the iron gate; and then the house itself, lighted up earlier than usual to welcome the travellers; the kindly faces of the servants, not excepting Mrs. Airey, who received her with a hearty embrace—O how natural did all seem to Georgina! She smiled and wept by turns, hovering all the while about her cousin, fearing lest he should find himself neglected in the midst of the little tumult of joy occasioned by her return.

"Mrs. Murray was here not an hour ago," said the housekeeper, as she conducted them to the library, where a bright fire was blazing, and tea arranged for their refreshment, "and brought these flowers," and she pointed to a vase of rare greenhouse blossoms upon the table.

"How kind," exclaimed Georgina; "and she was well?"

"Yes; and Miss Murray too, miss; they desired their love to you, and hope to call to-morrow."

She went to her old bed-room then, to change her dress before tea. Varied emotions of sorrow and gratitude and hope mingled in her heart, as Leonard's picture, hanging in its accustomed place, met her eye. Before rejoining her cousin she knelt and thanked her heavenly Father for bringing her once more back to her earthly home in safety, and prayed very earnestly for her brother, asking for continued submission and trust in reference to him.

She found Lloyd come down from his room, and in better spirits than she could at all have anticipated.

"Well, little Constance, you have a charming retreat here; but Leonard, I am afraid, will not thank you if he comes unexpectedly and finds a great cuckoo in the nest."

"You are no cuckoo at all," she said, laughing; "but you must be a reasonable and obedient man, and not expect to sit up to the table to tea to-night. Remember, I am doctor and nurse both now."

"Well, where do you wish me to sit?"

"Why, either on the sofa or in this very easy chair, which is Leonard's; and I shall bring you your tea on this small table. You are tired, you know."

"No, not so much as I expected; and it rests me to look round upon this room, and you. You are looking better already."

She busied herself with her tea things, and Lloyd watched her contentedly.

"What sort of a woman is Mrs. Murray?" he inquired, when tea was over, and Georgie had settled herself to her work.

"I think you will like her. She is very well educated and intelligent: she plays and sings very beautifully, and then is so gentle and motherly, and such a real, earnest Christian."

"What is that?" he said, carelessly.

Georgina looked up from her work, and did not reply for a moment. She had half forgotten to whom she was speaking.

"Am *I* one?"

O how could he ask such a question so indifferently! And the hope which she had fondly encouraged for the last weeks faded almost away as she answered seriously, "I think our own hearts must answer that question best."

There was silence for some minutes after this reply, only broken by Lloyd's humming the words of a song in a low tone. Then he continued the conversation about Mrs. Murray; but Georgie felt a little disheartened. She proposed, however, the accustomed reading before retiring to rest; and he made no objection. She chose the first epistle of St. John; and, when she came to the tenth verse of the last chapter, a response, as it were, to the urgent question which Lloyd had proposed to her with such apparent levity, she could not refrain from pausing a moment and glancing at his countenance. It was half turned from her; and on it was an expression of such extreme suffering that she could not venture to speak the words which had risen to her lips, but, ere he had time to notice the pause, resumed her reading; and, when it was ended, and she rose to say, 'Good night,' the look had passed away—his face was composed and unconcerned as before.

"O Lloyd," she said, as she took his hand at parting, "you cannot have any true happiness or rest, until the question you asked just now is settled. Out of Christ there is neither peace nor safety."

She had never spoken so plainly to him before; and even now the effort that it cost her made the color come into her cheeks, and her hand tremble nervously. He looked down upon her sternly, proudly, for a moment, then said, "Thank you," in a cold tone, which almost frightened her as she turned away and left him to himself.

As soon as she was gone he leaned his face upon

his hands and sighed bitterly. "O what a hypocrite I am," he murmured, "to affect indifference on a matter which is now the all-absorbing, all-engrossing subject of my existence!—the idea which swallows up all others, and casts an impenetrable shadow on all that once was beautiful and pleasant to me, and all that even now might soothe and interest. O life! O death! O eternity! I am fit for neither. I am a sin-bound man, and to-night have but added another to the great load which is crushing me to the very earth. Yes, the words of that book are all beautiful, but they are not meant for me."

Tears, drawn forth by the very anguish of his soul, fell on the book before him; while Georgie, in the silence of her room, was weeping and praying for one who she sadly imagined felt but little real concern and anxiety for his own soul's welfare.

Morning came—very bright and beautiful. Lloyd, who had passed a wakeful, restless night, was very late in coming down stairs. Georgina was waiting breakfast for him in the library, which, in the light and beauty of that early spring morning, looked even more cheery and home-like than on the preceding night. The sweet happy face of his little cousin, and her cheering, pleasant words, enlivened him; and he could not but smile in return as she welcomed him.

"You are better already, Lloyd, I believe. How did you sleep?"

"O, not particularly well; but that is nothing new."

"Do you think you shall feel able for a walk this morning? I want to show you all the beauties of the place; and you know, when the weather is warm enough, there is a charming fishing stream not more than a mile from here, where you will be able to amuse yourself catching trout, by the hour."

"That sounds inviting. And you can read: your voice would scarcely frighten away the fish, I imagine."

"Yes, or draw. I think I shall take sketches now of all the pretty places round. The air is exquisitely soft to-day. April is the loveliest month of all sometimes."

"So changeful," said Lloyd. "I cannot endure that in anything. I love the Mediterranean, with its smooth unebbing waters; the intense blue of a perfectly clear Italian sky, without speck or cloud or variation; the unfading green of the laurel and cedar-tree; and you, little Georgie, who are always constant."

"O no, not always," she said, very seriously. He took no notice of her remark.

"There is something to me so beautiful in the idea of unchangeableness—a person or object which is always the same—which you can count upon that it will not alter. What a pity it seems that in everything in nature this should be the exception, and not the rule!"

"Not even the exception," said Georgina. "It is a perfect impossibility. The beautiful tideless Mediterranean has its fatal storms and tempests: the calm blue sky is overclouded sometimes. And the evergreen of the cedar and laurel is not the same: the old leaves wither and die. It is a law of nature that everything here must change."

"'Tis a bitter law," said Lloyd, in a low melancholy tone. And Georgie longed to speak to her cousin of him who is the same yesterday and to-day and for ever, the Unchangeable One; and of the home incorruptible, undefiled, and that fadeth not away, prepared in heaven for those that love him; and of the rest, even here, which they who believe "do enter into." But she remembered her repulse the night before, and was silent.

Before the breakfast things were removed, a knock was heard at the door.

"It is Mrs. Murray," exclaimed Georgina: "I know her knock." And she sprang to her feet.

"Well, don't alarm yourself. Your face is becoming more the color of a flamingo than anything else. She will think we have been quarrelling." Georgie was calm instantly.

"Do you mind her coming in here?"

But it was too late. The door opened, and Mrs. Murray and Margaret were announced. The two friends had a long silent embrace; during which time Mrs. Murray, in her easy courteous manner, introduced herself to Lloyd, begging his forgiveness for this intrusion, as she had not the least idea he was in the room.

Then she turned to Georgie, and welcomed her fondly. " My darling child, how you are grown and"—improved, she was going to say, but stopped herself—"how well you are looking. Captain Archdale, I am sure we have to thank you for taking so good care of her."

" Au contraire," said Lloyd; " it is Georgina who has taken care of me : you will say I do her credit also, I think."

" A little more care will not hurt you yet, I think," replied Mrs. Murray, glancing at the thin white hand which he was passing across his brow.

" They tell me I need rest and change; and so I must believe them, I suppose; but I feel pretty well, only lazy and cross, eh, Georgie ?"

Georgina smiled; and presently Lloyd went out of the room.

" He is not strong, and cannot very well entertain strangers, dear Mrs. Murray," said Georgie, by way of apology.

" No; and we will not keep you long, darling; but we felt we must call and inquire for you both. He looks very ill, my dear, still. Is it not a great responsibility for you ?"

" But he is so much better. Six weeks ago he was a mere shadow : now his appetite is very good; and though he looks so thin, yet he is stronger, and, there are no alarming symptoms whatever. Aunt is coming soon, when the weather is a little more settled; and I trust, with God's blessing, he may go on well till then. But his spirits are depressed: he seems so low and restless at times."

"It is, perhaps, more mental than physical depression which keeps him low," remarked Mrs. Murray. "Is his mind at rest on the great question?"

"O no, I am afraid not. I fear sometimes whether he thinks of such things at all. But, then, he is so reserved; and, whatever he was going through in his mind, he would not perhaps speak of it to others, and cannot endure to be spoken to, on the subject either. Sometimes I do think that if he were happy in his mind he would get well sooner— that there may be some great load upon his heart, which he cannot tell to any one."

"Then you think that his illness and wonderful recovery have had the effect of awakening him?"

"Well, I have hoped so, dear Mrs. Murray. He is very different from what he was; but, again, I think that, after all, it may be merely physical weakness, and that if he had strength and energy his tastes would still lead him to be as gay and unconcerned as ever. But, O, I cannot tell! I wish Leonard were here."

It was the first time she had spoken her brother's name; and in doing so she burst into tears, and threw herself into Mrs. Murray's arms.

"Dear Mrs. Murray, the time has been so long."

"My poor child, I feel very much for you; but you must not be cast down. Your patience has had a long trial; but not at all longer than your heavenly Father sees best; and, when the waiting-time is over, and every purpose for which it has been sent is accomplished, how happy the meeting will be!"

"You do not think, then, that anything is amiss?"

"Not at all. It is more than probable they have been delayed at the Cape or elsewhere. I myself was once five months in returning from India."

"It is longer than that since I heard," said Georgie, mournfully.

"Well, darling, all must be, all is, well for you. You must have trust and hope, my child."

"It is a great joy to see you once more; and now that I am home, I seem all ready, waiting for Leonard at my post, do I not, Mrs. Murray?"

"I hope so, dear; and that reminds me we must not linger."

"Not yet, mamma," whispered Margaret.

Georgie glanced at her lovingly. "I will come and see you, Maggie, as soon as ever I can; but I promised Lloyd to walk at half past twelve, and he does not like to be disappointed."

"Poor Georgie!" exclaimed Margaret, as soon as they had left the house. "She must have enough on her hands, mamma: all this terrible uncertainty about her brother, and captain Archdale to take care of as well, looking so ill—so gloomy too, and haughty. He ignored my presence, mamma, entirely."

" He is unhappy, evidently," said Mrs. Murray, "his very smile told that; but if any one could soothe and benefit him it must be our little Georgie. Dear girl, how she is grown, and how lovely her sweet face is become!"

" I am afraid we shall not see much of her now," Margaret said with a sigh. And this proved to be the case.

" What an age you have been!" was Lloyd's somewhat impatient exclamation, when she joined him that morning in the garden, ready equipped for the proposed walk.

" I am very sorry; but the time did not seem long to me."

" I dare say not. Your paragon, Mrs. Murray, is a very nice woman, no doubt; and her daughter something like you, only not half so good; but I am too lazy to entertain people now, and too stupid to be entertained by them, with one or two exceptions, so that I don't care to be with any one fresh. I dare say they thought me uncouth enough for taking myself off; but I can't help it."

Georgie wished in her heart he could be persuaded to make Mrs. Murray one of his exceptions. She had so strong a feeling that she might be useful to him, but she could not tell him so. She felt also she must not expect to see much of her friends at present, as even this little absence had fretted her cousin; but she knew that her great duty now was to take care of him, and do what she could to interest and divert his mind. It required some denial not to be able to return Margaret's visit, or have the long outpouring for which both so much longed; but she had the inward satisfaction of feeling she was right, and that the path of duty, though trying at times, is ever the really happy one. And Margaret sighed sadly as she saw Georgie at her cousin's side pass in front of their cottage garden, and not turn in at the little gate, which was rarely passed by in former days. They met sometimes in the village; but Lloyd, though always courteous, never seemed disposed to linger or to accept Mrs. Murray's suggestion that a call at the cottage might afford him some little change, should he feel so disposed.

Mr. Harkness, the clergyman who had taken Mr. Grove's place for a time at the church of Beechwood, took an early opportunity of calling at the rectory. He was an old friend of Georgie's; and it was great pleasure to her to meet him again. Lloyd, who was in the room at the time of his visit, after a minute or two's chat, of a general kind, went out in a perfectly unceremonious manner, leaving Georgina to excuse him as she had done before.

"I should have liked a little conversation with your cousin," Mr. Harkness said, when he rose to leave; "but I suppose he is scarcely equal to it."

"I hardly know: he is very reserved."

"Yes, but I might talk if he did not choose to talk. He looks unhappy, Georgina. He has had a wonderful—little less than miraculous preservation; and God oftentimes, in his great love, deals thus to lead the wanderer back to him. He may need words of counsel and advice."

"I wish you could find the opportunity. Do come soon again, dear Mr. Harkness. He hears the Bible read constantly; and I believe reads it himself as well."

"Ah, well, dear child, human words cannot speak like that. I am thankful to hear it: read on; and may God bless you both." He laid his hand on her head kindly, tenderly; and Georgie smiled through her tears.

It was a beautiful spring: April was indeed very, very lovely. The cousins took long afternoon rambles together through lanes bright with primroses and stellaria, and woods where the anemone and sweet wood-sorrel and adoxa grew in all their wild luxuriance; and Georgie sketched, as she had said; and Lloyd sat silently with his fishing-rod, helping her when she needed help, till the sun drew near the horizon; and then they reluctantly bent their steps homewards.

Georgina read to him of an evening. It was strange the books she chose for the young officer, who, until within the last few months, had been full of the world and schemes of pleasure and dissipation: the "Pilgrim's Progress"—begun for the sec ond time—"Fox's Acts and Monuments of the Martyrs," and the "Prayers and holy Meditations of St. Augustine," with, from time to time, favorite portions from the beautiful Thomas-à-Kempis, Lloyd himself had given her.

They always had a fire of an evening, for "appearance' sake," as Georgie said laughingly; and Lloyd seemed perfectly contented to lie on the sofa near it, with Georgie on her low seat on the other side, reading in that soft clear voice of hers. He never made any objection to the books she chose, nor any remark on what he heard, except just to thank her; but she felt sure that he liked it, he listened so attentively. She always closed with the Bible. And Lloyd grew stronger and better from day to day; but a great cloud still hung upon his brow—the impenetrable shadow was yet thick around his soul. Georgie guessed how it was, and she longed and prayed for light to dawn, but waited patiently.

One night—it was the Thursday before Easter-day—in her reading she came to these words, "But now I dare not despair, because he, having shown himself obedient to thee unto the death, even the death of the cross, hath taken away the handwriting of our sins, and, fastening it upon the cross, hath crucified both sin and death." It seemed as though meant for Lloyd, and, glancing at his face, she saw that look of great suffering upon it that she had noticed once before.

"Dear Lloyd, are you in pain?" she said; "is your head worse to-night?"

He started a little, and then gave, O such a sad gloomy smile.

"You find out everything, little Constance," he answered. "My head is not just as it should be to-night: I will go to bed soon. What was that last sentence? Read it again, will you?"

She did so, and then closed the book.

It was the morning of Good Friday, and the bells were chiming for morning worship. Georgina came into the room where Lloyd sat on the couch, with her bonnet on, her books in her hand, and a peaceful smile on her calm still face. What a contrast to the dejection depicted on his!

"I do not like to leave you, now," she said, " with your head so suffering: let me stay."

" No, indeed, I will not keep you away again, especially this morning. I am better already, since breakfast."

" What will you do all the while?"

" O read, or have some music, or a turn in the garden. I shall not hurt: don't think about me."

But she could not help it. The look he had worn on the previous evening followed her even to the house of God: she could not forget it. When she was gone Lloyd walked to the window, and watched her retreating figure as long as it was visible. " O this wearisome struggle, will it never, never end? Can the peace she enjoys never be intended for me?

O Lord, who hast taught me to seek thee, hide thy-self no longer, but let me find rest in thee."

"I had hoped to see your cousin, dear Georgie," said Mrs. Murray, as they walked a little together on their way home: "he is not worse; or you would not be here."

"No, not materially worse, only the headache; and he would not let me stay away. Dear Mrs Murray, will you pray for him more than ever?"

She pressed the little hand, and they parted. Georgie lingered a little in the garden, and gathered a few flowers to make the room look brighter, as she thought of Lloyd's wearied, troubled face. "What can I do or say to comfort him?" she asked herself as she walked up the passage. She opened the door of the library quietly. Lloyd was there on the sofa where she had left him; but O what wonderful change had passed over him! His fine face, no longer troubled and restless, was radiant with a joy and happiness she had never seen there before; not the strange, wild enthusiasm that it had sometimes worn when he stood unconscious of all else beside before his easel, painting; nor the care-less gaiety and mirth which he was wont to assume when in the midst of company thoughtless and un-concerned as himself; but a peaceful settled joy, the source of which could not be mistaken. She stood for a moment at the door, with the conscious-ness of a great joy at her heart, which yet she

hardly dared to believe. He looked up at her, and smiled. The flowers dropped from her hand.

"O Lloyd!"

It was all she could say; but the tone conveyed the question that was intended. He answered as though she had spoken—

"Yes;" and then, pointing to the book before him, he said, "'He hath given me rest by his sorrow, and life by his death;' I have been to the cross, this morning, Georgie, and have left my burden there."

She came up to him, and leaning her face for a moment upon his shoulder, wept silently. They were tears of unfeigned joy and gratitude; and Lloyd, the once proud, scorning Lloyd, wept with her. And then he told her the long history of his past convictions, fears, and conflicts; how the burden of his sins had of late become so intolerable to him that life itself was a weariness, and how to no living being, not even to her, could he speak of it; and how he had endeavored to assume carelessness and levity, when all the while his heart was aching with the load of sin unpardoned, and the thought of the just anger of a long-neglected God. "And, when you read his precious life-giving words, something would whisper that they were not for me— that I had too long trifled with and neglected his offers of mercy; and so there could be no pardon for me. I thought upon my sins, my wasted life, my broken sabbaths, the thousand ways in which

I had broken the holy law, and everything seemed to say, 'No hope, no hope.' Sometimes, when you read of Christ's sufferings, and death, a gleam of hope would appear for a moment, but then vanish away again. I could not think that it was intended for me. O how I have longed and agonized for peace!"

"You have found it now," she said softly.

"Yes, all in him. I had been reading the fifteenth of St. Luke, this morning; how the father received the prodigal son, and not only forgave, but met and welcomed him; and I saw that my case was his. I cast myself upon Christ, just as I was; and now I feel that I am forgiven—that sinful, miserable as I am, there is room in the Father's heart and home for me; and that, through the perfect atonement Christ made upon the cross for all, even the chief of sinners, I can say now with St. Augustine, as you were reading last night, 'therefore, I dare not despair.'"

Much more he told her of the conflict and suffering he had experienced, and the sweet hope and assurance he now possessed; and, when he had finished, he said—

"And it is you, Georgie, that, next to God, I must thank for this blessed change. It was the consistency and blamelessness of your life that first led me to think about religion at all. I could not help admiring it in you, though my own heart long hated and despised it. Then your faithfulness in telling me of the great sin I was daily in the habit of committing, though I knew it to be wrong" (here Georgina wept again), "and your reading to me the word of God, and not giving me up, though I must have appeared so stupidly indifferent, that I only wonder how you persevered. You have prayed for me, too, I know. My thanks are very poor; but you will have your reward, my dear little cousin."

Her heart seemed too full to reply, and he went on—

"I am very sorry for the light, careless way in which I spoke of being an earnest Christian, the first night we came here, Georgie. I do not wonder that you thought me totally indifferent, though that was not the case; but I have got into the way, lately, of feigning carelessness when I felt the most. I could not endure the thought of any one's guessing my real feelings; and yet I wanted you to talk to me. I was vexed with the way in which you answered my seemingly thoughtless question: I thought you would have told me 'no,' plainly, and then I might have told you all."

"I am very sorry, dear Lloyd."

"Ah, but it was best as it was: it threw me back more entirely upon the word of God. I searched my heart more faithfully than ever, and prayed more ardently than before that the great question might be decided—that peace and happiness might come. O it has seemed a long time waiting; but I know now that my prayer has been heard."

The conversation was interrupted at length by the entrance of a servant.

"I shall go with you this afternoon," Lloyd said, as Georgie was putting on her things again.

"Do you think you should?" she said, half-hesitatingly, and yet with a very happy smile: "your head was so bad this, morning."

"Ah, it is better now. And do you think Mr. Harkness would come in this evening, if you were to ask him, Georgie? I should like to talk with him a little."

"Yes, I am quite sure he would; he inquired for you this morning."

O with what changed feelings did Georgina stand side by side with her cousin at that afternoon's worship. Deep gratitude, mingled with the yet-hardly realized joy that the wanderer had returned to his Father and his home, that the middle wall, broken down before, had been crossed over, and her cousin, no longer a stranger and an alien, had received the welcome and the blessing of a son and heir.

Mr. Harkness preached from the words: "In whom we' have redemption, through his blood, the forgiveness of sins." Lloyd listened with eager rapt attention to every word; all seemed to be spoken for him. At the close he appeared much moved.

"What a beautiful sermon!" he said to Georgina. "How is it possible I can have heard so many, quite as beautiful, doubtless, and remained unawakened?"

"In a person without ear, the most exquisite music cannot excite pleasure," she answered: "he may stand by perfectly unmoved, while a real lover of it has his soul so full that he can think of nothing else; and the impression made remains thrilling within him for long after. That is strange, but stranger still that the music of the Shepherd's voice, inviting his wandering sheep to return, should fall on their ears disregarded and slighted for days, and months, and years.

"But then, when they do hear it, it is real music," said Lloyd. "O Georgie, that text this afternoon—'In whom we *have* the forgiveness of sins'—my heart seemed to answer to it so thankfully."

In this manner they conversed till they reached the house; and soon after, in compliance with Georgina's request, Mr. Harkness came to the rectory.

"Shall I go?" whispered Georgina to her cousin, after he had entered.

"O, no," said Lloyd, "not unless you wish it. I am only going to speak of my new-found treasure, and ask advice and instruction and direction."

And as she listened to her once haughty cousin, meekly, and with the humility of a little child listening to the words of admonition which fell from the lips of Christ's minister, and answering with candor and simplicity the questions of examination which he felt it meet to put to him, Georgina's head sank yet lower, and tears of thankful joy again dropped from her eyelids.

When Mr. Harkness took leave of her that night, he said, laying his hand upon her head, " They that sow in tears shall reap in joy ;" and Lloyd looked up and smiled, for he, too, well understood his meaning.

23

XV.

RETURN OF TWO WANDERERS.

"Not thus let us meet—
　　Mid falling leaves
　　And sere frost-stricken flowers;
But when the leaf is budding in its freshness,
And the rich blossom putting forth its gladness.
Not thus let us meet:
　　It is too sad;
　　But, when the buried verdure
　　Is coming up to meet the joyous sun,
When the new spring looks round upon the hill,
Full of youth's buoyant promise and bright song,
　　Then let us meet." *

ERY calmly and peacefully passed the Easter day, and the succeeding Easter week. To Lloyd it was a season of unalloyed happiness. The new life, so recently begun in his soul, and untroubled as yet by the conflicts and temptations which his return to the outward world must necessarily involve, welled up so deeply and thankfully, that each day seemed more happy and joyous than its forerunner. And life, common every-day life, was no longer the dull and insipid thing of heretofore. One great object stood out plainly and stead-

* From ·Hymns of Faith and Hope." By Bonar.

fastly before him. There was a Master to be
served; a Father, who had loved and sought him
when wandering far from his presence, to be obeyed
and glorified; a Saviour, who had rescued and re-
deemed him, to be loved and gladly honored.
Saved and forgiven himself, the absorbing thought
now was, how to bring others to the same state of
happy peace and rest.

He chose the earliest occasion to write to each
member of the family at Leighton, and towards
the close of the week heard in reply from his
mother, father, and sisters. Lady Archdale wrote
thankfully and lovingly.

"Georgie, I did not know I had such a mother,"
he said, as he handed her the letter for her perusal.

He opened his father's then; and a glow of
color mounted even to his pale forehead as he
read:

"Over-wrought imagination, excited brain, natural enthusiasm of temperament, which would
gradually calm down as he was able to mingle
again in his old pursuits—"

"Nay," he murmured to himself; and a smile
succeeded the impatient flush which lingered but
for a moment. "The excitement, if such it be, I
trust will never pass away, the fire never cease to
burn until death quenches it."

The letters of his sisters caused him a touch of
pain, though he could not wonder at their tone and
language. Frances begged him to lay aside the

sober, methodistical notions which had so suddenly possessed his brain. "She could not spare him just yet," she said: "he must grow a little older before he turned pious—there was time enough yet." And she begged him to come away from Beechwood, and its gloomy associations, and return once more to his old friends and pleasures. Augusta echoed her sister's words, though both expressed their joy at the amendment he spoke of in his health, and their thanks to Georgina for having so far faithfully performed her trust.

And very thankful was Georgina to see the wonderful change for the better which had come upon Lloyd. It scarcely surprised her, though it was a subject for constant gratitude and joy. He no longer refused to visit Mrs. Murray; nor did he selfishly detain his cousin from spending as much of her time as she desired with her kind friends at the cottage. And he made Georgie take him to the houses of some of the poor parishioners; and, with all her thankfulness, she could scarcely repress a smile as her once-haughty cousin strove to bring his demeanor and conversation to the level of their comprehension and sympathy.

On returning from one of these visits, just as they reached the garden-gate, Lloyd said;

"Georgina, when I first went to Oxford it was with the idea that I might one day take orders. But I was not quite enough of a hypocrite; and my plans soon changed."

Here he paused; and, as his cousin made no reply, they walked up to the house in silence. But, as they parted at the foot of the stairs, he continued:

"Can it *ever* be too late to revoke a false step, or, at any rate, to atone for past error and neglect?"

"*Never*," she answered, in her clear decided tone; for she guessed somewhat of her cousin's meaning.

Thus passed the Easter week. On the Monday following, just as evening was creeping on, the cousins sat together in the library of the rectory. It had been a gustful, stormy day, for the season of the year; and, with the exception of a morning call from Lloyd upon Mr. Harkness, neither he nor Georgina had ventured out.

The cheerlessness of outward objects had made the latter more alive to the still heavy grief, which, poor child, was hidden away as secretly as possible in her nevertheless restless heart. Twilight deepened; and she ceased her work, but sat, silently and wearily, gazing through the window on the rain falling thick and fast, and the masses of dark clouds, which seemed to grow darker and yet darker as the light diminished. Lloyd was at the table, writing busily. It was two hours, now, since he had spoken.

"Lloyd, can you see?" she said, at last, with a little sigh.

23*

This roused him.

"No; I think I have been taking it for granted the last five minutes. What a chilly evening! And, Constance, you look benumbed, sitting so long by that window: we shall enjoy our fire now. Shall we shut up? Stay: I will ring the bell."

"No: I like to do all that myself," said Georgina, her face becoming a little brighter at the sound of a cheering voice. "And I am not benumbed, Lloyd: only I have been watching those grey clouds for such a time, and wondering how they can possibly pour down such torrents, and yet continue as heavy and grey as ever."

"I think a little of the grey was creeping over you, nevertheless," said her cousin; "and, to cheer you, when you have made all proper arrangements, we will have a little reading before dinner, from our favorite old saint."

The evening plan was changed now; Lloyd becoming the reader, Georgina the listener. Her arrangements were soon made. The fire blazed cheerfully, the lamp was lighted, and herself seated in her favorite position by the fire-side. Lloyd was in Leonard's seat.

"Where shall I read?" he asked.

"That beautiful piece on the heavenly country," she answered: "Leonard liked it so."

The heaviness seemed to pass away as Lloyd read:

"O everlasting kingdom, O kingdom, world

without end, wherein light is which alway lasteth, and the peace of God which passeth all understanding ; in which the souls of the saints do rest, and wherein everlasting joy shall be upon their heads, where they shall obtain joy and gladness, and sorrow and mourning shall flee away. O what a glorious kingdom is it where all the saints do reign with thee, O God, clothed with light as with à garment, having the crown of precious stones upon their heads! *There*, comfort endless, mirth without mourning, health without sickness, nay, without weariness, light without darkness, life without death, and all goodness without any evil, is. *There*, youth never cometh to age, life dieth not, beauty paleth not, love cools not, health decayeth not, joy wither eth not. *There*, neither pain is felt, neither groaning heard, neither sadness seen ; there alway they enjoy pleasure; and evil there is never heard. Wherefore, happy are they, whom God hath fetched out of this wretched life unto so great joys. Unhappy are we, who sail through the waves of this sea, and by these dangerous gulfs. Unhappy, I say, are we, whose life is in banishment, and whose way is perilous. We continue as yet in the streams of water, sighing after thee, the haven of the sea. O our country, O our quiet country, we ken thee afar off: we salute thee out of this sea, we sigh after thee out of this vale, and with tears we tug hard to come unto thee, O Christ, God of God, our strength and refuge, whose brightness doth enlighten our

eyes afar off, as the beam of the sea-star doth in
the dark clouds of the raging sea, that we may be
directed to thee, the haven of rest. O Lord, with
thy right hand govern thou our ship by the helm*
of thy cross, that we perish not in the waves, and
that the tempest of water drown us not, nor the
deep swallow us up ; but with the hook of thy cross
draw us back unto thee, our only comfort, whom
we behold afar off as the morning star, almost with
weeping eyes, looking for us upon the shore of the
celestial country. We abide in the troublesome
sea ; and thou, standing upon the shore, beholdest
all our dangers. O, save us, we pray thee, for thy
name's sake ! Give us grace, O Lord, among these
dangers to hold and keep such a course, that, each
peril escaped, we may come safe unto the haven,
both with ship and merchandize."†

Did Georgina's ears deceive her ? Were those
the sounds of carriage-wheels in the distance, or
merely the pattering of rain and rush of the wind
without ? The latter, perhaps ; for Lloyd read on
undisturbed.

"No : the sound came nearer—that surely was
the swing of the gate ! The color came all over

* The expression in St. Augustine is " clavo crucis tuæ,"
which should be rendered—by the *helm* or *rudder* of the
cross.

† St. Augustine's " Heavenly Meditations," chap. 35.
This book is not really by Augustine : it is a kind of collec-
tion from his writings, and those of other authors.

her face. She had been deceived once before, just at this hour, by the carrier's cart: it might be the same now. Still her heart beat violently; and she rose, her work dropping from her hands.

"O, Lloyd!"

"What, Georgie?"

"I think—I don't know; but there seems noise without, some one coming."

"I heard nothing, Connie: are you sure?"

"O, yes."

For now there was a loud knock and ring. Ah! well she knew that knock.

"It is! it is!" she cried. "O, Lloyd, help me to be thankful; for it seems too much."

She almost crushed his hand in hers; for he too, on marking her strange agitation, had risen, and come towards her. She did not rush into the hall: she seemed powerless to stir from the spot on which she was standing; for the overwhelming sense of joy was almost pain. The door opened; and at the sight of that dear loved face came also power to act. She sprang forwards, and, flinging herself into Leonard's arms, burst into a tumult of tears.

"Hush! hush! my darling," Leonard said; "it is all over now: God has sent me back to you once more. Not tears now, but thankfulness."

And yet his own heart felt a strange tumult and emotion, as he pressed his regained treasure closer and yet closer in his arms. A great deal of the sorrow, anxiety, and bitterness of the long separation was then more than compensated for; and a new joy was yet in store.

For some moments Georgina remained locked in that fond embrace, without thought of any other being upon earth, not even of her cousin. He stood there, close by, looking on the two, wondering at the strange depth of love and passionate fondness hidden under that usually calm and tranquil face.

He did not feel hurt at the apparent forgetfulness of himself: he might have done so, weeks back; but some of the old selfishness had vanished now. He thought of the long dull waiting time that his young cousin had known, of the patient trust and hope she had all the while exhibited, and of the joy that she must now experience. The same joy, though with perhaps an undefined shade of pain mingling with it, thrilled his own heart. He felt for the moment with her, and himself was forgotten.

She thought of him first.

"Leonard, dearest brother, we forget: here is Lloyd. Lloyd, forgive me!" And her eyes, still tearful, but beaming with grateful joy, looked up to his face pleadingly.

The cousins greeted each other warmly.

"We meet as brothers now," Leonard said. And Lloyd grasped his hand again; while the smile that lighted his fine countenance spoke more than words in reply.

There was a moment's pause. Leonard looked

down upon his sister, whose head still leaned upon his shoulder, and then at Lloyd. The latter spoke then; for, strangely enough, the inquiry he had thought would be the first had been forgotten until then.

"Is all right?" he asked eagerly.

Leonard smiled one of his beautiful smiles, and laid his hand caressingly on his sister's head.

"Georgina, my darling, there is a great joy for you."

"I have it," she replied, raising her eyes and head from the drooping posture she had assumed; as though at rest, standing there with him beside her: "more than I deserve."

"There is some yet for another," her brother said; and something in his tone made her unloose her hold of his arm, and look eagerly and inquiringly from him to Lloyd. Both smiled.

"I must leave you for one moment," Leonard said; and he went out into the hall. One moment of anxious excitement to Georgina, and to Lloyd as well; and then the brother reappeared, accompanied by—was it another Leonard? A tall manly figure, with the same wide brow, the same dark speaking eyes, though scarcely so grave and serious as were Leonard Archdale's.

There was a silence almost painful in its intensity; and the color came and went on Georgina's face as she looked from one to the other, as though entreating an explanation of this strange, strange mystery.

At length Leonard said, in a voice of deep emotion, and for the first time in her life Georgina saw tears in those steadfast eyes, " 'This thy brother was dead and is alive again : he was lost, and is found.' "

A sudden impulse made the sister cling again to her elder brother's arm ; but he unloosed the hold, feeling that she was no longer exclusively his, and led her towards the younger, who was gazing upon her with that look of earnest seeking love which was surely his, though he had scarce the right to claim it.

"Reginald," Leonard whispered, "your brother. You will love him, Georgie, even as you love me." And *that* was no light standard.

She did not say, "I will," in words ; but, as Reginal stooped to meet those outstretched arms, that fond loving face, and as the lips of brother and sister met in that first long sacred embrace, the vow was made deep in each heart that, until death should separate, the bond of so many years' separation, but united by the noble, self-denying, heroic love of the elder brother, should never, never be sundered. Without words the heart of each said that love restored at such a price, should never be dissolved.

There was much, very much to be told and retold that night, never to be forgotten in the lives of that little family group.

First, of the wanderings of the younger one, whose name even—so long was it since he had left

home and country, and so surely were the tidings
of his death long years ago accredited—was scarce
familiar to Georgina. And then of the deep love
and devotion of the elder brother; who, gaining a
clue, so distant and uncertain as to have been passed
over by the many, of his brother's existence far in
the interior of India, had left all that was dear to
him, his sacred toils, his home, his dearest earthly
love, and hastened to the rescue and recovery of
his wandering and erring brother. Distant was the
clue, and dangerous the search; but at last, in the
barracks of a small town far in the north of the
great Indian empire, stretched on his soldier's bed,
burning and delirious with an infectious fever, did
Leonard find his brother.

Racked with pain, at times unconscious, yet in
his more lucid moments did the young man speak
of his native land, and the home of his boyhood,
the loving parents, and the friends of his childish
years, whose hearts he had lacerated well nigh to
breaking by his waywardness, his rebellion, and his
ultimate desertion.

And there, as the shadow of death closed heavily
over him, as eternity with its untold solemnity
neared his shuddering view, the thought of meeting
his father's God, the God he had been taught to
kneel to and reverence in former years, but whom
he had since despised and slighted, overwhelmed
his trembling soul. O for a ray of hope! O for

24

one gleam of mercy to lighten the gloomy boding darkness!·

It came at last. Just in that moment of agonizing despair, when his lips cried out in terror, " What must I do to be saved? How, how shall I escape?" a voice, which sounded soothingly and like the music of a long-forgotten song, spoke gently to his ear the words, " Come unto me;. and I will give you rest...Return unto me, ye backsliding children, for I am the Lord your God...And, when he was yet a great way off, the Father saw him, and had compassion."

" Again, again," said Reginald: "speak those words again, and tell me there is hope."

Tenderly and faithfully did Leonard watch by that bed of suffering; and nobly was he rewarded. The life of his younger brother was given in answer to his strong and earnest prayers; and far more than this, the spiritual life, awoke within his soul. It had been a cold and stony heart; but the breath of the Spirit melted and warmed it. Much was forgiven him: and much in return, he loved.

As the touching tale reached its climax, and Leonard told of his brother hovering on the verge of death, and then slowly and languidly coming back to life, Georgina's emotion could scarcely be restrained.

" And then—" she murmured, as Leonard paused for a moment.

" And then," continued Reginald, taking up the

recital, and with a glance of inexpressible love towards his elder brother—" then Leonard was laid
down."

"What! in fever?" asked Georgina, slowly,
tremblingly, as though the fearful reality were even
then before her. "And I did not know of it! O
Leonard!"

" Yes, in fever," her brother answered ; who can
wonder, after braving all as he did for me, and his
strength reduced by the burning heat, as it was when
he came to V—— . But why speak of it, if it
troubles you ?" he continued, as the tears gathered
in his sister's eyes, which yet looked up with fearing scrutiny to Leonard's face, to see what traces
the fearful disease might have left. She had fancied
him a shade paler, and more worn than of old.

" No ; go on. I should like to hear all," she said.
" But why did I not know ?"

" It was better, much better as it was, my darling," said her brother. " That was, indeed, the
very reason I did not write. I must have mentioned my illness; and I wanted to be better—
well, first."

" And you were long in recovering ? You are
ill now? Tell me all, Leonard, I intreat of
you."

" I have, dear child. I am well, quite well. The
voyage, under God's blessing, has done everything in restoring me; and I feel as vigorous as
ever."

"But are you not paler, thinner?"

"Nay, Georgie, much stouter, as you would say had you seen me three or four months back. You need not be anxious on my account, dear, I assure you. Now, *Lloyd*," he continued, glancing towards his cousin : "*he* looks as though a little more nursing would not be thrown away upon him."

"Ah! but Lloyd is wonderfully better. He was saying, only to-day, he felt quite well. But he has been writing this afternoon so much—more a great deal than he ought."

Lloyd echoed Georgina's words as to the marked improvement in his health, and felt, indeed, as he surveyed the little family circle, that it was such as not to warrant a much longer tarry amidst it. He was able and anxious for work now; and the repose and quietude of the life he had lately been leading were no longer necessary. Once again life, earnest working life was before him; and with new feelings, new aims, and new purposes, did he look on into it.

He stayed a few days at the rectory after the brothers' return, during which time he was much with Leonard. Many long walks and rides did the cousins have together, with grave and earnest conversation, in which at first Leonard was the teacher and counsellor, and Lloyd the earnest listener. But, as his great natural reserve gradually melted away, and the beauty of his mind, with his lofty aspirations and longing strivings for the good and true opeued out to him, Leonard could not but gratefully admire and thank God that so much that was elevated, and pure, and noble, was henceforth to be consecrated to his service. And Lloyd did not fail to express to Leonard his sense of the deep debt of gratitude which, under God, he owed to the example and influence of his young cousin. He told all that had occurred, concealing nothing—his own kindly-intentioned, though mistaken endeavors, to lead her into gay scenes and company, with the idea that it might cheer and amuse her; her steadfast resistance; her calm, consistent life, and holy example; the patient endurance of unkindness and wrong, and the ultimate success of her perseverance and prayers.

" There seemed to me, even from the first time I saw her," he said, "a halo of calmness and peace encircling her, such as I had observed in none before, and the source of which I could not comprehend. I liked to fancy to myself that she held secret intercourse with angels or supernatural spirits, who diffused their calm and gentle presence about her, as we read of in old stories. I did not understand then that she did indeed hold constant communion with the highest of all beings, the great Invisible One, and that the light reflected here so beautifully was all derived from that source."

Leonard smiled as Lloyd spoke. He thought of his watchword, and he knew that his sister must have thought of it also."

Georgina meanwhile spent long hours with her soldier brother. The profession he had chosen in his early and wilful rashness was still the one he loved and desired to be engaged in; and, after a stay of some weeks at Beechwood, he was to join at C—— the regiment in which he had purchased a commission. So she saw comparatively little of Lloyd, but was content, knowing that her place was now more than supplied, and that this intercourse must be of benefit to him.

So, one lovely morning, early in June, Lloyd quitted Beechwood. He came into the library, where Georgina was before her easel, painting, to say "Good-bye."

"I am sorry, so sorry you are going," she said; and she took his hand affectionately.

"I shall often think of you, Constance. I shall have reason," he added, in a graver tone. "And now you must not be sorry, but pray that I may be brave and strong, and that God will use me in his service, and that I may live to him."

"I shall," she answered, in a low voice. And she thought of all her prayers—and what prayers—for him in days and months gone by. There was not need to tell her to pray on.

"Your pictures shall be sent you, Connie—all but one. I should like to keep one, if you have no objection."

"O yes; any you like," she answered.

So he gave her his hand once more, and they parted. Georgina stood at the library window, and watched him, as he had watched her on that Good Friday morning, and ther, with a short sigh, which presently faded into a smile, she resumed her work.

XVI

LLOYD'S SACRIFICE.

"Pleasure, and wealth, and praise no more
 Shall lead my captive soul astray:
My fond pursuits I all give o'er,
 Thee, only thee resolved to obey;
My own in all things to resign,
And know no other will but thine.

"Wherefore to thee I all resign;
 Being thou art, and Love, and Power;
Thy only will be done, not mine!
 Thee, Lord, let heaven and earth adore:
Flow back the rivers to the sea,
And let my all be lost in thee."

A WHOLE year passed by with very little of
outward stir or incident in the life of Georgina
Archdale. And yet such a peaceful, happy
year she perhaps had never known before. Her
old plans and studies and interests resumed, and
the new ties fastening closer and more firmly about
her heart, she felt increasingly how much she had
to be thankful for.

Lady Archdale paid her promised visit in the
course of the summer, bringing with her her
youngest daughter; and very pleasant was the
intercourse both to Georgina and the little Car-

oline, whose grateful and affectionate love to her favorite cousin the short separation had increased rather than diminished. With thankful joy Georgina found that the words of life she had so often read to and with this dear child seemed to have taken root in her heart, and, working surely but silently, were bringing forth the fruits of a careful and holy life. She was her mother's chosen companion now, having, ever since Georgina's departure from Leighton, taken up her post in reading the daily portions, morning and evening, from the sacred book.

With lady Archdale came the tidings of Walter's departure. His uncle had at length satisfied his wishes, bought him a commission, and he had sailed for India, the land where his father and mother slept, full of buoyant hopes and eager longings for the distinctions and renown which a military course seemed to open out before him. He wrote to Georgina, telling her with joy of the accomplishment of his hopes, and how bright and happy life had now become to him; only, he added, " I don't care to think too much about the past, or the distant future, for fear the dark shadow of former days should return."

Georgina felt that his anchor had fastened on a shifting sand, and she dreaded what the consequence might be, when the storm of temptation arose. She feared more for Walter when the prospect was perfectly bright and cloudless, than when the storms of adversity had darkened his path. She felt sure that he knew the way of truth, and that in his innermost heart he was persuaded that it was the only one of rest and safety; but she doubted much whether he had ever really desired to follow it, whether there had ever been an earnest and sincere seeking after God, or heartfelt wish to find him. His infidel views, she had long discovered, had been assumed, not from conviction, but from a sullen determina tion to banish all religious thoughts from his mind. He had ceased to bring them forward long before she had left Leighton, and only answered that he could not make himself feel or love, and that he must wait until God should see fit to convert him. Alas! he did not know how dangerous such waiting may prove.

Late in the spring of the following year, Georgina again visited Leighton. And again it was a wedding occasion that summoned her. Frances was to be married to George Forrester.

The wedding itself passed pretty much as the last had done: there was no saving of expense or display: the guests were numerous, and the party assembled by sir William's express desire on the following night, brilliant and distinguished. But there was a graver undercurrent pervading all, which perhaps none noticed so much as Georgina, who remembered so well her emotions on the former occasion.

And the one who was the gayest and most animated of all then, was absent now.

Lloyd, who was just on the eve of an important examinatioɪ, and who felt also that the gaiety and dissipation of such a scene, at such a time, would jar painfully on his mind, deeply occupied with the grave and solemn responsibilities before him, did not come to his sister's marriage.

The bustle and excitement past, things gradually relapsed into a more quiet and even course, although Augusta, now released from all governess control, and settled into the admired, but somewhat stately, Miss Archdale, could not be content without enjoying as much company, both at home and abroad, as her papa could possibly be persuaded to allow.

Georgina remained at Leighton for nearly a month after her cousin's marriage. The Hall seemed a strange and almost different place to her, with so many of its old inmates removed; and yet it was a pleasant time to her. Clara and Arthur Isbel was there, with their boy, a beautiful child, just entering on his second year; and Georgina soon formed a strong attachment to her cousins, who had strangely interested her on her first visit, short though the interview with them had then been.

The evening before the day fixed on for her return to Beechwood, Georgina sat in the drawing-room at Leighton. Her aunt was there on a sofa,

Clara and her husband, Augusta, Flora Legh and her brother, a young officer just returned from South America, with some other young people who had been spending the evening at Leighton.

Georgina sat in a recess of one of the large windows, her work-frame before her as usual: she was finishing a chair which Augusta had begun for her sister, but given up in despair. She looked a little grave and thoughtful as she bent over her work, and from time to time raised her head, turning it in the direction of the opened window and the park, and not towards her companions, who appeared very cheerful, and much amused by what the noisy young lieutenant was advancing.

For they were expecting Lloyd that night; and she remembered that other waiting-time; the long, lonely hours; the terrible suspense; the agonizing fear that had accompanied his arrival then. And yet, as the results, even of that terrible catastrophe, presented themselves to her mind, and she saw how sorrow had worked out joy, and fear and dreadful anguish had been succeeded by peace, and calm, trusting faith, the shade of anxiety passed from her brow, and her eyes were turned less frequently to the park-drive, and the white lodge in the distance.

Augusta came to the window at length, with Herbert Legh; and, just as she approached, the carriage came in sight, and she was the first to exclaim that Lloyd, after a six months' absence, was home again.

"How well he looks! how dear! how handsome! only a little too ecclesiastical," were her exclamations, as her brother entered the room; and Lloyd smiled his old bright smile, and greeted his mother and sister with a loving affection which was once unknown to him. And then he gave his hand to his old friend, Flora, who welcomed him warmly, and introduced him to Herbert; and then he asks for his father, Georgina all the while quietly waiting for her turn to come, as she sits half hidden by the muslin curtains in the recess of the great window.

"And Georgie, where is she?" he asked; and would have wondered, had he not known her well, at the apparent coolness which kept her there, while all the others had gathered round him so eagerly.

It was a year since they had met; and perhaps both were a little changed, Georgina at any rate. She was taller, less of the child, though not very womanish even now; and the color came into her cheek just as of old, when he sought her out; and she rose from her work to meet him. Sir William soon appeared, overjoyed to see his son; and the family were shortly afterwards summoned to dinner.

Later in the evening, Augusta proposed a turn on the terrace. It was a beautiful moonlight night, and the carved stonework of the fountains, and the white vases and statues in the garden stood out clearly and coldly in the pure light, casting fair shadows, and giving that radiance to the scene which perhaps has more of charm than the full genial glow and depth of sun-light. Her proposal was instantly agreed to, and soon cheerful merry voices resounded through the night air.

"Too cold for you, eh, Georgie?" said sir William, as, muffled up in her aunt's plaid, she emerged through the low open windows of the library into the broad terrace-walk.

"No, uncle: it is so very beautiful," she answered. "I love the moonlight: it is so pure and quiet."

"Then take my arm, little sentimental one," he said laughing. "You seem well wrapped, at any rate."

Lloyd was walking by his father's side, his arm linked in his; and for half an hour they paced thus, sir William telling his son of much that had occurred during his absence—improvements, alterations, the arrival of fresh tenants, and the departure of old ones; to all of which Lloyd listened with a cheerful interest, commenting and advising in a way which evinced such good sense and judgment, as surprised his father, who had been accustomed to meet with no sympathy whatever in his favorite schemes, from that quarter more especially.

At length sir William suddenly perceived the air to have become peculiarly keen, and, on reaching the hall door for the fourteenth time, turned in, to enjoy his evening cigar and nap, leaving the cousins to pursue their walk together. And Georgina gathered her plaid closer round her, and Lloyd's step became more firm and measured, and they passed one or two groups of cheerful talkers ere either spoke. And then Lloyd said:

"Constance, on Trinity Sunday I am to be ordained."

"So soon! I am very thankful." And every little word, as it came quietly from her lips, told that she was so.

But there was another turn up and down in silence; and then Lloyd said again,

"'Tis a solemn thing, Georgie, this taking the vows of God upon you, feeling that henceforth you are to be an ambassador between him and men. And I so unworthy, so undeserving of such an honor. The thought overwhelms me sometimes; and I tremble lest I should not fully have counted the cost, and weighed the tremendous responsibility."

He spoke low, but with deep and earnest feeling.

"'My grace is sufficient for thee. My strength is made perfect in weakness,'" repeated Georgina. "'Let him that heareth say, Come.' You have obeyed the call yourself, Lloyd; and your great desire now is to proclaim it to others. You have not sought self in this matter."

She thought of all he had renounced, and felt she could say this truthfully.

"No, I hope, I trust not. But if, through un-
faithfulness of mine, souls should be lost?—O
Georgie, it is this thought that is at times so insupportable!"

"I think," she answered, rather timidly, "that
you have no need to dwell too much on that. If
the faithfulness were to come from ourselves, then
indeed there would be fearful, awful danger; but it
is not so: all help aud power is treasured up in
Christ; and he will give out of his fulness. He
has helped you hitherto; and he will continue to
do so when your need becomes greater."

The simple trusting words fell soothingly on
Lloyd's ear; and he answered, in a less troubled
tone—

"Yes; and how delightful to know that, 'if any
man sin we have an Advocate with the Father.'
I have thought much of those words lately, not as
being an excuse or palliation for sin, as some
would imagine, but as comfort when the heart
is wrung with the remembrance of sins hated,
though indulged in, and bitterly lamented afterwards."

Lloyd then went on to speak to Georgina of his
future plans. He had quite made up his mind, he
told her, to take up the little living far away in the
north, which was in his father's gift, and which sir
William had, in former days, destined for Walter.
He had made inquiries, and found in what a sad
state of spiritual destitution the parish was; the

people for the most part poor and uninstructed, and the clergyman who occupied the temporary position of their pastor very far from faithfully fulfilling that solemn and responsible office. Lloyd felt that this plan of his would not meet his father's wishes; that, in consenting at all to his taking orders, sir William had in view some conspicuous and honorable office in the Church, where his son would receive the distinction and emolument worthy his high position in society, his native talent, and liberal education.

But what was all this to Lloyd now? Had he not sold his all, to purchase the pearl of great price? and what availed earth's jewels of honor and fame and distinction in comparison? Had he not given up his way and course into the hands of God? and should he choose the path which had the least of thorns and earthly entanglements besetting it? Did he not feel himself the least of all, hardly worthy to be called a minister of Christ's gospel? and should he choose a position where his learning, or talent, or wealth, might be courted and flattered, and so his heart led astray from its highest and purest motive? He shrank from the thought, and, as he told Georgina, firmly resolved, by God's assistance, to adhere to the plan he had named, which he felt sure had the direction and manifest sanction of his heavenly Father.

The conversation was interrupted at length by a soft voice near them,

" How unsociable you look ? If you are not too engaged, and will give me an arm, Lloyd, I will take just one more turn or two: my husband is gone in."

Lloyd placed his sister's hand within his arm; and Georgina, who perhaps felt that for her, too, the evening was growing chill, slipped in through the open library window, as she approached it the next time, and hastened up stairs to lady Archdale, to tell her of the calm glorious evening, and her pleasant walk.

She left Leighton the following day about noon, Clara and Arthur, who were travelling homewards, accompanying her half the way, as far as the town of W——, where Leonard was to meet her. She took a farewell turn with Carry through the gardens after breakfast, and was lingering awhile in the conservatory, where Hilman was preparing her a parting tribute of affection in the form of a beautiful bouquet, when Lloyd emerged from his studio.

He asked her to come in for a moment : he had something to give her. Strange feelings passed through her breast, as she entered for the first time during this stay at Leighton that apartment, and thought of all that had occurred there.

The room was unchanged—just as beautiful as ever, though perhaps a shade more orderly. The bright glowing pictures, with their massive frames, the ornaments so pure and classical, and the flowers blooming in the window recesses, how it reminded her of the first time she had stepped within its walls, and O how much had passed since then! Lloyd followed her glance round the room; and rather a sad smile passed across his face.

"It is very kind of them to keep it so beautifully, so exactly like what it was," he said.

"You have had pleasant hours in this room," said his cousin, rather at a loss what to say, and feeling that *she* had; ay, and painful ones too.

"Yes, *very;* and yet 1 would not have them all back, if I could, in exchange for one hour of the real pleasure I have known since. And yet," he added, "I loved my pictures very dearly, and my painting. Yes, I think that has been the only actual renouncement—giving up, that God has permitted me to make for him."

"And you do not regret it?" for Georgina knew full well *what* that giving up must have been; and it seemed for a moment a terrible sacrifice to her, and one that he need scarcely make fully, entirely. "Shall you *never* paint again?"

"I do not regret it. I think I shall never take up my pencil for mere amusement again;" and he spoke firmly—decidedly.

"Fra Angelico, the Beato," murmured Georgie in a low tone, and she glanced towards a little gem of this her favorite master's, which she had ever considered her ideal of all that was beautiful and sublime.

"Yes, he sanctified his profession," said Lloyd;

" and may God help me faithfully to follow mine, and give up cheerfully all that would hinder and distract. You know, Georgie, what an absorbing passion painting had become with me—milder terms would not be sufficient—how every other aim and idea was swallowed up for the time in that great object, how impossible it would be for me to be a moderate or apathetic painter. *You* would not wish it otherwise ?"

Georgie's conscience smote her : the thought that she should by one word have sought to dissuade Lloyd from the sacrifice he had so nobly resolved on, and which must have cost him so much, made her feel in her own eyes so weak, so despicable.

" Forgive me," she said, as her eyes sought the ground, and the color mounted to her brow.

But Lloyd had not viewed it thus : he did not think she would have felt with such interest on the subject; he had thought the sacrifice was only *his.*

" It is but little we can do for him, after all, Constance; and he has done so much for us : we shall not regret it by-and-by."

He spoke very kindly ; and then he took from a devonport at which he had been writing a small Bible. It was very beautiful externally, with gold edging and clasps, and the name of Georgina Arch-dale engraved upon the plate.

" I thought I should like to give you a Bible," he said ; " and *here*," he added, " in this room ; for I feel, Georgina, that, next to God, I owe you very much. In reading this you will sometimes think of me, and pray."

Georgina took the gift reverently and in silence. Perhaps her feelings were too much in the past, too deeply touched to speak. She seemed so far beneath him—him with his noble devotion and humility and gentleness, that was once so proud and scorning and self-satisfied. And to thank her! to say that any blessing he had felt, any happiness he had experienced, any usefulness that might henceforth crown his path, had the remotest connexion with her! No, she could not speak; but her heart sent a thrill of joy upward to her Father in heaven; and tears of gratitude dimmed her eyes, as she took her cousin's hand, and then, at a hasty summons from a servant sent to seek her, hurried from the room to prepare herself for her journey.

Lloyd was right in his surmises as to sir William's disapproval of the step he was about to take. But after much opposition he yielded to his son's quiet but fixed resolve; and, after his ordination, which took place on the following Trinity Sunday, and a temporary duty in the city where he had studied and been ordained, Lloyd proceeded to his distant home. It was for him a solemn day, that on which for the first time he addressed his flock—poor, for the most part, and few in number; but the words of truth came from lips powerful with the strength communicated from on high, and from a heart burning with the love of Christ, and the

desire for the salvation of his fellow-men. No
wonder that his congregation felt emotions long
forgotten kindling in their breasts. All listened
and wondered; some admired, and some retired
thankfully to their cottage homes, with the assurance that holier and better days than heretofore
were dawning upon them.

But it was through difficulties and disappoint-
ments many that Lloyd had to labor on. He had
not expected a smooth path, neither did he meet
with it. Mingled with the encouragements and
blessings—for these indeed were granted him, of
increasing and earnest hearers, prospering weekly
and Sunday schools, love and gratitude rendered, in
return for self-denying and diligent ministration—
came also the blight of expectation chilled, the sickness of hope deferred, the sting of misunderstand-
ing, and the heaviness of many a disappointment.
Nevertheless he found the faithfulness of the words,
" As thy days thy strength shall be :" with increasing work and effort came also increasing peace, and,
at the close of his first year's residence at Boultby,
no feeling of regret at the steps he had taken, or
the way in which he had been led, clouded his retro-
spective vision.

XVII.

THE WEDDING.

"And thus all cling unto each other;
For nought from all things else is riven.
Heaven bendeth o'er the prostrate earth;
Earth spreads her arms towards heaven."

IT was a beautiful morning in the summer, two years from the time when we last parted with Georgina Archdale, that we look upon her once more in the quiet garden of her brother's rectory. She was strolling from border to border, gathering flowers, and singing meanwhile to herself in a low quiet strain. She stopped suddenly, for footsteps approached over the soft turf; and, looking up, she saw her friend Margaret Murray.

"I am an early visitor, dear Georgie; but you will forgive me."

"Never too early here, Margaret; and now that your welcome visits are becoming numbered—but I cannot talk of that. I had been wanting you sadly, dear, and should have found my way to the cottage soon, if you had not made your appearance. I have had a letter from Leonard."

"Ah! no wonder you look so happy. He is enjoying his stay?"

"O yes; but I must tell you all about it. The letter is full of news."

The two friends walked, with their arms around each other, up and down the shrubbery.

"He is with Lloyd now in his parish at Boultby; and he says that Lloyd is so happy, so very happy in his work there, so loved and looked up to by all; But that he works so hard—*too* hard, Leonard is afraid. Leonard preached for him last Sunday, because he was not well. And next Sunday, Margaret, what do you think? Lloyd is to preach here; for he needs change, and is going home for a while, and stops at Beechwood just a day or two on his way. Does it not seem strange, dear Margaret, when we look back?"

Margaret paused a moment, and then replied: "Very. I did not think, when I first saw captain Archdale here so ill, and so haughtily unbending, that one day we should hear him preach in our own dear old church. What things, that we should deem incredible, God brings about, Georgie dear!"

"O yes; and, Margaret, I long to hear him preach. You can scarcely feel about Lloyd as I do; you did not know him in his gay reckless days. When I first saw him at Leighton, you remember, I dare say, what I used to tell you in my letters; he was the one to be courted and sought after in every ball and party."

"Yes, I recollect very well. And how afraid you used to be of him, Georgie! Are you now?"

"I think I am rather: quite a different feeling to
what it was then; because we have been such friends
since. But I think the feeling of extreme reverence
will never go away. O Margaret, he gave up every
thing so beautifully when he went to Boultby. He
is so refined, so sensitive, so fond of every thing
beautiful and artistic; and yet he gave all up, and
went to that dull remote village, just because he
knew it to be right. It is quite in the north, in the
coal country, I believe; and Leonard says the people love him so. But he never writes, hardly. I
have thought it strange sometimes."

"I am glad he is coming," Margaret said, when
Georgina, with a short sigh, ceased speaking; "but,
Georgie dear, I forgot, I have not delivered mamma's message. She is going over to S—— for a
shopping-day, and thought you might like to accompany us: we shall not be home till evening, as we
are to dine with our friends the Eltons. They will
be delighted to see you, mamma told me to say."

"I should have liked to come much, but am engaged to-day to Geraldine. She was here with colonel Blygh last evening, and made me promise, if
she called for me in the carriage at twelve o'clock,
I would have a drive, and return with her to the
Grange. I am very sorry; but you will explain to
Mrs. Murray, and thank her very much for thinking
of me."

"I will, dear, and now must say 'Good-bye,' or
she will be waiting."

And the two friends parted.

At twelve o'clock precisely a handsome carriage drove up to the rectory; and a tall graceful girl alighted, and made her way to the house. It was Geraldine, the only daughter of colonel Blygh, who, within the last twelve months had taken the large old manor-house, a mile or two from Beechwood, which bore the name of the Grange, and which had for some years been unoccupied. Not long retired from active service, colonel Blygh was a sincere and devoted Christian gentleman. His settlement in the parish was a great acquisition to the young rector, who found in him a zealous friend and helper in all schemes for the welfare and benefit of his parishioners.

His daughter Geraldine was no less an acquisition to Georgina and her friend Margaret. She was a blithe and happy creature, rejoicing in life, and in that also which alone can make life happy and joyous, the sense of peace and reconciliation with God through Christ.

Very frequent visits were exchanged between the rectory and the Grange, though Geraldine was more frequently the guest, as Georgina did not like leaving her brother alone, and she knew his innate distaste for visiting. Latterly, however, she had fancied this wearing away. He himself would occasionally propose an evening stroll or ride to the Grange. Some plan had to be discussed with the colonel, or with the colonel's excellent sister, aunt

Mary, as Geraldine called her, who resided with them. And, when there, he would remain, without great solicitation, to the social tea in the pleasant saloon, which opened out on the Grange grounds; and thus many happy evenings passed, the tie of friendship becoming more firmly drawn after each new meeting.

In the early part of June Leonard was summoned from home on business of importance connected with his parish. Affairs leading him to the north, he paid a long promised visit to Lloyd; and it was a letter with the details of this visit which had so excited Georgina's interest, the morning on which we have seen her. She could not refrain from alluding to it, as she drove with Geraldine towards the Grange, although Geraldine did not know Lloyd as Margaret did, and his coming to Beechwood could not be attended with any great interest to her.

But there was no lack of sympathy in the manner with which Miss Blygh received her friend's intelligence. As the friend and cousin of Leonard and Georgina, she could not but feel an interest in Lloyd's coming; besides, as she told Georgie, Margaret Murray had often spoken to her of his former visit to Beechwood, and told her, too, that he was the artist of some of those beautiful pictures with which the walls of Georgina's little study were adorned.

"So he will not be quite a stranger to me, Georgie," she ended by saying, "I should think he must be fond of Beechwood; I almost wonder he has not been here before."

"He is coming now," Georgina answered very quietly.

No one would have guessed the intensity of feeling which this coming, with all the old associations, painful and pleasant, revived thereby, awakened in her mind.

"From Saturday till Tuesday, you said, I think?'

"Yes; only those three days."

The time seemed long till those three days approached. Leonard had been absent nearly a fortnight.

Saturday afternoon came at last. Georgina had been with Margaret on the tour which that afternoon always brought with it, to the cottages across the common, where old John Hilman lived; and her friend had returned, to end the evening with her. Margaret's company was growing more precious than ever now, since Georgina was so soon to be deprived of it. Mrs. Murray was, with her daughter, going out to India, to join a brother, who had lately been bereaved of his wife, and whose children had been anxiously recommended to Mrs. Murray's care. The length of her stay was uncertain. It might be for years; and Margaret could not be parted from her.

The prospect of the long separation was peculiarly painful to the young friends; though, from many a past lesson, they had learned the fleeting transitory nature of earth's dearest ties and friendships; and they could look above for comfort even in this great trial.

They sat in the verandah after tea, in the quiet of that summer Saturday evening, and awaited the travellers. Their conversation turned on past scenes and reminiscences, until the sound of carriage wheels put a hasty end to it; and the next minute the figures of the two young clergymen were seen approaching through the shrubbery. They might have been taken for brothers, of equal height; and the resemblance Georgina had fancied she could trace to her brother years ago was deepened now in Lloyd's fine face, paler and more serious than she had ever seen it before. What Leonard had mentioned in his letter of his cousin being out of health struck painfully through her heart for a moment, and sobered the welcome which she bestowed on both. But the journey had been long and fatiguing; and she hastened into the house, to hurry the arrangements for the coming refreshments, leaving Margaret for the while to entertain her brother and cousin.

It was a Sunday full of interest, that following day, when Georgina for the first time heard Lloyd preach the glad tidings of the gospel in that church where he himself had first realized the blessedness of Christ's peace-speaking blood.

He sat alone in the rectory library after breakfast, until the hour of service approached. Leonard and Georgina had been, as usual, at the schools; and the latter returned to fetch her cousin. She tapped at the door, and on her entrance the grave, anxious look cleared away from Lloyd's countenance, and, with his Bible in his hand, he walked with her to the church. Leonard read the service; and Lloyd preached. With beautiful simplicity, and at the same time with that true eloquence which speaks to the heart, did he dwell upon his text, " He is our peace." It was a theme on which he was never tired to linger—he, who had known so bitterly what the world's peace is, who had struggled, and agonized so painfully, and tried so many channels ere slaking his burning thirst at the true cistern.

Almost the whole of the following day Lloyd and Leonard were abroad together. A visit had to be paid at the Grange, as well as to the humbler homes of many of the poorer parishioners, who welcomed Captain Archdale, as they still found themselves calling him, most sincerely. It was late in the afternoon when they returned, the dinner bell was sounding, and Georgina awaiting them in the library.

Dinner over, Leonard told his sister he had a call to make on a brother clergyman at a few miles' distance, which might detain him until quite late in the evening; and he set off, charging Georgina, who had accompanied him to the garden gate, to entertain her cousin during his absence. It seemed strange; but this charge seemed a difficult one to Georgina. She could not help wondering to herself, as she walked slowly back to the house, what change, either in herself or cousin, might have caused it.

During that stay of so many weeks at Beechwood, years before, she had never felt a moment's difficulty in acting the part of hostess; she had proposed walking, or reading, or music, just as she had fancied might best suit him; but he was her charge then. Now he might possibly prefer not being interfered with; he might wish this long evening for quiet or for study. But, in accordance with her brother's request, she repaired to the library, where she found, rather to her relief, Lloyd busily engaged writing a letter, with a brow quite compressed and anxious, as though he would not choose to be disturbed. So, taking up her work which she had left there before dinner, she was preparing to retire from the room, when her cousin looked up from his letter, and said quickly, "Why are you going, Georgina? I have scarcely seen you since I came."

"I thought I might disturb," she replied, hesitatingly. "Shall I come when you have finished writing?"

"No: stay now. I shall have finished presently; and I shall like to talk to you a little before I leave."

The old habit of obedience to Lloyd was still so strong, that Georgina felt almost as though she had transgressed, as she seated herself near the window, and busied her hands with the knitting on which she was engaged.

Lloyd finished his letter soon, and after giving it to a servant to post, he returned to the library, and came and stood in the window, leaning against the framework of the bay, and surveying the lawn, and the smiling prospect beyond.

"Boultby is not at all like this, Georgina," he said at length, after some time of silence: "it is bleak and barren; and what fine scenery there is! rugged and stern. The sea only five miles distant, edged with grey frowning rocks, against which large waves beat when the tide comes in, and the gale is high. Even on quiet days inland there is something tumultuous and restless on that coast."

"I did not know you were so near the sea," Georgie remarked, as her cousin seemed waiting for some response. "It must be very grand."

"And the people seem to partake somewhat of the character of their scenery. They are rough and immovable, not like the simple country people in these inland districts, whose hearts and homes seem so accessible, and whose very rusticity appears courteous."

There was another pause, which seemed to suggest a remark, and Georgina said:

"Still you are happy there, Lloyd : they are not *all* rude and inaccessible."

"There is very much to encourage," Lloyd answered ; "and I am, as you ask, Georgina, happy in my work. I believe it is the post for which God assigned me, and I cannot but feel happy in that. There is much to be done; scope for usefulness and serious effort at every turn. But I have my lonely moments at times—moments when I need a cheering voice and helping hand, when all looks cloudy, and it seems as though my unaided effort were of no avail. There were times, last winter, when I felt this need so painfully, that, on returning from my parochial visits I was depressed, nay, almost overwhelmed, by the void which the absence of human sympathy seemed to create."

"It must have been very lonely for you. Might not a curate be a great comfort and assistance?" suggested Georgina.

"And it may appear strange to you, Georgina," Lloyd continued, taking no notice of his cousin's suggestion, "that, in these lonely moments, these seasons of wearisome dejection, my thoughts have invariably turned in the direction of Beechwood."

"Strange that he should never have written," thought Georgina, as the remembrance of the only two or three short business letters which had reached the rectory for the past year and a half, came into her mind; but she only answered—

"Leonard, I know, has never availed himself of

such assistance, though at times he has talked of it; but this parish is so small, and he is strong."

"It has not been so much Leonard whose recollection has had strange power and control over me," said Lloyd, in a tone which sent a quick thrill through the heart of Georgina, as she bent yet closer over her work to conceal the old blush which she felt gathering across her face—"not so much Leonard, whose image, in these moments, desolate and gloomy though they were, had power to nerve my drooping energies, and kindle hope and trust within my heart."

He paused: and there was a lengthened silence, only interrupted by the hum of bees as they hovered past the open window, and the song of an evening bird in the trees beyond the garden.

"I have at such times fondly thought of one who was ever a true and faithful friend to me, and whom, whether the blessing of her love be granted me or no, I shall have cause to remember until death, with no ordinary affection and gratitude. I have sometimes, when wearied and discouraged with the care of outward things, wondered whether, if she knew all, she would be sorry—fancied, it may perhaps, have been but a fancy, a self-delusion—that she would come to me."

His voice was troubled with emotion. She could not bear to hear him speak so; a large tear dropped upon her work, which she held but loosely in her trembling fingers.

"Constance, is it too much to ask? Will you come?"

He sat down beside her, and held out his hand. She placed both her own within it, tearfully, but confidingly, as a child gives up its possessions unreservedly into a mother's keeping, saying only very gently, "I am not worthy, dear Lloyd."

Lloyd pressed them very closely, but for a while spoke not. Georgina felt that he was praying.

"It is no new thing, my own one," he said, fondly, when he spoke again, "this deep, absorbing love, which I feel for you in my heart even in my calmest and most religious moments. The growth has been long and very firm; the only chilling breath that has ever nipped it, the dreary thought that possibly it might not be reciprocated. But O, I should not have doubted. You have always been a minister of peace and rest to me, Constance, from that very night, now so far in the distance, when your sweet pale face first looked up to me in the drawing-room at Leighton, the eve of Clara's marriage, until even yesterday, when, in anticipation of preaching the word of life for the first time here at Beechwood, bewildering thoughts and memories of what had occurred here, rose thronging through my breast, making a din and tempest strangely discordant with the soothing and heavenly measures of the text I had chosen. But you came in, Georgie; and your face wore the same look as on that Good Friday morning; and the tumult died away, and the thoughts of peace only remained. I know and feel that God sends this human help; that it is not all earthly affection, but a foretaste of what we shall know hereafter in the perfect and unsullied love of heaven."

He drew her nearer; and, with her hand still clasped in his, they knelt; and Lloyd thanked God for this, the greatest of all earthly gifts with which he had endowed him, and prayed that their lives, soon to be one, might be wholly given to him and his service.

"But, Constance," Lloyd asked, awhile after, "shall you be happy, do you think, in the bleak, cold region I have been telling you of, where, for miles round there are no cornfields, no green meadows, no lovely, sloping hills and wooded valleys, but all is barren, and waste, and rocky."

"I love you, Lloyd," was all the answer she gave in reply; and with this answer Lloyd was well satisfied.

"Leonard," inquired Lloyd, as, when the evening was far advanced, the young rector returned to his home, "what punishment did the man deserve, in ancient times, who, after hospitable reception and entertainment, departed, robbing his host and benefactor of his penates?"

"Ah!" said Leonard, whose quick ear detected somewhat farther than the question at first sound might convey, "my memory fails me; ask Georgie."

But the smile sobered, as, at the thought of leaving him, the sister's grief burst forth, and she threw herself into his arms.

"Leonard, dearest brother, am I ungrateful ?"

"Nay, nay, Georgie," he answered, "I yield you up willingly : my affection and care will be worthily replaced; I can confide you to him without one pang of mistrust."

"Not as once before," murmured Lloyd, as Leonard placed his sister's hand in his, and gave them both his blessing.

The wedding was not very long deferred; for Mrs. Murray and Margaret were leaving for India at the close of the autumn, and their presence on the occasion could not be dispensed with. Sir William Archdale was very anxious that it should take place at Leighton; but this both Leonard and Georgina declined, the latter by far preferring the calm and quietude of the little country village to the show and grandeur of the Hall. At the same time all the family were urged to be present at the ceremony.

Georgina sat alone in her room on the morning of the eventful day, a bright and cheerful one early in September. Margaret herself had just put the finishing touches to her dress, which was pure white; and she had asked them to be left alone for a quiet half-hour previous to the arrival of the carriages.

There was unusual stir and bustle going on in the

27

rectory. Sir William and Lady Archdale were there, with Augusta and Carry; the two latter, together with Margaret Murray and Geraldine Blygh, acting as bridesmaids.

But Georgina's room was quiet, and as she sat there, quite ready and prepared, a waiting bride, deep, solemn, grateful thoughts passed through her mind. She had been led lovingly and graciously; she could trace a Father's hand so plainly during every step of the past five years; and, though trials bitterly, keenly felt at the time had befallen her, yet how greatly had blessing preponderated! The very trials had worked for her happiness, bringing forth rich fruits of gladness in her heart. And still one sorrow remained to be borne—the parting with her dear old home, and dearer brother, the guide and protector of her early years, and the loving friend and companion of later ones. For a time, at least, he would be alone; and the thought of this was a dash of bitter in her cup of happiness.

A gentle tap was heard at the door, and Leonard entered.

"My darling child, I am come to say good-bye here, where we can be still. You are happy, dearest sister, and peaceful."

"Yes, dear—only—I must leave you. You will be alone—you will miss me."

"Ah! no one can know how much," he answered, in a tone of deep emotion, as he bent down to the sweet face, upturned to his, and kissed it fondly.

"But, Georgie, there will be no parting by-and-by. We shall one day meet, to go no more out for ever."

"Yes," said Georgina, " Leonard, dear, it is not quite time yet; let us have prayer together, once more."

So they knelt; and again Leonard commended both his sister and himself to the protection and care of the invisible One.

When they arose there was a long but quiet embrace; and then there came another tap, and Lloyd entered. He had only arrived at Beechwood late the preceding night, and had not seen Georgina before.

" Georgie, darling, they are waiting, are you ready ?"

Leonard placed his sister's hand in that of Lloyd, and left them together.

When they were alone Lloyd took a tiny paper from his waistcoat pocket, and, taking the little hand in his, " Constance, do you remember this day four years? You once asked me to promise never again to allude to it, to forget it: we never shall do that. I know I am forgiven now. Georgie, you will soon receive this as a pledge." And he fitted the ring on the hand which still, on careful inspection, bore the marks of that cruel accident. He pressed it to his lips for a moment, and then, placing it upon his arm, he led her from the room.

The light from the old painted window in the chancel fell radiantly upon the white figure of the young bride, as she knelt before the altar and took upon herself the solemn marriage vow. She was very calm and still: how could she be otherwise, with that firm, noble heart, beating at her side, and that deep steadfast voice in her hearing, the tones of which fell on her ears as notes from a land beyond her present vision.

And long did the soothing and strengthening remembrance of that hallowed service rest upon her heart. Called to fresh duties and fresh responsibilities, she met them, not only with the help of him now dearer to her than any other earthly being, but with the remembrance of the earnest, devoted life and noble example of her tried and faithful brother. Still was his parting text her constant watchword. Happy in the affection of Lloyd and the pleasures and opening duties of a new life, she yet remembered, amidst all the scenes of home and friendship, and the care-demanding responsibilities of wife and mother, the solemn, searching injunction, so to walk as " seeing him who is invisible."

THE END.